P9-DZN-048

The Haunting of Charles Dickens

The Haunting of Charles Dickens

Lewis Buzbee

illustrated by Greg Ruth

NEW HANOVER COUNTY PUBLIC LIBRARY
201 Chestnut Street
Wilmington, NC 28401

FEIWEL AND FRIENDS
NEW YORK

A FEIWEL AND FRIENDS BOOK
An Imprint of Macmillan

THE HAUNTING OF CHARLES DICKENS.
Copyright © 2010 by Lewis Buzbee. All rights reserved.
Distributed in Canada by H.B. Fenn and Company Ltd. Printed in September 2010 in the United States of America by R. R. Donnelley & Sons Company, Harrisonburg, Virginia.
For information, address Feiwel and Friends, 175 Fifth Avenue, New York, N.Y. 10010.

Library of Congress Cataloging-in-Publication Data

Buzbee, Lewis,
The haunting of Charles Dickens / by Lewis Buzbee. — 1st ed.
p. cm.
Summary: Twelve-year-old Meg travels the rooftops and streets of 1862 London, England, in search of her missing brother, Orion, accompanied by a family friend, the famed author Charles Dickens, whose quest is to find his next novel.
ISBN: 978-0-312-38256-8
[1. Missing persons—Fiction. 2. Dickens, Charles, 1812–1870—Fiction. 3. Authors—Fiction. 4. Family life—England—Fiction. 5. Kidnapping—Fiction. 6. London (England)—History—19th century—Fiction. 7. Great Britain—History—Victoria, 1837–1901—Fiction. 8. Mystery and detective stories.] I. Title.
PZ7.B98318Hau 2009
[Fic]—dc22
2008028553

Book design by Rich Deas and Patrick Collins

Feiwel and Friends logo designed by Filomena Tuosto

First Edition: 2010

10 9 8 7 6 5 4 3 2 1

www.feiwelandfriends.com

For Julie

without whom nothing . . .

Whether I shall turn out to be the hero of my own life,
or whether that station will be held by anybody else,
these pages must show.

—*Charles Dickens*
David Copperfield

The Haunting of Charles Dickens

Chapter I

Another sleepless night

LONDON. Mid-summer night nearly upon us. Meg Pickel stood, as she had every night for six months now, at the edge of her family's roof-garden, and stared into the City, towards the massive black dome of St. Paul's Cathedral. It was nearly time, she knew, for the midnight bells to begin their ringing. Each night, in the brief moment before the bells first rang, the whole of the City grew unnaturally calm. Not a coach wheel turned, no horse collar chimed, not one child cried out for its mother—a perfect quiet.

St. Paul's sounded the first note, low and booming, as if the cathedral itself were an enormous bell struck by the City's legendary giants, Gog and Magog. Immediately the bells of a hundred other churches began striking all around Meg, a great hammering of bells, and soon the sky was nothing but bells, bells, bells. Like pebbles dropped into a still pond, each bell created a ripple of sound in the sky, great leaden circles that flowed outward. Meg leaned forward into the night, and the crashing ripples of the bells washed over and through her. Then the final stroke landed, and the bells stopped their ringing, and the leaden circles dissolved into air.

Midnight again. One day ended, another newly started. One more day without her beloved brother Orion.

This was Meg's favorite moment of the day, for in the great clang and crash of the bells, she could forget about her brother and the six months he had been missing, could forget about his handsome face and how it still laughed before her, even though he was not there. When the bells were ringing, she could stop imagining what horrible fates might have overtaken him. But the bells always stopped, and Meg was filled once again with nothing but Orion's absence.

Winding her way through the roof-garden's potted plants, she settled on a low bench—as she had every night for the last six months. She scanned what few stars shone, looking for the constellation that shared its name with her brother, Orion the Hunter. But Orion was a winter constellation and would not rise again until the autumn, when on clear nights, its bright and easily known shape—the three stars of Orion's belt—seemed to leap out of the sky. Tonight, though, the sky was a haze of soot and gas-light, and no constellations made their patterns known to her.

As she had done every night for the last six months, Meg turned her fancies to the many ways Orion might return. This was a game at which she excelled. If she could no longer imagine his return, then she had given up hope, and she would not give up hope—not yet.

Orion might, Meg knew, return in any one of a hundred different fashions. She had many versions of this story, and she whispered these to herself constantly, as one might sing a favorite song time and again.

In one version, Orion simply climbed up and over the edge of the roof-garden from out of the garish gas-lights of busy Cheapside. He told her that he had been chased by hooligans, but had managed to evade them. What Meg liked most about this dream was that she could pretend Orion had only been gone a few hours.

Meg also quite liked the version of return in which she saw him striding casually down the dark of Tonson Lane, humming a silly tune—Orion was always humming some silly tune, tunes he invented himself and which Meg still heard six months later. In this version, he simply walked in the print-shop's front door, while Meg watched silently from the edge of the roof-garden, waiting for the loud "Huzzah!" that would erupt from their family gathered by the hearth. She liked standing outside this moment and watching it unfold, like reading a scene from a novel.

Some of her imaginings were more incredible than others. In one, Orion came climbing out of the ancient plane-tree that bordered the eastern edge of the roof-garden. This was an enormous tree, whose crown shielded the roof-garden, and one of the only trees in this part of the City; Orion

would swing out of it on a handy vine, pretending to be a savage ape-man.

When her mind was most fevered by thoughts of Orion's return—*O please come back, Orion, please make our family whole again*—Meg envisioned a strange light in the sky that drew nearer and nearer, until the shape of a hot-air balloon made itself known, hovering delicately over her head. Orion, laughing, would slither down the mooring rope and into Meg's arms.

It never mattered to Meg how her brother returned, only that he did. Imagining his return allowed her a brief rest from her constant memories of the night he disappeared.

It was snowing that night, the first real snow-fall of the season. The fires had been banked against the cold, but no one had noticed the snow yet. Dinner was over and cleaned up, bed-time near, and everyone was reading under gas-light and candle glow. Aunt Julia sat near the stove with a large book about tropical orchids, tracing their delicate forms into her sketch-pad. Meg's father lay on the sofa, a newspaper peaked over his head; he was probably asleep. Tobias, her younger brother, lay on the hearth-rug with the one book he favored most, Malory's *Tales of King Arthur,* and next to him, Mulberry, the dog, head on crossed paws. Meg and Orion both sat at the dining table, noses buried in novels.

Such was the nightly custom of the Pickel house-hold, and even six months after Orion's disappearance, Meg could recall how much pleasure this moment used to give her. Since their mother had died, three years before, it had become Meg's responsibility—taken on her by herself—to latch all the doors, upstairs and down, before settling with her family for a night's read. It was as if by latching the doors she could keep the darkness away from the family, stall any possibility of one more family member being snatched. It gave Meg great comfort to accomplish this task, and when she remembered that six-months-ago night, she could still feel that comfort—what was left of the family was together and safe.

On that night, Meg was staring at the pages of *Robinson Crusoe,* one of her most loved books, but she was unable to concentrate—the letters simply refused to become words for her. Although he was doing nothing but reading, Orion was causing her great consternation, for he was reading the third volume of *Great Expectations,* the newest novel by Mr. Charles Dickens, their favorite author. That Mr. Dickens was also a long-time friend of the family, something of a god-uncle to the Pickel children, did nothing to soften Meg's desire for his newest novel.

You see, Mr. Charles Dickens was often a guest in the family print-shop, for he had been purchasing his special writing paper from Campion Pickel and Co., Printers, since the time Meg's grandfather had run the shop. His visits to the shop, then and now, were never brief and never quiet; Meg loved to listen to his stories, and he often helped her with her home-school work—he was particularly good with Latin, though not so much with Maths. He was fond of all the children, Meg knew, but he had taken a special liking to Orion in the last year, and the two of them were often found huddled together over sheets of scribbled-upon paper.

Aside from being a family friend, Mr. Dickens was also one of the most famous people in all of England—and for Meg this meant all of the world. She knew of his fame only what other people said about him, not what she witnessed. The famous Mr. Dickens seemed a wholly other person from the one who used to bring Meg endless boxes of Turkish Delight.

But so much of who Mr. Dickens was, friend or celebrity, had nothing to do, for Meg at least, with how she felt about his novels. Mr. Dickens, the writer, was only found in his books. This Mr. Dickens, the writer, was not a man, but a world. Each new book of his was an event of great excitement in the Pickel house-hold.

On the night he disappeared, Orion had been tormenting Meg by the simple act of reading *Great Expectations* as slowly as possible. O the agony of having the book you most want just out of your grasp.

Meg's father had brought home *Great Expectations* only the week before. He had traded the three volumes of it for some print-work to be done at a later date. While there was never much money in their house-hold, there were always books. In the printer's trade, in which Meg had grown up, books were like water from a mountain spring, flowing freely everywhere. Meg grew up reading the novels of Mr. Dickens, as had Orion and Tobias. The first book she recalled reading on her own was *Oliver Twist,* that tale of a pitiable orphan's despair, a pity only relieved at the end by Oliver's adoption into the house of the kind-hearted Mr. Brownlow. There was a constant flood of books in Meg's house, new books coming in and finished books going out, but the novels of Mr. Dickens always remained.

When the publication of *Great Expectations* had been announced, Meg and Orion decided not to read it in its serialized form, the thirty-six weekly installments appearing in Mr. Dickens's own magazine, *All the Year Round.* Meg and Orion would wait, instead, for the bound volumes to appear, once the serialization was complete. Mr. Dickens, they both agreed, was simply too frustrating a writer. He would lead you into a chapter, which you would follow with great enthusiasm, only to find yourself on some cliff-edge and having to wait days for the next installment. No, when Meg and Orion began a novel by Mr. Dickens, they wished to read the entire book as quickly as possible, and with very little disturbance from the outside world.

When their father brought home *Great Expectations,* Meg and Orion decided who would read it first in their usual manner. They played Rochambeau for dibs. Orion won the Rochambeau—scissors cut paper—as he always did, and Meg could still remember the look on his face at that moment, kind but superior, as though he had played a trick on an unusually clever dog.

So Orion would begin the first volume, and Meg would start the minute he finished it. For days they both ignored their home-studies, with their father's permission, and drowned themselves in Mr. Dickens's world.

But by the time Orion got to the end of the third volume of *Great Expectations,* he began to—without mercy—taunt Meg. The day before Orion disappeared, she had finished the second volume—Pip had just discovered the source of his great expectations to be the fearsome convict Abel Magwitch—and now Orion was reading as slowly and methodically as a spider spins a web. If he read any slower, Meg thought, he'd start reading backwards. He was torturing her.

Meg looked down at the suddenly dull pages of *Robinson Crusoe,* then looked up at Orion reading Mr. Dickens. Every once in a while, Orion would laugh out loud, or gasp in horror, or wipe away a tear as he read, each gesture overdone so she would know exactly what she was missing. This behavior of Orion's drove Meg to the edge of her wits. It was all she could do to keep from yelling at him; her foot was beating the floor as if it were Orion's accomplice.

"Listen," Orion said of a sudden, in a stage-whisper.

The entire family looked up, including Mulberry the

dog, who seemed somewhat ashamed that he hadn't first heard whatever noise Orion had.

But it was Meg, not Mulberry, who barked.

"What?" she said crossly. "I don't hear anything."

"Precisely, Meg-ling. Not a sound."

"Why, thank you, dear brother," Meg said with a nasty hook in her voice.

Mulberry cocked his head from one side to the other, trying to locate the noise.

"But *why* is it quiet, dear sister?"

"Because . . ." Meg said. She had nothing to say to Orion at that moment except *Give me that book!*

"Because it's snowing!" yipped Aunt Julia.

And Mulberry barked, and they all jumped up and ran out the door to the stairs and into the snow on the landing and up onto the roof-garden, where, indeed, it was snowing, and beautifully so.

Mulberry barked and barked—O that was the noise, he realized, the super-silence of snow—and tried to catch the fat flakes with his snapping jaws. Tobias, as a nine-year-old boy must, by his nature, gathered up and packed snow-balls and pelted everyone. Meg simply watched in silence as the snow fell over London and transformed the black and brown world of the roof-tops into an immaculate forest of white chimneys and spires.

It was such a beautiful sight that even Tobias stopped to admire it.

"This is what I think," Tobias announced. "I think that

snow is when you take the moon to a nutmeg grater, and it turns to snow and lands everywhere."

They all laughed and nodded, and Meg looked at Tobias with a new appreciation. He was correct; the snow looked exactly as he said. Even though he was her little brother, she realized, he could be rather clever.

"And with that," Meg's father said, "I suggest we all return before we become moonlight ourselves. The snow will be here tomorrow."

Only Orion stayed behind. At fifteen, he was old enough, their father said, to make his own decisions, which rankled Meg. Yes, she was younger than her brother, she would admit to that. But she was also a girl, and therefore, much more mature and reasonable. This was a fact Meg considered obviously obvious.

Meg stood at the top of the stairs and watched her family go down and re-enter their warm rooms, Mulberry herding them along.

"Orion," she said. "Please come in, you'll catch your death."

"O, Meg, you humbug," he said. "Don't worry so. I'll be down in half a tick, I promise."

"It's cold and late, Orion. What keeps you out here?"

"I've thoughts to think, and they require solitude. Shortly, I promise."

Meg didn't want to leave him there. It went against her instincts—everyone should be together and inside. This was the only safety against the darkness, against losing more than had already been lost. They had lost Mother, and an unnamed brother, and those two losses were too much already.

The image of Orion alone on the snowy roof-top would haunt Meg forever, she knew, as unchanging as a photograph. He stands in the snow, looking over his shoulder as if already going away, and the look in his eye is curious. He's seen something in the world his sister hasn't seen yet, and he's determined to go after it. Just before she turns to go in, he winks at her. In that wink was a secret she has not solved in six endless months of decoding.

But Meg turned and went down the stairs and pulled the door closed behind her, leaving her brother alone on the roof. It continued to snow all night, and in the morning Orion was gone, his bed unslept in. He had disappeared.

Meg has been sleepless every night since.

O she can fall to sleep. Even on the first evening of the day Orion went missing, with everyone in the family flustered and confused and frightened, Meg fell asleep early. But she woke near midnight, and could not find sleep again until just before dawn. And for six months, each night has been the same.

Each night she wakes and begins her rounds, always near midnight. On first waking up, she lies in bed and waits for the house to settle, the deep breath and snore of the family—O how her father can snore! She tries to will herself back to sleep, but this effort only wakes her more. Finally she gives up and rises, a spirit about night roaming the dark rooms. She goes to Tobias's chamber and listens outside his curtain for his soft breathing, waits for the sudden shift of his restless legs. Then she pulls his curtain aside and peeks in. There he is, asleep, as safe as a baby but as vulnerable, too. She glides to his window and tests its latch. All's safe here. Then she does the same for her father, his proud snoring a testament to the depth of his sleep. And does the same for her aunt, who has a way of mumbling to herself in her dreams. She latches these windows, too, as well as the windows in the kitchen and the windows and doors of the print-shop downstairs.

Her first round complete, Meg climbs up to the roof-garden and dreams of Orion's return. And waits and waits through the long, chilly hours. Then she goes downstairs again, first to the print-shop, then to the bed-chambers, and when the last window is checked once again and the last door re-latched, she climbs into bed. With the sky growing lighter, she finally falls asleep, satisfied that her home is intact, at least for one more night.

It has been six months of no sleep and no Orion. How much longer can Meg live like this?

Meg stood up from the bench and pulled a handful of leaves from a silly old shrub—*Stupid, stupid shrub!*—and threw them down as if to shatter them. But they did not shatter or make any noise, and this only made Meg angrier. She stamped her feet, then stood, her arms folded, and gazed with fierce eyes at the midnight world.

And suddenly she had a thought she had not had since

Orion disappeared. She wanted more than anything in the world to finish reading *Great Expectations*. Orion had carried the novel's third volume up to the roof-garden with him the night he disappeared, and he had taken it with him, wherever he was. Meg hadn't read a single word of any book in six months. It was all fine for Orion to go off and get kidnapped or run away to sea or whatever it was he was doing, but he could have left the book for her at least. Selfish brat of a brother, that's what he was.

Wherever Orion was, he had *Great Expectations* with him, and she would find him, she was determined, if only to retrieve the book that was so rightly hers. She wanted more than anything to finish the story that Mr. Dickens had so rousingly begun. It was not right to have a story interrupted.

Meg took a deep breath.

The book was merely a symbol, she knew. If Meg could get the book back, she could retrieve Orion, and that was all that mattered.

She stared into the warm London night, the roof-tops of the City spread before her, a dark map for which she had no legend. Orion was out there—she knew it, felt it. But how to find him, where to begin? London was too huge.

"Stupid, stupid London," she said. Right now Meg hated everything—London, her home, the stars she could not see, and most of all, the waiting.

It was precisely at this moment, the moment of her greatest despair, that Meg saw the strange green glow from the sky-parlor of Satis House. It was the only bright light in the dark map of London's night, and without hesitation she moved towards it. The green glow was a beacon, and it was calling her, begging her to follow it. It was time to stop waiting for Orion's return, she thought in an instant. It was time to go after him.

Chapter II

In which two of London's sleepless meet precariously, only to discover a mutual friend

THERE ARE AT LEAST two planes of existence in London—there are many more, truth be known, but we shall satisfy ourselves with two for the moment. The first plane is most obviously that of the streets, where throngs of humans march and rush by day, and skulk and steal by night, where carriages and omnibuses career and collide.

But there is a second plane, a more elevated one, a less crowded one, and that plane is up here on the roof-tops. A second surface of the earth, at least here in London. The jagged roofs are all squeezed together, like pieces of typeface in a composing stick—not a lick of space between them. And it seems possible—Meg has imagined this since she was a child—to walk across all of the City from one roof-top to another, never setting foot on solid ground. The world up here is complete.

But while Meg has always wanted to step from her

family's roof-garden onto the roof-world, caution has held her back. Tonight, however, caution would not stop her. Orion might or might not be in the direction of Satis House, but it seemed to Meg as good a place as any to begin her search for him. There was no telling where the journey would lead her, but she knew a first step had to be taken. The time to move was now.

The green glow from the sky-light was an illuminated emerald placed handsomely on a black velvet cloth, and it transfixed Meg. The once-glorious Satis House, separated from the world by high and rugged brick walls, had always been shut up, to Meg's knowing. In all the years she'd watched the place, no light had ever shone from its cracked and dirty windows.

Aunt Julia had told them all the story of Satis House, and its legend was known throughout the neighborhood. It had belonged to a jilted spinster who lived alone there many long years, and when the spinster died, she left her considerable fortune to one purpose—to keep up the house and ensure that it would be occupied by no one. What a waste of a perfectly fine house, Meg often thought. Behind the crumbling masonry, it was easy to see how beautiful the house had once been. After her mother's death, when Meg was but nine, she had often used Satis House as a diversion from the pain of her loss. Meg would imagine the house refurbished, made glorious again, and her own family living in it, each with his own bedroom, each with his own work-room or play-room, and her mother, of course, dressed in a fine gown and greeting an endless parade of visitors. Meg gave up this fantasy not long after she invented it; it was clear no amount of wishing would bring her mother back.

Meg stared at the green glow. It was utterly irresistible, though it gave her a case of the creeps.

Meg climbed atop the roof-garden wall and stood balanced over all of London. She plotted her course through the chimney-forest, then lowered herself to the neighboring roof and began to make her way.

The roofs nearest to Meg were flat like hers, and she nimbly skittered across them. Though no moon was out tonight, the City of London was never cave-black dark; the thousands of gas-lights that dotted its streets were illuminated 'til past dawn. The yellowish glow of the City covered the roof-world with a fine dust of pale yellow, and it was easy-safe for Meg to pick her way.

When Meg reached the narrow ravine of Curll Court, the landscape changed dramatically—as when, Meg thought, in novels, characters crossing a desert find themselves confronted by perilous mountains. Between her and a foot-bridge that would carry her across Curll Court loomed a bank of roof-tops so steep they seemed a wall. Meg stopped, scouted up and down, and soon discovered, as the intrepid explorers in novels always do, that there was no way under or around or through this obstacle. There was only over.

She put one foot against the lead roof and tested it: sturdy but slippery. She then leaned against the slanted roof on her hands, and crawling much like a spider, worked her way to the peak and threw one leg over. O, Meg thought, if only she were a boy—no, not to be a boy, but to dress like one. Breeches were more suited to this journey. A girl's dress could be a pretty and desirable thing, Meg considered, but a boy's breeches, well, they could give you speed, agility, recklessness: freedom.

Meg allowed herself to slide to the roof's edge, stopped from falling four stories by a decorative molding. She looked down to the dark street below and was surprised to find herself un-frightened. She knew she could do this.

Only a few yards away, the arched foot-bridge over Curll Court waited. She inched to it carefully, lowered herself over the roof's edge, and dropped like a sack of potatoes to the foot-bridge. She crouched and looked about, waiting to see if her loud thump had roused a neighbor.

Then she ran across the bridge, where she boosted herself onto a breeze-way railing, found a foot-hold on a richly carved post, and threw herself, in one motion, onto the next roof.

Here Meg stood, straight and tall, her arms akimbo, looking back at the print-shop where her family slept. She had only come a little ways, measured by a map, but it seemed quite far. Not because of a trick of the eye, but because she felt she had left some old portion of herself behind—that's how far she'd come. She'd left behind the Meg who only waited; it was a new Meg out here on the night-roofs.

"I will find you, dear brother," Meg said aloud. And then she said the words again, not because the night hadn't heard—the night heard everything—but because she liked how it felt to say them. Then she added, "And when I do find you, Orion, I'll get my book back, too."

She set her course for the green glow of the Satis House sky-parlor. Up and over roofs, around chimneys, balanced on low walls, across eaves studded with bits of broken glass—studded so to keep night-crawlers like herself away—she moved across the roof-world.

Meg took one last little leap over a narrow gap, and she was on the Satis House roof. It was Meg's fortune that Satis House had no leading on its roof, but was instead shingled with old wood. The Satis House roof was far steeper than she'd imagined, and without the shingles' overlaps and grainy texture, she'd have no foot-hold and might never get to the sky-lights where the green glow wavered.

Crouched spider-like again, Meg inched her way to the lower edge of the sky-light. She attached herself to the window's frame and pulled up until she could peer down into the sky-parlor.

Perhaps it was her vantage point—watching the scene from above—or perhaps it was the queer green light that suffused the scene, but Meg could make no sense, at first, of what she saw in the sky-parlor.

Circles, that's what she saw. One large circle, in the middle of which was a smaller circle, and surrounding the larger circle, more small circles. But these outer circles were moving, nodding and swaying. The circles around were connected by thick lines that over-lapped, some dark and some pale.

O, she realized, hats! Hats crowded around a table, men's hats and ladies' hats, and the circle in the center of the table was no circle but a crystal ball. Two women and three men were sitting around the table, all holding hands, all seemingly concentrated on the crystal ball. The green light shone solely on the table; the rest of the room was a murky dream.

One of the circles now re-captured her focus: a lady's hat. Meg had never seen such a contraption. It was nearly like a Christmas tree, tall and sculptural, and hung, it appeared, with golden ornaments. A hat it must be, but if a hat, a ridiculous one.

What were those people doing? Meg wondered. She stopped her own question with a most obvious answer. She was watching a séance. These hats, and the people under them, had gathered in this sky-parlor to speak with the spirits of the dead. Meg knew about séances from her reading, and had always thought them quite unreasonable. She had spoken to her dead mother many times in the last three years, and while such conversations always soothed her, her mother never responded. The only reply to Meg's words was a resounding silence.

Another of the dark circles looked up—a man's face—not looking up at Meg but towards the other side of the house. The man had a moustache as furry as a monstrous caterpillar. It made him appear rather ridiculous, but his expression chased away Meg's mirth. This was an angry and watchful man.

A noise made Meg raise her head—a scraping sound and a muffled gasp, not from inside the old mansion but from out here, from the other side of the roof's summit. Clearly it had been made by some creature, though human or otherwise it was difficult to discern. Meg didn't know which would frighten her more, a strange animal or a strange human. She decided, despite the chills that crept up her arms, that she would rather be the surpriser in this case, not the surprisee.

Inching away from the sky-light, Meg crawled to the mansion's highest point, where she rested between two tall chimneys. She waited for her loud heart-beat to quiet. Then she peered around the edge of one chimney.

A man appeared to have glued himself face-first to the roof just below the edge of the sky-light. Perhaps, Meg thought, he'd fallen from a hot-air balloon and landed—*splat!*—right here; perhaps he was dead. But no, his head, hat-less, lifted slowly and turned from side to side. Then the man rose to his hands and knees, tilted himself forward, and peered, as Meg had done, into the sky-light's green glow.

Who else would be out past midnight, crawling the surface of the City's roof-world? Who else would be drawn to this strange green glow? Her questions were answered anon; the man looked right at Meg.

His face was a face Meg knew only too well. This was

a face all of London knew only too well. This was a face known all over England, throughout Europe, up and down both the Americas—this was, to put a point on it, one of the most famous faces in the world. And it was also the face of her god-uncle, friend of the family, valued print-shop customer, and bearer of endless boxes of Turkish Delight.

"Mr. Dickens!" Meg shout-whispered.

The man recoiled from the sky-light, gazing all the while at Meg, and he slowly raised himself to his knees. He covered his eyes with an open hand, as if it were midday and the sun blinded him, then squinted into the night.

Mr. Dickens's face lighted with recognition, and he seemed to mouth Meg's name. But instead of speaking, he put a finger to his lips, then beckoned Meg to join him. She turned feet-first and scooted down the roof. Mr. Dickens held out his hand to her.

In a throaty whisper that rattled with caution, he spoke. "Is it you, Miss Meg Pickel?"

"Yes, sir," she whispered. "And is that you, Mr. Charles Dickens?"

"Why, yes, one and the same, Miss Pickel. A pleasure to see you again," he said, and he held out his hand once more.

He shook her hand as he always shook it, as she'd only seen men shake hands. He shook her hand as if they were equals.

"And your father, I trust, is well?"

"Yes, sir. Quite well, thank you. And you, sir?"

"I'm also well, I'm happy to say. It is a lovely night, after all." A short squall of concern crossed his face. "Your father, does he know that you are here at this hour?"

"No, sir, I am afraid he does not. Nor would he be pleased to know it. But you, Mr. Dickens, what brings you out tonight?"

They sat as if on a picnic blanket, their backs to the sky-light's green glow.

"I do not sleep well these nights," he said.

"I have not been sleeping well either," Meg said. "And I was in our roof-garden and saw the glow from Satis House, which I beg to say—"

"Yes," he said. "Exactly what brings me here, too. What a serendipity."

How odd, Meg thought, that they should be conversing as if they had simply crossed paths on the street.

To remind them where they were, and at what time of night, St. Paul's, followed by the City's hundred other bells, struck one o'clock.

Meg and Mr. Dickens flattened themselves against the roof. Now they turned onto their stomachs and inched towards the sky-light, peering over.

"What is it, do you know?" Meg asked. "Is it a séance?"

"I do believe it intends to be."

"But why here?" Meg asked. "In this deserted old heap?"

"What better place than a deserted old heap?"

Both looked down on the scene in the sky-parlor.

"Do you see," he said, pointing, "that woman in the

flowing shawls? She is, I believe, the medium. She is the channel, or so she would have you believe, between the world of the living and the world of those who have already lived quite enough."

"I've read about séances," Meg said. "Tables rise from the floor, walls emit groans, doors are knocked upon by invisible hands."

"Yes, but almost always a sham, I'm afraid. I'm guessing that the rather larger woman in the rather ridiculous hat is the relative of the deceased, most likely her late husband. And she has paid these fine people handsomely for the pleasure of one last chat."

The longer Meg gazed into the sky-parlor, the clearer the scene became to her, and from her vantage up high, surprising elements appeared. She saw now that the eerie glow originated in several spots, each from behind a large piece of furniture.

"This strange light," she said quietly. "It's not really so mysterious, is it?" She pointed to a heavy cupboard.

"Not mysterious at all," Mr. Dickens said. "Bravo, Meg. In fact, far from mysterious. I'd recognize that glow anywhere. It's lime-light, as used in the theater. Only someone has added a pinch of some metallic powder, hence the green portion of the glow. There is no haunting here—only stagecraft."

Above a set of high windows, heavily draped, Meg could now make out a rope and pulley. The rope crossed under a rug and snaked under the corner of the table.

"And that rope," she said. "Is that a trick, too?"

"Aye, Meg, a trick. Though not a very good one. I expect that table to start a-bucking and a-knocking any second."

"But why—" Meg's question was cut short by a sudden commotion in the sky-parlor. The table around which the nodding circles were gathered began to rise from the floor. Squeaks and groans were heard. The medium in her gypsy shawls rose and she seemed about to speak, when a sleek black shape leaped over the table, and the green glow extinguished, as if a chill wind had entered the room. Meg thought the shape that crossed over the table was that of a cat.

All was blackness in the sky-parlor now, but what light had left the room was replaced by screams—both female and male—and the knocking of chairs, followed by the falling to the floor of those same chairs.

A soft blue light then filled the room, and upon this illumination, the screaming figures in the sky-parlor froze, as in the game called Statues. The light that filled the room was a pure blue-white, akin to the glow of all the stars in the sky. Meg looked around to find the hidden source of this new light, but could not.

"Aha!" Mr. Dickens exclaimed, and his long hand pointed to a far corner of the sky-parlor. There, peeking from behind a tapestry, was the laughing, impish face of a young boy, a boy certainly younger than Meg's younger brother, Tobias. The boy held in his arms a black cat, whose head he stroked. The look on the boy's face was, Meg decided, delighted and demonic at once.

Strangely enough, it was the most obvious detail about the boy that registered last with Meg: The boy was the source of the room's blue-white light. Yes, it's true: The boy was glowing. Several more instants passed before Meg was able to calculate what this glowing meant.

There were now more figures in the room than had been there previously. The gypsy woman and the widow were there, each leaning on the other, and the man with the caterpillar moustache, and the other two men at the table, but they were joined now by two boys, both close to Orion's age.

And in the blue light, Meg thought that the taller of the two boys *could* be Orion. She could not see his face from where she gazed down upon him, nor did she recognize his hat or clothes. But these are not our only clues for recognizing those we love. It was in the way this boy held his shoulders, and in the shape of his hands where they darted about. These were the qualities that brought Meg to see Orion. Could this really be him? She wished to call out to him, but was frozen.

And then the blue-white boy leaped out from behind the curtains—as at a surprise party! He unloosed his cat, whose black shadow raced about the room, across the floor, and up the walls faster than the fastest steam locomotive. The boy screeched to a halt and stood with his hands on his hips, head back, laughing.

It was clear to Meg who this boy was, *what* this boy was: a spirit, a true spirit, a ghost. It was also clear to Meg that the members of the sky-parlor séance had come to the same conclusion. The petrified looks on their faces told her that, while they might have come to the sky-parlor for a séance, the arrival of a true spirit was not on that evening's program.

The petrified faces fell to screaming, hands swung blindly in the air and feet began to wheel, and soon the figures in the sky-parlor—the women, the men, and the two young assistants—ran as quickly from the room as the laws of nature would permit. It was a shame that none of them looked back, for they would have seen the blue-white boy chasing along after them and having the grandest fun imaginable.

Then the room was dark again, though the sound of the chase continued to travel down and through the house.

The séance-gang was fleeing, running pell-mell down the stairs and through the mansion's empty rooms, and if she had seen Orion, then he was leaving, too, and she might never see him again. Meg froze.

Meg turned to speak to her companion, tell him about Orion, or what she thought was Orion, but Mr. Dickens was unapproachable. He had fallen onto his back and was howling with laughter.

It was too late, anyway. If Orion had been here, he was gone now, out into the endless streets of London. But Meg was calm. If it was Orion she'd seen—and she could not be sure at this moment—then at least he was still alive, and she could still afford to hope.

From the far side of Satis House a commotion arose, the clatter of voices and foot-falls. It was the sound of the séance-gang emptying out onto the street. Meg and Mr. Dickens listened as their hurried steps clacked down the pavement. Yes: hope.

Mr. Dickens was still laughing.

"Such a spirit, Meg."

"And do you think that it was a true spirit?" When Meg spoke, she discovered that a petite "ha" of Mr. Dickens's laughter had crept into her own voice.

"And what do *you* think, Meg? *Was* that a true spirit?"

"Without a question. I've seen many boys in my life, but no living boy who ever glowed with such a color."

Mr. Dickens rose to his feet, knocked roof-dust from his knees, then offered his hand to Meg.

"That is my delight, Meg. They came to this house promising spirits to our undoubtedly wealthy widow. The only spirits our séance masters believe in, I daresay, are the spirits of pounds, shillings, and pence. *Voilà!* A true spirit arrives. Even the widow, gullible as she is, was not expecting that. O rich, Meg, quite rich that."

A silence settled between them. Meg opened her mouth to speak, but no sound came forth. She was dying to say out loud what she thought she had seen—or rather who: Orion—but could not make herself speak. It seemed dangerous, all of a sudden, as if uttering his name would make that possibility vanish.

"I cannot tell you," Mr. Dickens said, "how much I needed to see what we've just witnessed." Another small laugh erupted from him. "Just the ticket. But I must get you home now, intrepid girl. Or your father will never excuse me."

"But you see—"

"On the way you can tell me what you need to tell me."

Mr. Dickens led Meg gingerly to a corner of the roof and an old exterior staircase, the way he'd come up. He held out his hand to her, to help her navigate the stairs, but she refused him—not out of rudeness but because she was quite capable and wished to prove it. She had come this far on her own.

Meg led her companion through some narrow passages around Satis House—passages only the neighborhood children knew of—and from there they headed back up Tonson Lane. Mr. Dickens stopped to set a match to a rush-light, the bundle of sticky reeds throwing off a weak, warm glow. Enclosed in the bell of this feeble light, they made their way to Meg's home. Something about the enclosing light, the dark homes and alleys all around them, made it easier for Meg to unburden her heart and to explain how she came to be out at this hour.

She told her midnight companion all about Orion, about her determination to find him. She did not tell him that she thought she had seen her brother at the séance. Her certainty—though not her hope—had left her for the moment. Maybe tomorrow.

Mr. Dickens listened to her story. Then he stopped and faced Meg, who naturally stopped, too.

"Orion has been gone six months?"

"Yes, sir," and when she said this, Meg thought she would weep. She had not wept in the longest time.

Mr. Dickens looked struck. He hung his head.

"I have been away so long, I did not know. Six months? An eternity. Our dear Orion?"

Meg watched the news of Orion's disappearance sink into Mr. Dickens. His voice caught in his throat. His shoulders fell. He looked up and away from Meg, staring far down the alley, far beyond what the human eye could see. And then, in the next moment, Meg saw Mr. Dickens pull himself up, re-animated.

"We will find him, Meg. Must. For you and your family, we must. And I shall help you. His recovery might just save all of us. Will you help me find him, Meg?"

"Yes, sir," she said, and she did believe him. His words brought tears to her eyes: hope.

"There, Meg." Mr. Dickens wiped away her tears. "That will do us no good. Tomorrow, we have work to do."

He turned, and Meg turned, and they continued through the dark night.

At last they stood under the sign of CAMPION PICKEL AND CO., OCCASIONAL PRINTERS.

"Meg, you tell your father I'll stop by for a visit

tomorrow. It seems I'll be needing a fresh supply of his special paper. I once again have something to write about—Orion! I'll order my paper first, and then we shall tell him all that we saw tonight. And then"—he touched the side of his nose with one finger—"we shall set about bringing Orion home."

"We will all be happy to see you, sir."

"Now off to bed. And to sleep, too."

Meg let herself into the sleeping house. She latched the door behind her, but did not check any of the other windows or doors. Everyone who was still here when she left was still here now; she heard it in each one's breathing. Only Mulberry stirred at her approach but, good dog that he was, immediately slept again.

She crept into her own bed, still in her dress, pulled the covers under her chin, and prepared herself for another sleepless, tormented night. The image of her brother—*Was it Orion, truly?*—in the Satis House sky-parlor presented itself before her mind. Yes, it could have been him, she thought, Orion. But that was the last thing she thought that night. Sleep gathered her quickly in its arms and rushed away with her at once.

Chapter III

A visit from the Great Man

MEG'S FAMILY'S BUSINESS, Campion Pickel and Co., Occasional Printers, is very near Cheapside Street, but it must be made clear that Cheapside is anything but cheap. In the year of our story, the twenty-fifth year of our Queen's reign, her silver jubilee year—that is, 1862—Cheapside celebrates more lavishly than any other quarter of England. Its shops are rich and varied—goldsmiths, haberdashers, dress-makers, linen-drapers, purveyors of exotic birds. Its broad avenue is not yet broad enough to accommodate the cabs, carriages, and omnibuses that bring customers to these shops. Cheapside is a mirror of London proper—commerce and commotion. Only the high, thin steeple of St. Mary-le-bow church, with its dragon weather-vane, and the Cheapside plane-tree, with its round crown of green, remind us that there are things in the world besides commerce and commotion.

Campion Pickel and Co., though a house of commerce, receives very little of Cheapside's commotion. Walking east from St. Paul's, on the northern side of Cheapside, one finds the narrow entrance to Tonson Lane, where Campion Pickel and Co. may be found, as it has been found for nearly two hundred years. But be watchful, for the entrance to Tonson Lane might easily be mistaken for an un-shut cupboard door, and the careless traveler might stroll right by it.

Too narrow for wheels, no omnibus dares go down Tonson. No rich-man's carriage either, for the rich-man is ever careful of the fine paint and décor for which he's paid so richly. A hired Hansom cab may venture down Tonson Lane, but it may not venture out, for there is no space to turn around in, and the horses of Hansom cabs seem to know only one direction—forward, and quickly so!

Once one enters Tonson Lane, the bustle and glitter of Cheapside fades instantly. The shop-fronts of Tonson do not offer the most fashionable jewelry from Paris, nor men's hats in extravagant heights and shapes, nor gowns of copper or emerald or scarlet silks, nor drapes in velvet brocades, and certainly no macaws or toucans squawking angrily in their gilded cages. No, the shops on Tonson are of a more mundane nature—knife-grinders, lock-smiths, chair-menders, purveyors of books, and Meg's favorite destination, Monsieur Sept-Onze the Chandler.

Two shop-fronts north of Cheapside is Meg's family business and home: CAMPION PICKEL AND CO., OCCASIONAL PRINTERS; CARDS, MENUS, INVITATIONS, FUNERAL MEMENTOS,

AND THE LIKE, AT YOUR REQUEST. To ensure that the customers of expensive Cheapside might find Campion Pickel and Co., etc., a painted wooden sign shows its best face to Cheapside.

Meg loved this sign. For her it was no advertisement; it had always meant home. Only since Orion's disappearance had the sign brought her any sadness, for the sign was decorated with an image of Orion the Hunter, his bow pulled taut. Meg's brother Orion was not named for the celestial Orion, but for their grand-father Orion. And he was named for the first Orion, that is, the Orion Pickel who built this print-shop off of Cheapside after the Great Fire of 1666. The Christian name on the sign has changed through the generations, but the symbol of Orion the Hunter, its nine stars tracing the regal outline of the constellation, has remained. Each time Meg entered the print-shop, she was reminded of who was not to be found inside.

The visitor to Campion Pickel and Co., gazing through the window of the shop's public face, could never guess that through the faded curtains behind the counter, on this very day, the Great Man of London, Mr. Charles Dickens, was sitting now with all the Pickel family. They were discussing—much to Meg's chagrin—that most humble and elegant of materials, without which life in bustling and glittering London would be impossible: paper!

But before we turn our attention to Mr. Dickens on this morning, we must first take notice of a small oak chair occupied by Meg. Meg's countenance was placid; she

Campion Pickel
&Co.

seemed satisfied to be sitting in her usual chair. Yet Meg was not satisfied at all. While she usually loved to listen to Mr. Dickens go on about anything in the world, she would rather have had him going on about Orion and Satis House and . . . Orion.

Last night, Mr. Dickens had suggested to Meg that it would go easier on her father if they spoke of simpler matters before resorting to tales of spirits and séances and disappeared brothers. Meg had agreed readily, but was sorry now that she had. Please speak of Orion, she wished to blurt, but Mr. Dickens seemed settled on speaking of paper.

"Ardoise!" Mr. Dickens said, slapping his chair's arm. "I must have my *Ardoise,* Campion, and I must have it soon!"

Meg, Aunt Julia, and Tobias sat in various chairs around the larger chair in which Mr. Dickens sat as guest of the house. Meg's father, shrouded in his leather apron, worked at the enormous black-iron printing press. Mulberry the dog rested at Mr. Dickens's feet.

"You shall have your paper, Charles," Meg's father said. "*The Montaigne* has just docked. I can have it by sun-down. How many reams?"

"Twenty!" Again Mr. Dickens slapped the chair's arm.

"Twenty?!?" Meg's father turned from the printing press. "Why, that's ten thousand sheets. How many novels are you planning to write? Ten at a time?"

A smile leaped from Mr. Dickens's salt-and-pepper beard. He held up one finger.

"Only one, Campion. One novel a time. But a writer is

not a writer if he doesn't waste ten sheets of foolscap for every one he keeps."

"Or *she* keeps," Meg said. Her tone was a bit stiff. Mr. Dickens looked at her, smiled.

"Correct, Meg. Or *she*."

"But tell us, Charles," Meg's father said. "Why *Ardoise*? In all the years you've purchased paper from our family, you have only ever purchased *Ardoise*. Though you are a man of means, it's cost you a pretty penny."

Meg, Aunt Julia, and Tobias all leaned forward. Mr. Dickens did that to people when he spoke. People listened carefully, hungrily. Even grumpy Meg leaned forward. It was hard to resist Mr. Dickens.

"Ardoise," Mr. Dickens said. He said the word as if it had a sweet taste to it. He leaned back and to the side in his chair. His body told Meg, or any listener, that *Ardoise,* whatever it might be, was an item that brought immense pleasure to him.

"Ardoise, you see, isn't only paper. In fact, it is hardly paper at all, it is so extraordinary. *Ardoise* is a vast plain of fresh snow, a newly frozen pond, the ultimate morning-blue sky. Across the blue-tinged field of *Ardoise* my pen does not skip or gouge—it flows. But it does so with the tiniest scratch of the pen's nib, as—if I may return to my bungled metaphors—the sharpest skating blade catches an edge for traction. A confident flow that permits no smudging. It is a perfect paper, my *Ardoise*."

Meg nearly applauded. Mr. Dickens was renowned for

the public performance of his own works; all around the world audiences were brought to tears, laughter, gasps of horror when he read from *A Christmas Carol* or *Oliver Twist*. Meg had never seen one of his performances, had only read admiring reviews in the newspapers, but today she felt as if she were seated in a theater. And he was only talking about paper! His hands carefully described the movements his words predicted; they flowed through the air, gouged the ice, smoothed the creamy texture of the paper. And his voice! It glided along the new snow, rose in admiration of *Ardoise,* despaired at the defects of other papers, and when Mr. Dickens discussed the catching of the pen's nib, his voice caught the peculiar texture of that sound, the scratch of pen on paper.

Impatient as she was, Meg was also leery of telling her father about last night. While her father might be glad to learn that she had seen Orion—she was positive of it this morning!—he could only know this if he knew she'd been prowling the roof-world by herself. Since Orion's disappearance, her father had bristled at the mere idea of any one of the family leaving home unattended. And it had been past midnight when Meg was out. What would he make of that? There would be trouble for her in it.

"And you," Mr. Dickens erupted. "You, my old friend Campion, and your father, too, only you know of *Ardoise* and where to get it. I swear, if *Ardoise* suddenly sprouted like leaves on the Cheapside plane-tree, I'd still come here to have it."

Not more paper! Meg's knees rattled her chair.

"And did you know, it bears no water-mark, no sign at all of the paper-maker's hand? It is a paper made only for writing. And *Ardoise* is the perfect size. Seven inches by nine inches is the paper I need. There are larger foolscaps, I know. But if you don't restrict the size of your foolscap, how can you restrict the size of your imagination? Now, foolscap, there's a ripe word."

Meg felt a scowl crossing her face; Aunt Julia must have caught it.

"Meg, dear," Aunt Julia said. "I believe the tea's ready. Would you kindly?"

Meg flashed out the print-shop's back door, up the stairs, and into the family's rooms. She came back into the print-shop bearing a tea service of cups as mis-matched as the chairs on which the family and its guest sat.

Mr. Dickens was still talking, but not yet about last night. Would he never get to the point!

"Can't you just see him by his name? Prentiss Foolscap, journeyman printer. A grand name for a foolish character. As it should be."

Meg's father chuckled, repeating the name under his breath. He'd stepped away from the printing-press and pulled up a stray chair. Meg set the tea-tray on a nearby workbench.

"Miff or Tiff, Mr. Dickens?" she asked.

"Miff, please, Miss Pickel."

Meg poured around, Miff-ing and Tiff-ing. Each member of her family had a strong preference, believing that milk in the cup first, followed by tea—that is, Miff—or tea in first, followed by milk—that is, Tiff—improved, if not one's whole mood, at least the flavor of the tea. Meg, like Orion, preferred Tiff.

There was silence while the company took its first sips. But it was clear that Mr. Dickens was going to speak again, raising one finger to alert his audience. Meg had to cut him off. She'd done her duty; she'd been courteous, she'd poured the tea. It was time to talk about last night.

"Now Prentiss Foolscap—"

"Mr. Dickens," Meg said, and rather much too curtly. Aunt Julia shot her a look that hovered between angry and amused. "May I ask how you've been sleeping?"

Mr. Dickens turned and fixed his gaze on Meg. A sly smile peek-a-booed from under his moustache.

"A provocative question, Miss Pickel." Mr. Dickens sat back in his chair and picked up his tea again. "Perhaps you'd best answer it."

Anxious as she was to get to the story of last night, Meg had not expected to begin.

"Well," Meg said. She sat up straight and nodded both at her father and at Aunt Julia. "Well," she said again. "Father, Aunt Julia, I must tell you in all honesty—Mr. Dickens has not been sleeping well, not at all."

Meg's father and Aunt Julia shared a quizzical glance. Mulberry removed himself from Mr. Dickens's feet and went to Meg, placing one paw on her knee and staring up, as if her serious tone worried him. Meg scratched his scruffy head.

"It's true, I'm afraid," Meg said. "Mr. Dickens has not been sleeping well, not one bit. And neither have I."

The work-room was all silence.

"And there lies the tale," Mr. Dickens said.

It took quite a long time to tell the entire story. Meg and Mr. Dickens frequently looked back and forth from one to the other, though Meg felt more secure telling the story when she was not looking at anyone.

Mr. Dickens spoke, as he always did, with great animation. His hands flew, his language flew, and the story seemed to inhabit the room.

But Meg would not be overpowered by the Great Man; it was her story, too. She described the ghost-cat, the caterpillar moustache, the gypsy's shawls, the hideous gold-ornamented hat of the grieving widow, the obvious sham of the séance and how the widow had surely been hood-winked. She wanted very much to continue from that point, to tell her father about Orion, but still she hesitated. She had nearly convinced herself she'd seen him, but when she heard the words in her head, she grew less certain.

Aunt Julia put down her tea. Mulberry looked from face to face, one eyebrow raised in doubt. And Tobias wore a look that was, at once, astonished at Meg's derring-do and frightened for its consequences.

Aunt Julia spoke.

"But Charles," she began, leaning forward and patting him on the knee. "You still haven't said: Why is it you cannot sleep?"

"Julia Spragg," Mr. Dickens said, a-twinkle. "You were never one to let a good story get in the way of the truth. Very well. It's as simple as—" He snapped his fingers. "I cannot sleep because I cannot write. *Great Expectations* is quite finished, a perfect grave-stone of a book, dead and such. And no new novel has risen up to greet me, and that is a state I cannot abide. So I do as I have always done. I prowl the City at night, until I trip upon a story. And I do believe I have tripped upon it."

Meg was waiting for her father to speak. She knew that Aunt Julia had spoken first so that her father would have time to collect himself.

"And you, Meg," her father said finally. "What makes you sleepless?"

Meg paused; gathered.

"It's Orion, Father. I cannot sleep for Orion." It was all she could manage to say for now.

"I see," he said. "And I under—"

"And here is our real story, Campion," Mr. Dickens said. He stood and went to Meg's father. "Orion, that's the real story, and it breaks my heart. You know how fond I have grown of him, what promise he shows as a man of letters. I am tempted to be cross with you, that you did not come to me for help. You know I would have done anything in my power to help. And I will. But I cannot be cross with you. You are much too saddened by this, and I am guilty of being away too long. My word on it, Campion. I will do all I can."

"Charles, I . . ." But her father could say nothing more. Meg saw the dark cloud lower around him, the cloud that had surrounded him these past six months.

"We did everything we could, Charles," her father squeaked out. "He's gone, Charles, disappeared. It is too late for help."

A thousand versions of these same words flew through Meg's head—the only thing her father had said in six months. She would not listen to them any longer.

"I saw him, Father," Meg said, and the rush of these words surprised even her. "Orion. He was at Satis House, I'm certain of it. He was a member of the séance-gang, one of the boys. You remember, Mr. Dickens, they came in at the end. I didn't say anything last night, but I'm sure of it. If you had been there, you would have recognized him, too, the way he moved, held himself. He was there, Father. He is alive. We must go find him."

A phrase often used in such instances is so quiet one could hear a pin drop. The quiet that now engulfed the work-room of Campion Pickel and Co. was so overpowering that one might have heard the ghost of the shadow of an idea of a pin dropping. Yes, that's how quiet it was. Even Mr. Dickens was quiet.

Meg nearly wept at her words, but held herself. If she would do what she wanted, she needed to show strength.

She was determined—had been so since she awoke this morning—to return to Satis House at night, with or without Mr. Dickens. Orion was surely no longer there. But the séance-gang had left so quickly, perhaps they had left behind some clue, some evidence of Orion's whereabouts. Yes, she would return to Satis House, alone or otherwise.

Her father looked up at her; there were tears in his eyes.

"You saw him, Meg?"

"I believe I did, yes."

And that was all the conversation they needed, Meg and her father. He was not a man of many words, but the words he did speak spoke loudly. He was asking her if she was telling the truth, and she told him, as much with her tone as with her words, that she was.

"Let me guess: Satis House. You wish to go back. You wish to start your search there."

Meg nodded.

"And if you'll allow it, Campion," Mr. Dickens said, "I shall accompany her. She'll be safe with me."

"No question of that," Aunt Julia said. "You are a good friend, sir. Campion, we must let them. If there is any chance at all that he was there, we must find out. I say yes, let them go—no, command them to go. Meg believes she has seen Orion!"

Her father stood, looked down at Meg, and then at the wall of the work-shop. He seemed to expect to find a window there, but there was none. She knew this gaze of her father's, a gaze that saw both near and far. He was making a decision, and it was a difficult one.

He smoothed his waist-coat with the palms of his hands. He had made up his mind.

"It's decided then," Meg's father said. He was standing straighter now, his face clear, open. The cloud had lifted. "Tonight, I assume, if I know my Meg well enough, and if I know my Charles well enough. You are both impatient."

Meg thought that Tobias had fallen asleep in his chair, he'd grown so quiet. But he sprang up now.

"I want to go, too, I want to go, too!" he was yelling. This set Mulberry to barking and leaping. Mulberry was always keen for an adventure.

Plans were made—no, Tobias would not go, only Meg and Mr. Dickens together—and tea was had, and for hours, it seemed, the story of last night was told again and again, if only to get to that part where Meg saw the long-lost Orion. If only so that each of them could ask Meg one more time, "And do you really think it was him?"

She did think it was him, and she said so every time.

Eventually the excitement and noise faded. It was time for the evening to end.

"Charles," Meg's father said. "Are you staying in London? Tell me where, and I'll have your *Ardoise* delivered. Or shall I send it on to Gad's Hill?"

"Ah yes, Campion. No, not to Gad's Hill." He paused. "But I'm afraid there's more than one mystery about. I'll pick up the *Ardoise* myself. I'm afraid I cannot tell you where I lodge. Please, all of you, if you'd be so kind, remember this: You have not seen Mr. Dickens in a very long time."

Mr. Dickens stood and drew an imaginary cape about him. Then he ducked, theatrically, out of the print-shop's back door.

Meg watched the door shut behind him. She wondered for a moment what Mr. Dickens was hiding that he had to be so mysterious. But that thought soon fell away and was replaced by the one and only thought that mattered—Orion. They *would* find him.

Chapter IV

A dark night with some startling illuminations

When Mr. Dickens returned to Campion Pickel and Co., just after Meg and her family had finished with supper, the sky was that twi-light purple-blue that only the sky can create, a color unmatched elsewhere in Nature. Dusk it was, when Mr. Dickens arrived, when the world of day and the world of night collide.

Meg was anxious to leave for Satis House straight off, but there were the "niceties," as her father called them, to be attended to. Greetings, polite inquiries—such conventions bewildered Meg at times like these. Why couldn't they simply get on with it, for heaven's sake? Why the civility when there were more pressing matters? First, they were off in search of Orion, and shouldn't that demand urgency? Second, they were returning to—and entering!—a decaying old heap of a mansion that was clearly home to at least one spirit, and this made Meg eager to proceed, lest she should lose all courage. But no, her father and Aunt Julia and Mr. Dickens insisted upon playing at dull and silly grown-up chatter. Grown-ups were often too thick for anyone's good.

Finally, the niceties were concluded—even Mulberry had demanded a thorough head-scratching from Mr. Dickens—and all was set to go except—

"Meg!" Mr. Dickens cried as if he'd seen a spirit already. "Do you have your notebook and your pen?"

He pulled from his vest a portable inkwell and several sharpened goose quills.

"But why should I need a notebook? I've a very good memory," Meg replied.

"Because we are going on an adventure. We must keep note of all that we see—anything might be a clue. The smallest grain of dust might lead us to your brother. A notebook is a caution against forgetting."

Since Orion had disappeared Meg had written in a notebook every day, and what she wrote was a record of everything she could remember about her brother. The way he slurped his soup, looking around slyly as if no one noticed; the day he slipped on the ice outside the Guildhall, bruising himself badly, but still laughing; the concentration on his face when he set a line of type; all she could remember, no matter how miniscule. She had lost her brother—for now—and was determined to keep her memories alive. The actual notebook, too, helped keep Orion alive to Meg, for he had made it for her. It was a tall, bulky notebook, whose boards were covered with stitched-together leaves from the Cheapside plane-tree, which he'd then covered with a clear resin. The binding that held the rough pages was simply twine passed through holes in the boards and pages. Small branches from the plane-tree ran under the twine, for a decorative touch. Paper, Orion told Meg when he gave her the notebook on her last birthday, paper came from trees, and he had wanted her notebook to look as much like a tree as possible. Meg had practically filled its pages in the last six months.

It was this notebook Meg retrieved, in a heart's beat, from her chamber upstairs. She had also placed three carpenter's pencils in the pocket of her dress.

Mr. Dickens pulled Orion's notebook from under Meg's arm. He examined it thoroughly, and with obvious admiration.

"It's beautiful, Meg," he said. "And most original. I've half a mind to steal it from you."

"It was a gift from Orion," she said. "He made it for me."

"I see," he said, admiring the book once again, turning it over in his hands, not so much for the beauty of the thing, Meg imagined, but with respect for Orion.

She eased the book from him.

"However," Mr. Dickens said, "it's too large for our purposes. Your notebook, while beautiful, is a desk book, a house book. A reporter of the street requires a book that's as nimble as she must be"—Meg smiled when he said "she"—"and I should know. I've been recording the streets for nearly four decades now. Here."

He withdrew from an inside pocket a narrow tablet bound in green cloth. Rather than opening right to left, this notebook opened bottom to top. Mr. Dickens held the tablet in his left hand, between thumb and crooked fingers. He aped writing across it with his right hand.

"A reporter's notebook," he said. "It's small, easily concealed, and fits in one hand. The perfect device for our adventure. Here. This is yours."

"Thank you, sir." It was plain to Meg how perfect this notebook was. She slipped it into her pocket, and her pocket accepted it as a glove accepts a hand.

"And your pen?" he asked.

"O I never use a pen," she said. "I always use a pencil."

She took one of her sharpened pencils from her pocket and handed it to Mr. Dickens.

"You see," she said, "you never have to fuss with ink, or clean up spilled ink, which is inevitable. And as Father says, pencil will last much longer than ink. Ink will fade, turn brown, eventually disappear. Not so with the writing from a pencil. A pencil is the perfect writing instrument. You may have this pencil, if you like. A fair trade, sir."

"Is this true, Campion?" Mr. Dickens asked.

Her father laughed and shrugged.

"Meg knows all the printers' secrets, Charles. She is quite correct. Eternity belongs to the pencil."

Mr. Dickens took the pencil and rolled it in his fingers.

He stared at it as if it were a treasure from the tomb of an Egyptian pharaoh.

"Meg Pickel, Meg Pickel," he said. "I am astonished. Campion, Aunt Julia, regard. Mulberry, Tobias, look on. A miracle. I have been a reporter, a recorder, and a scribbler since I was sixteen, and it has never occurred to me once to use a pencil. And yet the pencil has always been there—hidden in plain view. This is a revolution, is what it is. This is perfection; this is a pencil! A fair trade, indeed!"

Everyone was laughing, except Mulberry, who wagged his black-and-white tail.

"And now may we please go?" Meg asked.

"Ahead, Meg, lead on."

And it was a good thing that Mr. Dickens had agreed to leaving just then, for Meg was half-way out the print-shop door.

After Mr. Dickens left them that morning, Meg had done her best to occupy herself. She did her chores, she did her reading, she ran her father's errands, she helped Aunt Julia with the roof-garden, she played both Skittles and Lamp-post Swing with Tobias, she spoke and nodded to all she met. But these were the gyrations of a marionette. All day Meg was nowhere in the world but inside herself.

And what was inside her all day was a buzzing wasp-nest of words. *Satis House, Orion, séance, spirit, secrets, widow,* etc., a hive of words all bumping and humming and leaving and returning—*zzzt, zzzt, zzzt*—nothing but words, and each word following a different flight in her imagination. It was too crazed a jumble to make sense of the words. The only stillness in her that day was a picture, as clear and sharp as a daguerreotype: Orion seen from the Satis House roof. She glared and glared at the image, but could not set it in motion, could not make it turn its face to her. She believed it was Orion she saw last night, and yet she was afraid she only believed this because she so wanted it to be true.

Now, under the cavernous blue-purple sky, Meg and Mr. Dickens spied Satis House, still shrouded in black. They would not venture the roof-world tonight. Mr. Dickens was certain that another, safer entrance could be found, and Meg's father had insisted upon this.

They strolled down cozy Tonson Lane, enthralled by the warm, lovely evening. Yellow gas-light and candle-glow flickered from the upper rooms; all the shops were closed. The only sounds were the calls of the cart-men on their final rounds—Fish! Strawberries! Pies! Muffins!

"Meg," Mr. Dickens said. "Why did you not tell me last night that you had seen Orion? Are you certain?"

"I am as certain as I can be," Meg said. "But I am afraid, too."

"And why is that?"

"Either way, it portends ill," she said. "If I did not see Orion, then he is still lost to us. And if I did see him, then he is a party to criminals and fake séances. Neither of these possibilities gives me much joy."

Meg had not known she felt this way until she spoke the words. She was so excited at the thought that she'd seen her brother again—that he was alive!—she had not entirely reckoned what that might mean.

They stopped some distance from Satis House and stared up at the decaying old heap. Mr. Dickens put a reassuring hand on her shoulder.

"I know your brother," he said, "and he is no criminal. If he was at the séance last night, it was against his will. You know that, Meg, as I do, deep in your heart."

A breath of cool, chilled air swept through her: relief. It was true; Orion would never act dishonorably, unless he were coerced.

"What do *you* think happened to Orion?"

"I no longer can guess at it," she said. "We stopped such guessing games a long time ago. For weeks after his disappearance, it was all we talked about at home. Runaway? Kidnap? Murder? We invented every possibility for these scenes. But we soon stopped such stories. And for all those weeks we searched and searched, running ourselves ragged. But to no avail. Orion would not be found. He is simply gone, Father says, and he refuses to entertain any other notion. We must accept, that's what Father says. So we are quiet now; only mourn."

"Ah, yes, your father," he said. "He almost seems to have disappeared, too."

It was true. A man who looked very much like her father ran the print-shop, kissed her and Tobias on the head, helped them with their home-studies, but he hardly seemed their father anymore. Another loss for the family. If they could find Orion, perhaps Father would return as well.

"And you, sir. What do you imagine has happened to Orion? I know your books; you've seen so much of the world. You know London. What's happened, pray tell me?"

Mr. Dickens shook his head and turned again to Satis House.

"I have seen the world, true. And such knowledge can be frightening. Runaway? Kidnap? Murder? Any or all is possible. I understand your father's sorrow and why he will not dwell in such possibilities, which are endless. So I try to be guided by what I see, and only that. What I saw was what you saw, and that will have to do for us both. Let us believe with all our hearts that it is Orion we saw, and we shall follow 'til disproved."

It was strange yet comforting to have this discussion with Mr. Dickens. He invented such stories for his novels, each a fabrication. But she and Mr. Dickens were speaking of a true story, a real brother who had gone missing. The world of novels and the real world seemed to be coming together. This gave Meg renewed hope. In Mr. Dickens's novels, happy endings, especially for those characters of good hearts, abounded.

Meg nodded, looking at the ground now. Then she smiled.

"Yes, let's believe that I saw him."

"Very well, but standing here won't help us. On." Mr. Dickens set off again. "Let us find evidence; let us be detectives. Belief can only do so much."

They closed the distance to Satis House, not speaking, and stopped below it. The mansion rose dark and crooked against the sky.

"Why *Satis* House?" She put an emphasis on the important word, making the inquiry clear—why was the house so named?

"A true question, Meg. It is a puzzling name, isn't it? Sounds ugly on the ear. Let's think."

His hands behind his back, Mr. Dickens looked up, as if the answers were written in the heavens. Meg looked up, too—no stars. London's gas-light glow obscured them.

"*Satus*, from the Latin," he said, "meaning 'enough.' Satisfied, satisfaction, sated. Perhaps a house that was meant to be enough."

"Or not enough?" Meg proposed. "Which is why it's abandoned? When I was a child"—Meg blushed in the dark; she felt childish saying this—"before I could read, of course, I thought it was 'Saddest' House. The saddest house that ever was."

"That may be wrong in its spelling, but certainly correct in its meaning. It is the saddest house."

"But it makes a good place for a séance," Meg said, "doesn't it? I should think no one has used this house for years. Who would even know?"

"No one," he said. "A perfect ruse. Our fake mediums could never have expected two sleepless humans and one sleepless spirit to join them."

From this vantage, from below rather than from above, the Satis House seemed much more imposing. The wall that guarded it seemed mountainous, and the iron bars and bricked-up windows of the lower floors seemed medieval. Saddest Castle, Meg thought.

"The time has come," Mr. Dickens said. "Our adventure awaits."

"Open sesame," Meg said. But the wall refused to open. They would have to take the fire-stairs again.

"Aha!" Mr. Dickens said and scooted them into a narrow opening and down a narrower passage between wall and house. Both Meg and Mr. Dickens turned to the side, flattened. It was near-black in the passage, and Meg was on the verge of requesting a retreat, when Mr. Dickens found a door with one window-pane broken out. He reached into the jagged space and the door creaked open.

"Servants' entrance. Always your easiest entry."

Meg huddled next to him and peeked into what seemed the kitchen. All was black. This would be an opportune moment, she considered, to turn around and go home. It is at such moments that the wise, standing on the thresholds of decaying old heaps of mansions, turn and leave, rush back to their homes and retreat under their bed-clothes. It takes a dose of thoughtlessness to go forward at such moments. And thank heavens for that, for no books would ever be written if it weren't for those characters who did not look before they leaped.

Mr. Dickens pulled two rush-lights from his pocket and handed one to Meg. He struck a match against brick, lit the bundled reeds, and our heroes were trapped in a globe of yellow light.

The dismal, disused, discarded kitchen soaked up the frail rush-light as the desert sands soak up rain. The kitchen illuminated, but grudgingly. *Dismal, disused, discarded,* these were the only words to describe the scene. Pots, pans, cups, plates, utensils of all sorts lay scattered everywhere, and on top of these, and every surface of the kitchen, the thickest coating of Nature's own dust.

Mr. Dickens stood transfixed for a moment. Meg was anxious to continue. If she didn't keep moving, she worried, she might end up forever in this lost kitchen, coated with dust herself.

"The sky-parlor," Meg said.

"Yes, then. Up we go."

They entered a dark hallway, then turned, then another but broader hallway, then turned again, and came finally to a grand hallway, where they found the main stairs, which rose, wide and regal and disused, up through the center of the house. Meg and Mr. Dickens did not speak, only watched, as if their own voices were now dismal, disused, discarded.

At the foot of the grand stairway, a coffin-case clock had stopped at twenty minutes to nine, though it refused to say on which day it had stopped, nor whether it was twenty minutes to nine in the morning or in the evening. Meg wondered who had last wound it.

Silently they agreed to go up the stairs, so up they went, step by step, and round and round. The dust had so conquered this house that neither its stair-steps nor floorboards creaked, and neither did their foot-falls make a sound.

At each landing, their feeble lights showed little of the floor on which they trespassed, only the shadowy shapes of walls, doors, possible rooms. At each landing Meg saw only one thing, a coffin-case clock, enormous, identical to the first clock, and like the first clock, frozen at twenty minutes to nine. And at each landing, as the darkness increased behind her, as she moved farther from the open kitchen door and deeper into the unknown, the more frightened Meg became.

Without thinking, she took hold of the sleeve of Mr. Dickens's coat. He patted her hand.

"Thank you, Meg," he said. "I am in need of a little comfort."

Meg felt at that moment what her own fear had kept from her: Mr. Dickens was shaking. It was an unusual comfort for Meg to know that Mr. Dickens was frightened, too. It made her feel less foolish, though not so comforted that she abandoned all caution.

Once more, without a word between them, they agreed

on a course of action, and were now stepping—or running, truth be told—up the grand staircase.

At the fourth turn of the stairs, they finally reached the sky-parlor.

The last violet light of the summer sky mingled with the yellowish glow of London's night-light and cast a distinct, though not unlovely, hue over the broad room. The two enormous sky-lights seemed, tonight, to glow from the outside rather than from inside. The coffin-case clock on the landing here also read twenty minutes to nine.

Meg and Mr. Dickens stepped into the hush of the sky-parlor.

"Well, Meg," Mr. Dickens said, his voice cracking. "What do we do now?"

"I suppose we look for clues," she said. "Anything that might lead us to Orion, make us certain that he was here. Perhaps the identity of the séance-gang. Through them we might find Orion. And let us hope that the clues don't come looking for us."

"Spirits, you mean? You're afraid of them?"

"Yes."

"Don't be," he said. "I have met, I'm happy to say, many spirits in my time. And none has ever harmed me. Nor frightened me. I'm much more frightened of the living."

"Not afraid of spirits?"

"A spirit knows to whom it speaks. It may want to frighten you—if you are in need of frightening, as happened at the séance last night. Or it may wish to speak with you. Spirits can get terribly lonely, and often have much to say."

"Do we call out for the boy's spirit? Ask him about Orion?" Meg could scarcely believe she was speaking so calmly about spirits—a matter that would seem to call for great excitement. But there was comfort in the matter-of-fact tone with which Mr. Dickens spoke of the spirits. O she was still frightened, but, reasonably so.

"No. We wait. This is his realm. In the offing, we look for clues." Mr. Dickens looked down at Meg, put his hand on her shoulder. "Are you ready for this, Meg? There is no harm in using discretion, you know."

Meg looked about. A good part of her wanted to leave immediately; the other good part of her wished to stay. She took a deep breath and straightened her shoulders. That was all it took.

"We must stay," she said as boldly as her fear permitted.

The room opened up before them, revealing itself. It was filled with furniture, pieces of every kind of furniture against the walls. In the center of this city of furniture, the overturned séance table lay, still connected to the rope that ran behind the drapes. Mr. Dickens went to that, knelt, and began to examine the table. He was already taking notes.

"Voilà," he said. "Our first clue, a calling card."

He held out the tiny card to Meg. She read the name on it: MRS. JOHN PODSNAP, BELLE FONTAINE PLACE.

"What do you think?" Meg asked, handing the card to Mr. Dickens.

"Our widow, would be my guess. Con-artists rarely leave their calling cards."

"We should pay a call on this lady," Meg said. "Perhaps she will know where Orion is."

"A cozy idea, but I'm not so certain our Mrs. Podsnap would be happy to see us. By now, I imagine, she knows she was duped. Her shame might only lead to silence. It's not her we need, it's those who shamed her, our séance-gang."

Mr. Dickens went back to work. He was examining the pulley mechanism on the underside of the table.

Meg knew that he was right. If they could find the séance-gang, they would be that much closer to Orion. Still, she took out her notebook and pencil, and scribbled the name "Mrs. John Podsnap."

She looked up and was drawn to a long dinner table shoved under the short eaves of the slanted ceiling.

There was, it seemed, an impressive centerpiece on the table, and Meg squinted to see its shape in the dim light. She stopped dead. The centerpiece was moving, she thought, pulsating as though alive. Her breath caught; her blood froze.

It was a cake, and Meg almost laughed when she realized what she was looking at. A cake! But it was a very old cake, a very old bridal cake, and the white shroud over it was the gauzy net of many a spider's web. And what made the cake pulsate so was the movement of the spiders who had spun the web. The spiders were speckle-legged, with blotchy bodies as big as shillings, and they worked in quiet.

Meg knew, without knowing the day on which it

happened, the time, at least. This cake had been here since twenty minutes to nine on some day long ago.

In the silence, she could almost hear the spiders spinning, and out of that silence, she heard the mice in the walls, and the *tap-tap* of one lone beetle skittering across a marble hearth.

Meg turned to tell all of this to Mr. Dickens—he was still on his knees by the table, still taking notes—when the servant's bell above her rang out, and in the next seconds, other bells rang out through the house.

Mr. Dickens stood, and Meg ran to him, the two of them surrounded by the automatic bells. As suddenly as they began, the bells ceased.

Meg looked up at the sky-light, her eye drawn by a movement there, and Mr. Dickens looked up, too.

From the great center-beam of the roof a woman in white hung from a noose, swaying ever so gently. Meg opened her mouth to scream, but the woman in white was gone, vanished. Meg figured it was a passing cloud and a trick of the eye. At least, that is what she hoped.

"Calm, Meg," Mr. Dickens said, his voice a soft breath. "It's just a test. The spirits are testing us. Remember, they will not harm you. Can not."

"I'm not afraid. Simply startled. As are you, I think. Look."

The black cat-shape Meg had seen last night crouched silently before them. Blacker than any black in this London night, so black that its black was almost a form of light.

Rather than frighten her, the ghost-cat's presence soothed her, and Meg sensed, too, that Mr. Dickens was breathing easier. And rather than streak across the floor, tonight the ghost-cat merely padded towards Meg, circled twice around her ankles, and settled imperiously at her side. Meg felt the faintest brush of fur against her dress's hem.

But there was not time to pet the ghost-cat, for the ghost-boy was stepping forward to meet them now. He was evolving from plain air the way mist evolves on a clear window. The more of him that appeared, the brighter the blue star-glow of his apparition.

He stood smiling, legs apart, seemingly quite satisfied with himself. Meg and Mr. Dickens were not smiling, but gape-mouthed, their legs locked.

"Welcome, welcome," the boy cried. "Guv'ner, miss. So nice of you to come. I was hoping you might."

He flourished his soft cap and took a deep bow. Meg thought his manner charming, but not quite natural.

Mr. Dickens stepped forward.

"Good evening," he said. "And many thanks for your most gracious welcome. We hope we do not intrude."

"O not at all," the boy said, a moon-smile on his face. "Watch this."

Like all young boys striving to be polite, the ghost-boy could only maintain his reserve for so long before he had to move again, and he flew about the room, round and round. Meg and Mr. Dickens, delighted, watched. He landed in front of them again, quite proud of his achievement. Meg sensed the ghost-cat near her feet. It bristled at the ghost-boy's behavior.

"This is my friend—" Mr. Dickens began.

"O but I know who you are. You are him and she is her. I know all about you."

"And you are?" Meg asked. The question popped out of her. She found she was not afraid in the least.

"Why, I am a spirit!" Again the ghost-boy swelled with pride, and his blue-white, star-white glow glowed more brightly.

"Surely you have a name. After all, I am Meg Pickel, and this is Charles Dickens."

"Yes, it's true." The ghost-boy was bouncing now, a little jig. "I do have a name. But I have forgotten it. I have been dead too long. I need no name now. I am a dead-child, that is all that you need to know."

"But how shall we call you then?" Meg stepped towards him. "Every creature has a name."

"Then call me Dick Whittington," he said. He snapped his fingers, and the black-cat leaped, in one fluid arc, to his shoulder. "And this is my cat."

"And what shall I call your cat?" Meg asked, almost laughing.

"Why, Dick Whittington's cat should be a good enough name."

Mr. Dickens stepped forward.

"Are you the same Dick Whittington," he asked, "who

would become mayor of London? The same Dick Whittington we still speak of centuries later?"

"Not the same," he said, "but same enough."

"No other name?" Meg asked with impatience. He was, like all boys, rather infuriating. Why wouldn't he speak plainly?

Dick Whittington's blue-white twinkle dimmed.

"I think I was once called Peter."

Then he flew around the room again, around and around furiously. The cat re-joined Meg, licking its ghost-paws in a show of embarrassment.

Dick Whittington stopped before them again. Meg thought of him there, his hands on his hips, as the impetuous leader of a gang of lost-boy pirates.

Mr. Dickens began to pace. He was concentrating furiously, stabbing at his notebook with his pencil.

"How did you come to be here, Dick?" he finally asked.

"I died."

"Of what?" Meg asked.

"Of what all children die of, I suppose. No one to look over me."

"You're an orphan then?" Meg asked.

"O I was and I am and will be forever. Orphaned as a child, I came to London to seek my fortune, and wound up in the kitchen here, working for the baddest of bad men. He never fed me, he only worked me. When I was ill with what did kill me, he ignored me. But I was being killed before that."

Meg fought back the swelling in her heart.

"I am sorry for you, Dick Whittington," she said.

"O ho!" he cried, and flew again, and while he flew he continued to speak. "Don't be sorry for me, miss, nor you, sir. I am happier now as a spirit than I ever was in life. As a spirit, I don't toil, I don't weep, I don't hunger. As a spirit, I can be a boy again, and I am, and I play all day, play for all time."

"And do you not miss this earth?" Mr. Dickens asked.

"Not one moment," Dick Whittington said. "What is to be missed for a child on *your* earth? The orphanage? The work-house? The mill? The being all alone? No. I've seen what life can do to children. No, sir, I beg of you, allow me to remain dead. I shall be a free child, at play, and I shall play for all children."

"But you can't mean that," Meg said.

"I do, and mean much more than that, but there's no time now, miss. Let me say what I must before I fall back to the other side."

"I thought you were forever," Meg said.

"I am a child, and so have only a little time. A little time I had on your earth to make myself known, and a little time each night to make myself known again."

Dick Whittington was almost calm now, and Meg thought, seemed a little less brilliant in his star-light glow.

"Tell us, then, Dick," Mr. Dickens said. His notebook was poised and ready.

"You both came here," he said, "looking for something for you both. The two may be one and the same. I can only say this. What you search for in the sky, miss, is to be found at your feet."

"A riddle, Master Whittington?" Mr. Dickens asked. "Surely you must—"

"A riddle, yes, it's all I have. I am a child. I love games. And you, after all, are a very clever girl—" He looked right at Meg. "Now good night. I am off to play with my others, my happy companions."

The blue-white light that was Dick Whittington increased in intensity until he was nothing but blue-white light, and the entire room glowed, which, Meg thought, was a glow that must be like the glow inside of a star. The ghost-cat whooshed away down a hall. And then Dick Whittington's light expired, and dimness recaptured the sky-parlor.

Meg turned to Mr. Dickens, but he was walking away from her, traveling in circles, his eyes glued to the floor.

"At our feet, Meg. He said what we searched for was at our feet."

In the faint glow of the crackling, dying rush-lights, Meg saw what she was looking for yet had not expected to find. Sometimes, the pattern is before us, and it only requires the smallest concentration to find it.

What Meg saw on the sky-parlor floor was the constellation Orion. In a cleanly swept corner of the floor, smudged

unmistakably with soot, were the nine obvious points that made up the constellation of Orion. Orion the Hunter. Orion her brother! It was the mark he used on all of his notes—notes left about the print-shop and in the upstairs rooms. It was Orion's mark, and so it was Orion, and so there was only one conclusion: He *had* been here.

Chapter V

Having seen a spirit without a body, we now hear of a body without a spirit

MEG WAS ONLY PRETENDING to sleep, curled 'neath one of her aunt's shawls, an embroidered pillow under her head. Her father, Aunt Julia, and Mr. Dickens were speaking, low and confidential, and the sounds of their voices comforted her. When she and Mr. Dickens returned from Satis House—a thorough search offered no other clues—they divulged, in one short burst, the good news: They had found Orion's mark! Tobias was already asleep in his chamber, so the rest gathered on the roof-garden for further discussion. Exhausted from the excitement of the evening, Meg lay down on her favorite bench.

It had always been a secret pleasure of Meg's, a moment like this, listening to the unguarded conversations of those who thought you were asleep. It had long been a comfort, when her mother was alive, to listen in on her parents. Meg often fought against her bed-times, not out of mere stubbornness, but because she didn't want to miss out on a word of anything. Her favored spot was the braided rug before the hearth-fire. It was of little matter to Meg what her parents spoke of, as long as she could hear it. Her mother loved to talk on about the future of the print-shop, how the children would continue it, and when her mother spoke of such things, Meg pulled this all-but-certain future, woven from her mother's deep voice, around her like a blanket.

Tonight was a very different night, of course. Her mother's voice was absent . . . but the comfort was still there. And the future, too, Meg considered, for they had been speaking of Orion's imminent return. At one point she actually did sleep, which she knew because she woke to find the subject of the conversation changed. Mr. Dickens did most of the talking now, a not unusual occurrence.

"You see, Campion," Mr. Dickens was saying, "I am in France right now. You, Julia Spragg, speak to me not here in your lovely garden, but speak to me not at all. How is that possible? I am in France, I tell you, and I can prove it. Some weeks ago I left Gad's Hill, told everyone I was off to France for a 'research expedition' and hired a Hansom to Dover with a fully laden trunk. Once at Dover I boarded the ferry, had my documents inspected and stamped. The ferry's horn blew, the gulls responded with disdain, and the channel crossing began. But you see, I am not on that ferry, though my papers tell a different story. I have a good friend at Dover, Mr. Avery Binder, a man so charged with official scraps of paper, so overly fond of these scraps, that they spill from all his pockets—and he has many pockets—like stuffing from an old kid-skin doll. Mr. Binder has no care for what his scraps of paper represent, only that he be allowed the stamping, signing, sealing, and shuffling of those scraps. For a small consideration, Mr. Binder signs and stamps and shuffles my papers, and to all the world I appear to be in France.

"But of course, I am nowhere near France. As the ferry pulls away, I am—despite what my papers say—on the Dover Road, again in a hired Hansom, wheels thundering, blinds drawn, headed back to London. No one, not even you, can prove that I am in England—even as you speak to me!"

When Mr. Dickens spoke of the thundering coaches, his hands clopped the arms of the wooden chair, and when his voice rose—"even as you speak to me!"—Meg could see, though her eyes were closed, the glee and sparkle in his eyes.

"Why such secrecy, Charles?" Aunt Julia asked. Her voice was calm, collected.

"Indeed," Mr. Dickens said. "If I tell them that the Great Man—meaning myself; why do they insist on calling me that?—is merely at ease, at odds, at leisure, then they hound me. They all hound me—my friends, my family, readers, and those lowly beasts, my publishers. But if they believe I am engaged in 'research' for some new book or other—and that is what I always tell them—then they allow the Great

Man his privacy. They leave me alone only as long as the promise of fresh ink and spoiled pages persists. I see it plain in their faces. 'I'm to France,' I say, and they all think, 'O goody, let there be more of *Two Cities*.' How they would love that. Perhaps *A Tale of Four Cities* would please them, or *A Tale of Eight Cities*."

Aunt Julia stirred; rustling skirts told Meg this.

"That's only half an answer," Aunt Julia said, in a scolding tone. "And you know it."

"Yes, Charles." Her father spoke up from his long quiet. Her father would be leaning back in his chair, withdrawn, his favored pose of late. Meg remembered with a wince how he always used to perch on the edge of his chair during any conversation; these days her father was, alas, nothing but reticence. "You tell us all the 'hows' of your predicament. But none of the 'whys.' We're friends here, and you wish to tell us. Otherwise, why start the story?"

"Caught out, my friends," Mr. Dickens said. "Caught out well and true. So: the truth."

A warm breeze sailed across the roof-garden.

"I am haunted," Mr. Dickens said plainly. "I am haunted and sleepless and air-less and less-than-less. I am, you see, nothing. And if I am to be nothing, then I should be nowhere—neither in England nor France. Haunted and haunting."

"You are searching," Aunt Julia said. "But for what?"

"I wish I knew, Julia, I truly do. I am searching, but for what, I don't know. I am haunted because I am hollow. Meg and I tonight saw a spirit without a body. For you see, I am a body without a spirit."

Mr. Dickens's voice had lost all its shine and verve, Meg heard, and was now flat, dull, exhausted.

"But, Charles, why?" There was a stitch of pain in Aunt Julia's question.

"I wish I knew," he said. "I am, after all, or so they say, the Great Man. I have everything. Money. Though never enough of it, I've discovered. Fame. Why, everyone knows me everywhere, but that is not as pleasant as it sounds. Industry? I never tire of that—my magazines, my books, my readings, plenty to do. Friends I've got by the bushel, though friends who want some piece of me—my money, my fame, my industry. That is having no friends at all."

The roof-garden was all quietude. The only sound Meg detected was the keen sadness in Mr. Dickens's voice. Then Meg heard Aunt Julia shift, readying herself to speak, but Mr. Dickens began again, his voice a creaking door.

"And a home, yes, a home, and a grand one—Gad's Hill Place. Did you know that I'd first seen Gad's Hill when I was a child, when my father had no penny to his name? One day, when we were out walking from Gravesend to Rochester, I spied that house on the hill and admired it no end. My father—dreamer that he was—told me that if I worked hard enough, one day I might possess it."

Mr. Dickens coughed; paused.

"How surprised he would be to learn that I did come to live at Gad's Hill, more surprised, perhaps, that I had fixed my eye on't that day as a child, and never looked away. I have my Gad's Hill, and it has many rooms, and moreover, those rooms are filled with life. My sons, my daughters. My wife. But my family, I discover, do well enough without me. There are parties and visitors and servants to occupy them. It was different when the children were younger, but now I only get in the way."

Meg opened her eyes a sliver. Mr. Dickens was turned away from her father and her aunt, staring at the dark map of night-London.

"Why London?" Aunt Julia asked. She leaned forward and touched Mr. Dickens's hand.

"I have had to lose the disguise of the Great Man so that I may be the boy again. I have come to London to be a boy lost in the streets and to see the streets again for the first time. When I was a child wand'ring London, the City fed me, filled me with more than food. It gave me me. It gave me an entire city to populate with characters and stories. London made me."

He sighed, and gravely so. Meg had never known Mr. Dickens to sigh.

"Surely, Charles," Aunt Julia said, "you must write again, that's all."

"I do hope so. Yes, a new book is always the cure for a writer's withered soul."

"Have you found your new book yet?" Aunt Julia asked.

"Perhaps." This was the strangest of all of Mr. Dickens's speeches tonight—it was too brief.

Meg sat up and looked at Mr. Dickens. His eyes were unbearably sad.

"At Satis House?" Meg asked. "Is that, *perhaps,* where you, *perhaps,* have found your new book?"

"Meg, welcome back," her father said.

"O I do believe she's been back for some time," Aunt Julia said, the smile in her voice apparent.

"Yes, Meg," Mr. Dickens said. "Satis House has kindled some fire in me. Your brother has kindled some fire in me."

Meg stood and stretched; yawned. She felt rested, freshly awake. Meg went to her father and stood behind his chair, her hand on his shoulder.

"I wager you this, Pickel family. If I can help you to retrieve Orion, then I will have found my next book. And if I find that next book, then I will have found myself—I will become un-haunted."

"And what did you find for your novel in Satis House?" Meg asked.

"It was the ghost," he said. "The spirit-boy, the boy-spirit. A ghost can ruin any novel, if it's a ghost simply to have a ghost. A ghost must be *the* ghost, must have a purpose beyond haunting. The ghost of Dick Whittington, that's the ghost for me."

Mr. Dickens's voice had come to life again, a voice of sharp, bright lights in the quiet night.

"Now, Charles," Aunt Julia said, "are you insisting upon this ghost? A phantom, a specter? Truly?"

"Yes, Julia," he said. "Meg and I saw this spirit, and yes, we spoke with him. You are a brilliant thinker, Mrs. Spragg, possessed of a fine, scientific mind. You are right not to trust our story. But it is undeniable."

While Meg had pretended to sleep, she considered Dick Whittington's spirit. She *had* seen it. It was impossible to deny. She thought she ought to be more suspicious of her own senses, but found she could not be. Dick Whittington was a ghost *and* he was real.

"True, Aunt Julia," Meg said. "I would not lie to you."

Smiling, Aunt Julia eased back into her chair.

"But what?" Meg's father asked. "What about Dick Whittington's spirit has sparked your imagination, Charles?"

"Orion," Mr. Dickens said. "I saw how life crushed, literally, young Dick. I am determined that no such thing befall our friend, our brother, our son—Orion."

Meg clutched the back of her father's chair. She looked up at the sky—no Orion there. Not until November. The only traces of Orion tonight were the chalk smudges on the floor of the sky-parlor. Orion had left a message for Meg. He must have known he was close to home. He must have hoped, beyond reason, that Meg, or someone, would spy his mark. And she knew how it was possible for him to send the message. Who would ever suspect that nine chalk smudges were a secret, coded message? Orion, Meg had to admit, was wise that way.

Mr. Dickens stood then. He hooked his thumb into his waist-coat's watch-pocket. He paced a small circle among the gathered chairs. Mulberry, roused from rabbit-dreams, rose and trotted next to him. Mr. Dickens was preparing to speak.

"Dick Whittington rattled my old cage," he began. "He reminded me of my deepest passion, that is, the children of this world. He recalled to me my deepest anger, that is, how much of our society treats—or should we say mis-treats—its children. You saw him, Meg, all play and joy. In his after-life, as a spirit, he is free to be the child he should have been in his living-life. But in his living-life, he was forgotten, abandoned, ignored, worked close to death, and then, sick from work, cast off into death. He was nothing to anyone in this world. And if that doesn't break your heart, then you, too, are already dead, and deservedly so."

Mr. Dickens was not speaking to Meg, nor to anyone on the roof-garden. He was speaking to everyone.

"I had," he said, "a childhood that was often bleak itself, and so know something of that pain, that fear, that isolation. But when I see Dick Whittington, I know my own pain was nothing compared to that of others. And in knowing this fact, my heart breaks even more for those less fortunate children."

There was a long silence. Mulberry looked up meaningfully at Mr. Dickens. Mr. Dickens looked down at

Mulberry, leaned over and scratched him behind the ears. The two seemed to agree to continue.

"I have tried my best to wake my readers from their dead hearts. I have attempted—in every word I've penned—to argue a kinder world for our children. But Dick Whittington, he has rekindled my anger, especially as seen in the mirror of Orion's fate. My purpose on this earth, I know, is far from complete."

"Surely you've made changes," Aunt Julia said. "Surely the world is improved today. In some part thanks to you."

"Yes, Charles," her father said. "The debtors' prisons are gone. The work-houses abated and improved. We've clean water in London, more schools for the poor. Isn't ours a better world?"

Mulberry raised his head and seemed to ask the same question.

"Better, yes," Mr. Dickens said. "But not yet good."

Mulberry sat on his tail, his shoulders high, his ears alert. He barked once, and Mr. Dickens went on.

"I had forgotten, so caught up was I with the world. Forgotten that children work sixteen hours a day for scant wages, if any. Forgotten that they sleep in squalor, dress in squalor, live in squalor, and call that squalor home. Forgotten that their parents, children of squalor themselves, treat them to harsh hands and harsher words. I had forgotten that children disappear. Forgotten that the spirit of Dick Whittington has been killed in too many children. And worst of all, I have forgotten that I should try to help them, that it is my duty. But thank goodness for Dick Whittington. He has recalled me to life."

Mulberry wagged his tail with great force.

"But surely here in London—" Aunt Julia was cut short by Meg's outburst.

"Surely yes," Meg said. "Surely here in London, I have seen it. I, I am fortunate. But every day, as I run errands for you or Father, as I pass down the bye-streets, even on the prettiest corners of Cheapside, I see what Mr. Dickens has forgotten. Children who beg—beg, mind you—for a farthing, and getting that farthing, say thank-you in all sincerity. And not getting that farthing, they think to themselves, this is what I deserve: nothing. They are there, and Mr. Dickens has forgotten them. And if he has forgotten them, then all of London has forgotten them."

Mulberry was swaying now from side to side.

"And what of London!" Mr. Dickens fairly barked. "If all of the children of London were fed and clothed and schooled and sang 'Margery Daw' each night in featherbeds of gold and ivory, we would still have forgotten. Forgotten that England's reach is vast. Forgotten about Liverpool and Manchester and Brighton. Forgotten about all the children of our empire—China and India and all the world. We would still forget all the Dick Whittingtons we have stolen from their lives."

Yes, Meg thought, that is what happened—Orion was stolen from his life. Orion was stolen from Meg's life. She knew it, and in knowing it, knew once again that she must steal Orion back to her life. She looked out into the yellow darkness of London. Orion was somewhere there.

Mulberry pawed at the crushed granite, as if digging for something.

"We're all haunted, my friends," Mr. Dickens practically sang. "By what we forget. Now that we are un-forgetting, we must cease to be haunted. We must act."

Mulberry moved to Meg's father's chair, his snoot on her father's arm. Mr. Dickens, too, moved to her father's chair, and squatted in front of it, his face inches away from her father's.

"We must find Orion, Campion," he said. "You and Julia and myself, and Meg—Meg most of all—we must find Orion!"

Her father stood awkwardly and moved away from Mr. Dickens, his back to him. Aunt Julia leaned forward, suspended. Mr. Dickens waited. Her father turned.

"Charles, don't be so melodramatic. This isn't one of your novels."

"Not yet it isn't!"

The first bell of St. Paul's struck, and all the bells followed, and the chiming continued to twelve. The time was being called, unavoidably. The leaden circles, once again, dissolved into air.

Mr. Dickens and Meg's father faced each other.

"You are right, Charles," Meg's father said, stepping up. "I had forgotten, too, and forgotten too soon."

Mulberry's barking filled the air.

"Tomorrow then?" Aunt Julia asked.

"Tomorrow, yes," Mr. Dickens said. "Tomorrow we find that gang and bring Orion one step closer to his home."

"Today," Meg said. "It's already today."

And indeed it was.

Chapter VI

A brilliant sun precedes the rain

WHEN MEG BLASTED into the print-shop, looking about for Mr. Dickens, she found only disappointment. She had been all motion since she snapped awake that morning. She stoked and fed the hearth-fire, and then fed the family—warmed milk and hot rolls. She studied her Maths and Latin, as her father insisted upon, then flew off to run errands for Aunt Julia. It was as though by hurrying through her chores, she might make the clocks run faster. Now she was done, and ready to strike out on today's adventure. But where was Mr. Dickens? She could not believe that he would be late.

There was a visitor in the print-shop's work-room. This stranger and her father stood bent-headed over the proof-sheet of a funeral program, and Meg knew at a glance that this was not Mr. Dickens. However, her disappointment was coupled with some surprise, for while it was not unusual to find a stranger in the work-room, the appearance of this stranger was stranger than most.

He was yellow. Yellow all over. His trousers were yellow, his coat was yellow, his waist-coat was yellow, his shirt-collar and tie were yellow, and yes, even his shoes were yellow. But the yellowest aspect of this stranger was his yellow hat, and by being such a grand, high, and curvaceous hat, was all the yellower. No one, certainly no man in Meg's London, wore such a color. Meg was so startled by the appearance of so much yellow she felt as though she'd fallen through some long tunnel in the earth only to land at a rather mad tea-party.

Her father and the man in yellow both turned to Meg—she had made quite a brash entrance. A pair of yellow-tinged tortoise-shell spectacles framed the man's face. Meg feared her mouth gaped wide, and she was correct in her fear.

A voice called to her from the whirlpool of all that yellow.

"Meg, there you are," the voice said. "Are you ready? The day waits. And so does Orion."

The man in yellow was—

"Mr. Dickens?" Meg called. She stepped one inch closer. "I, well, I, what I mean to say is . . ."

"Yes, Meg, 'tis I. It's a disguise. Remember, I am not here. I am in France. The Great Man must not be seen. I do not wish to be seen."

Meg's father was laughing.

"While I agree," Meg said, "that you are wearing a disguise and that I did not recognize you, I must also point out that your disguise draws attention to itself." She paused; laughed. "Draws attention to itself in a very loud manner."

Mr. Dickens took off his hat. He looked more himself now.

"But that," he said, "is my purpose. Wherever we go today, people will not see me; they will only see my disguise. The wife will tell her husband, 'I saw the most curious man all in yellow today,' and she will not know she has seen the Great Man. She will only see Mr. Yellow. An obvious disguise is often the best."

"I did not know him at first myself," her father said. "Mr. Dickens is a man of the theater, and he knows his disguises."

"Shall I have a disguise, too?" she asked. "Purple, perhaps?"

"Not today. Now grab your notebook and pencils. We're off to see to the purchase of fine wine."

Wine? They were to shop for wine? This must be part of Mr. Dickens's plan, and for the moment, Meg would have to concede to it. Her first thought was to get out of the print-shop as quickly as possible and begin their journey.

Meg's father came to her and placed his hands on her shoulders. For a moment she feared he would tell her he had decided against her leaving, and she ought rather to remain at home, locking doors and latching windows to the end of her days.

"Be cautious, Meg," was all he said, and he kissed her forehead. When he pulled back, he gazed at her with solemn eyes, but in his gaze she thought she saw a glimpse of her father that had long been missing. Was that hope she saw there?

"We won't be long," she said.

When Meg and Mr. Dickens stepped into bustling, glittering Cheapside, the street and the sky seemed to glow with the yellow of Mr. Dickens's disguise. It was, Meg thought, as if Mr. Dickens himself were the sun.

Cheapside was all motion. Six-wheeled horse-drawn omnibuses flowed in both directions in the center of the broad avenue, each of the buses packed like a crate of oysters. In the lane of traffic next closest to the sidewalks were the private carriages of Cheapside shoppers and the small dray-carriages of delivery vans. Then still closer to where Meg and Mr. Dickens walked, the two-wheeled Hansom cabs stopped and started, weaved and darted, delivering their fares only to pick up others and fly away again. On the sidewalks, the wheeled carts of vendors—flat-fish, breakfast rolls, coffee, baked potatoes—strolled up and down, and between the carts and the store-fronts, hurried and harried Londoners weaved in and around one another.

And the motion of Cheapside rose sky-ward, too, the

buildings striving for the heavens, pushed up, it seemed, by the shop signs and the advertisements nailed to, glued on, and painted over every possible surface. The letters and logos pulled the eyes up—DAILY TELEGRAPH; MARRAT & ELLIS, OCULISTS; TO LEASE, TO LET, TO BE SOLD; BRYANT AND MAIS MATCHES; BOVRIL; HELMORE COAL OFFICE; YORKSHIRE RELISH; STICK NO BILLS.

It is a truth universally acknowledged that within the hub-bub of any grand city, a pair of friends might find a quiet bubble within which to cocoon themselves from all commotion. It is not that the walkers create, by force of concentration, such a bubble of silence to inhabit; the commotion itself creates such bubbles. Stand by a rushing brook or near the crashing ocean, and you will see bubbles. It was in one such bubble of silence that Meg and Mr. Dickens found themselves. All the way from Cheapside down Queen's Street, until they reached the docks and the Thames, Meg and Mr. Dickens were able to speak, as if in private, while the river of London flowed noisily around them.

"Shall we find him today, do you think? Orion. Is today the day?" Meg crossed her fingers—O that he would say yes.

"No," Mr. Dickens said squarely. "We will not find him today. However, most likely we will begin to find him."

"Why again do we go to this wine merchant?"

"For information. For a first step. We know—*know,* Meg—for certain that Orion is all caught up with our séance-gang. But look around you, all of London! Where to begin? So, we seek information, and I have a fine source for that. My good friend, my old and dear friend. He is, as you'll see, a man who seems little disposed to joining life, and by his very idleness, is able to hear all that happens around him."

"What will he tell us?"

"He will certainly give us no direct answer today. Instead, he will say that we must seek out someone else. And when we seek out that someone else, he or she will direct us yet in another direction. We take the first step. No journey ever had a happy conclusion without a first step taken."

Meg so wished to find Orion this day, or yesterday, any day but tomorrow. It ought to be easier—and quicker—to find Orion. If only Dick Whittington would materialize at this minute, Orion on his arm. Or the police, they should go once again to the police. Ought not the police help to find Orion? But her family had gone to the police, the day Orion disappeared, and again each day for weeks after. The only help offered by the police was summed up in one officer's observation: "Boys will be boys."

"And are we assured," she asked with gravity, "that your old and dear friend will lead us in the proper direction?"

"No, we are not. But we must start somewhere. We will toss this coin into the wishing-well, and should fate deny that coin, we will toss another coin and another, until either our wish is granted or our pockets emptied."

They turned onto Queen's Street, narrower than

Cheapside, but due to its narrowness, Queen's Street seemed all the busier, the commotion more frantic, and the bubble of privacy that much more private.

More at ease now, Meg let Mr. Dickens talk about all they saw, pointing out this building and that, this character and that, turning the streets of London into one of his novels. In his bright yellow suit, Mr. Dickens might have been, Meg reckoned, the owner of an elaborate candy manufactory, and she the lucky girl awarded the first tour of it. Mr. Dickens turned every object of his attention into an irresistible confection.

They made their way to the docks, to the dock-side of the Thames and the great ebb and flow of the river, the great ebb and flow of the world.

Turning north towards Blackfriar's Bridge, Meg and Mr. Dickens followed a narrow street, curving downhill, until they reached the last row of warehouses before the Thames. They stood in front of a narrow façade hung with an even narrower door.

Meg could almost see and feel the shop they were about to enter. It would be overall as narrow as the door, with skinny aisles, and countless shelves that rose to an impossibly high ceiling. There were many shops like this in London, and they were all dark and dingy, and smelled of dark and dingy odors. So it was with even greater surprise that when Meg opened the door, her expectations found themselves tumbled.

The wine-vaults' ceiling was indeed high but never

narrow, rather as broad as a horse paddock. And there, at the back of the wine-vaults, was the Thames. There was no back wall, whatsoever, to the place. The river flowed right up to it, and the river's wind blew right in. With the first fresh gust on her face, Meg was struck by the novelty of this place.

When running errands for her father and aunt, Meg was always warned to avoid dock-side—it was a dangerous place. There were many dangerous streets and by-ways in London, but all in all Meg had been—until Orion disappeared—a girl of the London streets, free to roam alone, at least during day-light. In the last months, her father had severely restricted her travels, and now she rarely left Tonson Lane unaccompanied. In fact, she rarely left Tonson Lane at all, nor did anyone else in the family. It wasn't so much that her father wished all to be at home should Orion re-appear; it was more that her father was afraid to lose anyone else. Being out and about this morning with Mr. Dickens, and seeing London afresh under his keen gaze, had lifted Meg's spirit, brightened her eyes. And now this—she'd never seen such a surprising place, this wine-vaults that opened on the world.

Then her thoughts turned to Orion. Had he seen such new and surprising places in the last six months? Meg missed, so very much, looking at the new things of the world with her brother. Only last summer Orion had surprised her with a day's outing to the Crystal Palace on Sydenham Hill. It was a treat—no occasion—for his beloved sister. Only the two of them went, much to Tobias's chagrin and Mulberry's sulking. How he'd scrimped together the money for this extravagance, Orion would not say. The money made no matter, Orion told her, but later, after his disappearance, Aunt Julia revealed to Meg that he had saved an entire year to afford the excursion. Meg had wept when Aunt Julia told her this.

It had been a perfect summer's day—clear and bright, warm but not hot—and they arrived at the Crystal Palace when it opened at nine, not leaving until near midnight. They marveled at the size of the glass-paned pavilion—next to it, St. Paul's was a hut—and the enormity and beauty of the vast, landscaped grounds. There were fountains that splashed the gates of Heaven, and boat rides in idyllic man-made lakes, and a zoo with camels and tigers, and the preserved bones of giant lizards that no longer roamed the earth. "I'm done," Meg had said finally. "I cannot go on one more amusement, nor gaze at another marvel. Take me home." It was the best day of her life, and she'd known this while it was happening.

All of this memory flooded Meg in an instant, as memories must, and in that instant she wished, too, that Orion, wherever he might be, was at least seeing more of the world than the Satis House sky-parlor. He was too curious a boy to be kept in a dingy room.

Mr. Dickens recalled Meg from her reverie, urging her forward. As they crossed into the wine-vaults, a voice of incredible power reached her ears.

"Ho, ho, ho," the voice cried. "What have we here? 'Tis the sun, my lords, the sun. Shield your eyes. 'Tis Roaming-O, as the bard wrote, and he's brought Juliet. What light through yon wine-vault breaks."

And from this voice, as if emerging from a fog, came its source.

"Good day, sir and miss. Kenneth Hardlywaite, *marchand du vin,* at your service."

Kenneth Hardlywaite wore a black-and-white-checked coat, a black waist-coat, and in the lapel of his coat a white chrysanthemum the size of a cat's head. His smile was enormous, his face was ruddy, and his voice was a storm to itself. He seemed, to Meg, a man on the verge of exploding.

"How may we help you today? Colonel Mustard, is it?" Mr. Hardlywaite said.

"My name is Slaughter," Mr. Dickens said. "Osgood Slaughter."

"A name to die for."

The two men shook hands. Mr. Hardlywaite stared deep into Mr. Dickens's eyes.

It was clear to Meg that Mr. Hardlywaite saw through Mr. Dickens's outlandish disguise, and that he recognized the man beneath it. It was clear to her, as well, that Mr. Hardlywaite, in seeing through the disguise, intended to honor it. 'Twas Hardlywaite's impish grin that betrayed his intentions.

"And this," Mr. Dickens said, "is my niece, Miss Meg"—he paused—"Miss Meg Chercher."

Meg recognized her false name; it was French for "to search."

"Welcome to Hardlywaite's," the voice said. "Where we can hardly wait to help you. Allow me to pour you a taste of our Chateau Y'quem, a magnificent—"

"Your hospitality is most welcome, sir," Mr. Dickens said. "But I'm looking for an old friend. Mr. Micawber. Is he still in your employ?"

"Employed here he is, Mr. Slaughter. And why shouldn't he be? No one else would employ him. Seek out the man in this warehouse doing the least amount of work, and you will have found my trustworthy Micawber, for he can be trusted to never work."

Mr. Dickens performed an extravagant bow.

"We are eternally in your debt, sir," he said.

Meg and Mr. Dickens prowled through the cases and bottles until, in a corner far from the Thames and its breezes, they came upon a stout-ish, middle-aged person in a brown short-coat and black breeches and tights. His head, which was a very large one, and shining, had upon it only as much hair as an egg would. As if to provide an egg-cup for such an eggy head, the man's shirt-collar was broad and tall. He leaned upon a jaunty sort of walking-stick, with two rusty tassels hanging from its knob, and across his waist-coat hung, on a tarnished chain, a quizzing-glass.

He was remarkable in his appearance, to be certain, but it was not his appearance that convinced Meg this was the sought-after Micawber. It was the intent idleness of the man. In the frantic scramble of the wine-vaults—crates being loaded and unloaded, the incessant clinking of bottles, and always the loud, traveling voice of Mr. Hardlywaite—Micawber was the one still object.

"Mr. Micawber, I presume," Mr. Dickens called out.

This greeting caused a series of movements to erupt from Micawber's person. His shoulders leaped up, his hands flew like a pair of startled birds, and his jaunty stick, freed from its captor, clattered to the floor. Even in his movements, Micawber managed to accomplish nothing.

"Ahem," Micawber said. "That is my name." He reached up to tip a hat that was not there. He stared at his empty hand for a moment.

"A word with you, sir?" Mr. Dickens put a confidential finger to one side of his nose. Micawber, looking about for agents of espionage, did the same.

"And would that one word," Micawber whispered, "be the one word that is your name?"

"Osgood Slaughter," Mr. Dickens said, "is the name I use today, but perhaps you know me by another name?" Mr. Dickens removed his yellow hat.

"But, sir," Micawber said, "if I do not yet know you, and have only heard your name today, how am I to know you by yesterday's name?"

"Perhaps your quizzing-glass would be of help to your memory?"

Shocked to find the monocle hanging from him, Micawber picked it up with wonder. He then affixed it to his right eye, and squinting with his left, examined Mr. Dickens's face. He dropped the quizzing-glass and stepped back.

Anxious as she was to get on with their mission and ask questions about Orion and the séance-gang, Meg couldn't help but be captivated by this rather silly man.

"You see, this glass is merely an ornament. I see less with it than with my own two eyes, and so my examination was inconclusive—in short, I have no idea who you are."

"But you do, Wilkins," Mr. Dickens said. He now removed his yellow tortoise-shell spectacles.

"Mr. Dickens!" Micawber fairly shouted. "You startle me so."

"Ix-nay on the Ickens-day," Mr. Dickens said. And he tapped his nose again. "I'm in disguise, don't you see."

"And a fine disguise it is!" Mr. Micawber turned to the warehouse. "I'll be the first to say it, and say it to anyone, this is a most extraordinary disguise, is it not?"

"Wilkins Micawber." Mr. Dickens hushed him with a whisper. "I beg of you."

"O yes, a disguise. Of course. Mum's the word. Say no more. Say. No. More."

Mr. Dickens introduced Meg, then spoke of their mission. He emphasized the séance—the phony séance. Would Micawber know of anyone in London at this time who might be conducting such séances? Without mentioning Orion, Mr. Dickens pressed upon his old friend the urgency of the situation.

"Would you know of such a man or such men?" Mr. Dickens asked.

"Mr. Muckle!" Micawber yelled, and Meg reached for her notebook to write down this name. But Micawber bolted away from them on his pin-like legs. For every step he took, his body created enough motion for four such steps.

"Mr. Muckle. Please, dear. Please, sit down, Mr. Muckle. Allow me, Mr. Muckle!"

Micawber was hurrying towards a thin, frail older gentleman who wore dark glasses and was waving about a long white stick.

Micawber moved towards the blind man, hoping, it was clear to Meg, to reach him before his stick reached one of the pyramids of wine bottles. She had only known this Mr. Micawber for one moment, but she was already certain that the wine bottles would fall, no matter how hard Micawber tried to stop them.

Muttering "Mr. Muckle, dear O dear, Mr. Muckle," Micawber reached him and seated him on a stack of wine cases. The wine was safe for now, Meg thought. But surely not much longer.

"I want my wine this minute, get me my Château Lafite." The man was seated now, but his white stick waved about.

"Yes, Mr. Muckle, dear. Right away, at once."

Fiddlesticks, Meg grumbled to herself. Why this interruption? They were here to find Orion—or at least the first information that would lead them to him—but now this.

She crossed her arms and pulled on a sulky frown. Then Meg relented her posture. Mr. Micawber was too entertaining, too hapless, and the scene with Mr. Muckle too hilarious. In fact, the scene was precisely like a scene from a novel by Mr. Dickens himself. In Mr. Dickens's works, the main character was always in search of something or someone, but every room the main character entered on this quest was filled with characters who had quests of their own. Eventually, in such scenes, the main character—Pip or David or Nell—would achieve their goal, but not before the other, more eccentric characters had a bit of fun.

Micawber slid to one side, reaching for one pyramid of bottles, when he noticed Mr. Muckle's stick moving towards another pyramid, and so Micawber followed the stick and guided it to an airier portion of the warehouse. But the stick found yet another pyramid, and tinkling against the uppermost bottle, loosened the rest. As if he'd been saving all his energy from years of idleness, Micawber was instantly at the pyramid, and caught six of the falling bottles before they hit the ground. It was an amazing feat of juggling—that two arms could catch six bottles in flight—and Micawber stood with obvious pride, clutching the errant bottles.

Alas, a seventh bottle had also been jostled, and now it fell with a great crash and splat on the warehouse floor. The pungent aroma of wine clouded the air.

"Boy!" Micawber yelled. "Clean up in Bordeaux!"

As though he were irritated by every bottle of wine in

the world, Micawber allowed the first six bottles to join their ruined cousin—*crash* and *splat*! He stared down at the red-wine's mess, and raising a shoe to his knee, swiped one stray drop from it. Then he dusted his hands and walked away from the mess.

Mr. Muckle stood with no ceremony, said to the air, "Ah, yes, a fine bouquet, that Lafite. Have it delivered." He made his way out of the wine-vaults, his stick waving about. Meg saw that Mr. Muckle's white cane protected him from the dangers of the world, even though it seemed a danger of its own.

"Ah, where were we?" Micawber said. "Indeed. Ghost-talkers, dead un-deaders, mediums at large—in short, a séance. As always, when you come to me, Mr. Dickens"—he touched his nose again—"you come to the right man. It's as if you know everything I know, everything in my breast. It is—in short—as if you created me, sir."

Micawber puffed up now at his own words.

"To wit," Micawber said. "While I have no personal history with the place—I am a sober, modest man, my dear girl—I have heard tell of an inn where such things may be procured. In short—the Six Jolly Fellowship Porters, where the house specialty, of late, seems to be séances and other spiritual scams. Quay-side off Nellie's dry-dock. Ask for Miss Jenny Wren. Tell her Og Ogleby sent you. Or so I've heard."

Meg was writing it all down. Finally, a place to go, a name—the next step towards Orion.

"I am your humble servant, Wilkins," Mr. Dickens said with a bow. "And as a show of my appreciation, please deliver five cases of your finest and most expensive to Gad's Hill for me. And Wilkins, I prefer my wine *inside* the bottle, and the bottles, for that matter, intact." Mr. Dickens pushed a gold sovereign into Micawber's hand.

When the money was safely stowed, Micawber looked right at Meg.

"The signs, my girl," Micawber said. "Mind the signs, I tell you. As a man who has never paid any mind to the signs about him—ask my wife, my creditors—I urge you, dear child, to mind the signs."

"Sir? I'm sorry, sir?"

"Mind the signs, dear girl," Mr. Micawber said flatly. "Simply a solid piece of advice in any one life. Micawber ain't good for much, but advice he has plenty."

He patted her on the head. Normally Meg would recoil from such a gesture, thinking it too patronizing of children. But Mr. Micawber was so charming and so without guile that she accepted his pat gracefully. She smiled and curtsied.

Meg and Mr. Dickens pushed off, navigating the cases and pyramids of wine with great care.

There had been an unexpected severity in Mr. Micawber's gaze when he spoke to her. She had no idea of what he spoke, but she knew that she would heed his advice. Whatever it meant.

As they were about to exit the wine-vaults, Mr. Hardlywaite called to them. He was seated before an old wine cask upon which was spread a tray of shucked oysters and a large glass of honey-colored wine. They stood before him, and surprisingly, Mr. Hardlywaite spoke softly.

"I know you, Mr. Dickens, and you know me. No disguise can hide you. Because of our mutual esteem, and your loyal patronage, I have a special gift for you today. Let me give it freely, but ask no questions."

Mr. Hardlywaite slurped down an oyster.

"You were seen, Mr. Dickens. At Satis House. There's talk about. I've heard no mention of the girl, though she seems to be involved. But you were seen, my friend, and recognized. Just this morning, you were looked for. Take good care."

Meg felt a new, chillier wind invade the wine-vaults.

Chapter VII

Shadows and signs

THE SKY ABOVE THE WINE-VAULTS was much changed when Meg and Mr. Dickens stepped outside. The sky to the north of the City seemed stood on its edge, no longer hovering over the City, but a black wall of cloud marching steadily towards the Thames. There was a cooling breeze in this storm, a relief from the grey and tepid morning. And in the relief, a promise. A storm like this could wash away the terrible soot-color and soot-odor of London's infernal summer. Tomorrow, the sky might be blue again.

But for now, rain and storm. Cracked lightning froze the sky, north by King's Cross, followed shortly, as is the nature of this phenomenon, by mumbled thunder.

"This way, Meg," Mr. Dickens said. "Nellie's dry-dock isn't far."

"But your outfit, your disguise," Meg said. "Surely if we're being searched out, as Mr. Hardlywaite says, then your disguise is now too obvious."

"Remember, Meg. They are looking for Mr. Dickens, not a man in yellow. And I do believe my purchase of Hardlywaite's finest wine will be enough cause for both Mr. Hardlywaite and our dear Mr. Micawber to forget that we were seen this morning. A little money can do wonders for the memory. It can make some men forget what they know perfectly well, and can make others remember what they never knew."

Meg was not convinced of this, but she bowed to her companion's experience.

They stuck close to the sides of buildings, trying to find shelter under the over-hanging eaves and to avoid the mud of these narrow bye-streets. It was not easy to stay dry, however, for dock-side was as thick with citizens of London as the sky with rain-drops. Such a squall, Meg thought, should have driven all to the comforts of home, but the streets were filled with people caught up in their business. And the moored ships nearby, their masts a crowded forest of skeletal trees, continued the loading and un-loading of those goods going out into the world and coming from it.

Mr. Dickens led the way. He offered Meg his coat, but she shrugged off the gesture. It was only rain, after all, only water.

As they slunk down and through the twisting bye-streets,

Meg found herself revisiting Mr. Micawber's cryptic advice. Mind the signs, he'd said. Mr. Micawber, all could see, was a harmless man, and a silly one as well. A harmless, silly man. And yet his voice had taken on a serious, almost eerie tone when he'd advised her to mind the signs. She knew she *must* mind the signs, whatever they might be; perhaps one bore Orion's name.

In a most unexpected turn, the world had molded itself to Meg's thoughts. When she looked up from her rain-bent attitude, all she saw were signs.

Every wall, every siding, every window was covered with signs. Advertisements, yes, of the kind she'd seen in Cheapside this morning—food and jewelry and books and theater plays. All of these signs implored you to want something, wanted you to purchase their goods. Shop-signs called out from every address and window—the names and businesses of attorneys and pawnbrokers and public houses and physicians, and all of these signs, too, wanted something of you. They asked you to enter, to change your path, perhaps your life.

But the most common sign in this dock-side region was what we call a notice. There were notices offering passage to faraway lands—APPLY ALL ABLE-BODIED SAILORS—how Meg wished to be a sailor at such moments. Notices that warned against certain behaviors and practices—loudness and drunkenness chief among them—all signed by the local police or magistrates. There were notices offering rewards for the return of—whatever it was that was lost. A particular sympathy colored Meg when she read the LOST notices; she knew what it was to lose something, someone.

In and around the posted signs, she discovered less apparent ones, signs that gave her new hope. Chalked upon any blank space were messages—messages drawn with hope by the hopeless. "My dear Sadie," one said, "off to Australia on the Gander, home soon a rich man, Harold." "Stella is a fine blonde dog, return her here." "Tuesday noon Blackfriars pay in full." "Heartless world no more Ed'd Pearce." "The owl tames no man." "Johnny, I love you." "Albert D. is still alive and was here yesterday."

There had always been such messages on walls throughout the City, but while she had always seen them, Meg had never truly considered them before. All of London was a world of words—the wants and desires and fears and negotiations of all her fellow citizens were displayed in plain sight. London was a book to be read.

Meg stopped to search one wall that was nearly covered in chalk. She was looking, of course, for Orion's mark. If he had left his mark at Satis House, perhaps he'd been leaving it all over the City, on wood and stone, on wall or window, for all these months, trying to contact his family. Looking for them! If so, the family's staying at home—for security, as her father reckoned—had been a mistake.

Two emotions arose in her—first, despair that she and her family had wasted too much time; and second, hope that Orion's mark might still reveal his whereabouts.

One cryptic message, in a pale green hand, called most

urgently to her—"Handsome did not but does will out all most handsomer." Whatever the message meant, it was obvious, from the slant and speed of the writing, that this was as urgent a message as the distress call of a floundering ship. It hit her then, a grand idea, and hit her full on. If Orion could send a message to her, then she ought to be able to send a message to him.

Meg looked up expecting to find Mr. Dickens farther along, but he had also stopped. He stood before a vacant building-site, around which a crude fence had been erected. As there were no eaves here, he was getting soaked. He turned to Meg and beckoned.

"See this, Meg! But do not be frightened." He pointed to a large white broadside, most of which was taken up with two simple words—BODY FOUND!

Meg breathed in sharply.

"No," he said. "It's not Orion, no cause for alarm. See the date. This was posted weeks ago, and we believe Orion still lives."

She nodded, but slowly. For a moment Meg pictured Orion laid out on a table at a coroner's inquest, his face laughing but still, his lips blue and frozen. She shook the picture from her mind.

"What of this broadside?" she asked.

"I do believe I've found my novel," he said.

"But surely one sheet of paper does not make a novel. It can't be as easy as that, can it? One glimpse of a posted broadside?"

"Who says it was easy? To get here, today, to discover this singular sheet of inspiration, consider what I've been through. I've been sleepless for months, isolated from friends and family. I've wandered roof-tops, spoken with spirits, and discovered, with great sorrow, that our own dear Orion is missing. How is that an easy journey? It took much hazard and effort and time to get me to this spot."

Meg considered Mr. Dickens, who stared at the broadside as if it were speaking aloud to him. Anger flashed through her. How could he be concerned with a novel when they should both be concerned only with Orion? The very idea of a novel seemed to her, at this moment, nothing but foolishness.

She was about to tell Mr. Dickens this—and with great force—but she softened. Watching Mr. Dickens as he stared at the words BODY FOUND! she saw that Mr. Dickens's search for his new novel was as important to him as her search for Orion was to her. Each person, each human, had his own search, her own quest. She could not deny Mr. Dickens this truth. And besides, it did not mean he cared only for his novel. She knew he cared for Orion's safety; after all, it was for Orion they were out this morning. The two searches—hers and Mr. Dickens's—were the same, one supporting the other. If Mr. Dickens was helping her to find Orion, surely she could not grudge him his new novel.

"What do you see of this new novel?" she asked.

"Just imagine. Opening scene. Dock-side, late at night.

Foggy, of course. A boat-man hauls a name-less body from the Thames, and this broadside appears shortly—BODY FOUND! How intriguing is that? The novel hinges on this point. Who is this body, who are his mutual friends, and how are these friends inter-connected? Once again, my thanks to London, for her continued inspiration."

Meg stared at the broadside. It was the standard size, eleven inches wide by seventeen inches tall, and the headline filled most of the sheet in letters several inches high. Below the headline was a brief caption that instructed all interested parties to the nearest police station. The broadside's message was bold—one could not fail to see it.

"Yes," Meg said. "Yes, of course. It's what we must do. Mr. Dickens, don't you see? If Orion can send us a sign, then we can send a sign to him."

Meg could nearly see the broadside already, could picture herself gluing up copies all over London. An advertisement for her brother. *To* her brother.

"Ingenious, Meg. Of course! But tell me, did your father never advertise for him?"

"Small notices, in the papers. But too small, I fear." She formed a little box with her fingers to show the size.

"And now, the largest newspaper of all—London's walls. We shall publish our notice, then—WANTED: BROTHER!"

Meg yanked the broadside from its glued-to spot, folded it in quarters, and slipped it into her pocket.

"Father and I can design it, you see, and then Tobias and I—"

"A splendid idea, inspired. However, we must hold that thought. A matter of some danger lurks."

Mr. Dickens's gaze returned to the fence, and Meg followed suit.

"Yes?"

"Do not turn, Meg. Pretend only to be speaking with me about these fascinating notices. There is, behind us, through the crowd, a man who believes himself hidden in a dark passage. He wears a brown suit and a grey hat, and he is keeping a close eye on us. He is under the impression we do not see him."

Meg nodded. She could feel, from across the way, eyes boring into her back.

"Now, Meg. I am going to offer you a shilling, which you'll take with the gratitude of a beggar girl—which will confuse him. Proceed to the bottom of the street, that's Nellie's dry-dock. On the river-side, you'll find the Six Jolly Fellowship Porters. Seek Miss Jenny Wren. I daresay she'll look after a poor girl on her own. Stick to her. I will arrive in good time."

Meg nodded again.

"Buy yourself something to eat. I know this is a daring move, but you are safer ensconced with Miss Wren than chased with me. If I do not return within the half-hour, take a cab home. Then contact the authorities on my behalf."

He turned to Meg, fished a coin from his waist-coat, and handed it to her—it was a sovereign, not a shilling. She had never held this much money before.

The notion of being all alone here—dock-side!—crashed over Meg, yes, very much like the lightning that crackled the sky, and a thunderous rumble of fear swept through her.

"You can do this, Meg. I won't be long. Miss Jenny Wren. Remember."

Meg expelled a long breath and tried her best to smile. She could do this.

"Now be gone," Mr. Dickens fairly yelled, playing his part. "And not another pence from me, you hear."

Playing the part of the forlorn beggar girl, Meg offered a feeble curtsy, then skipped off. At the bottom of the narrowing bye-street, she turned and saw Mr. Dickens scurrying away, the man in the brown suit and grey hat following. Mr. Dickens slipped into an alley and was gone.

Meg ducked out of the rain and into the Six Jolly Fellowship Porters.

A great cloud hung in the air of the Six Jolly Fellowship Porters, bringing to Meg's mind the great cloud of smoke, all man-made, that often hung above London. The chimneys that belched the tavern's smoke, however, were not those of coal-fires or manufactories or iron-horse trains, but rather long-stemmed clay pipes. Every customer was attached to one of these pipes, and there were many, many customers. A clatter of voices, like a second cloud, also obscured the air.

Of the many customers packed into the cozy room, not

a one looked up at her entrance. Businesses more urgent captured their attentions, and this ignorance of her put Meg at ease. She shook the rain from her hair and dress as best she could and stood to one side of the entrance, adjusting to the dim light.

Each of the tables, none bigger than a dinner plate, was occupied, by men, of course, men in dark and shabby clothes, men all hidden under lowered hats, men drinking from tin mugs and smoking, men conspiring. For all the noise and smoke and people, the Six Jolly Fellowship Porters seemed intent on secrecy.

Unseen and safe in her corner by the door, Meg looked about for Jenny Wren. At what seemed a considerable distance from her comfortable nook, Meg spied a tin-topped bar, and behind it the unmistakable silhouette of the bar-keep, and the bar-keep was unmistakably a woman. This must be Jenny Wren, and so summoning her courage, Meg made her way across the crowded, conspiring tavern, and with impressive speed. She hopped onto the one free bar-stool, a rather rickety one.

The bar-keep's fierce grey eyes melted when they fell on Meg. She reached out a tiny hand and placed it on Meg's, which soothed her. There was something unusual about the woman—Meg couldn't put her finger on it—but her presence was warm, protective.

"And what have we here?" the bar-keep cooed, as though speaking to a kitten. "What tide has washed you to this dangerous shore, my love?"

"Are you Miss Jenny Wren, please?" Meg's voice was shaking.

"Her I am, but no question was ever an answer. Calm now, you're safe. Who are you, girl, and what brings you here?"

"My name is Meg Chercher. My uncle will call for me momentarily."

"Bad for your uncle, then." Miss Jenny Wren continued to wipe the same tin mug with the same filthy rag. "For a moment in this place can be an eternity." She looked square at Meg. "Are you certain of that truth?"

"Yes, ma'am," Meg said. "He'll be here instanter."

"Then some vittals and coffee to hold you over. You're damp as an eel."

Miss Jenny Wren disappeared from sight. Which is not to say that she walked away from the tin-topped bar to some other room. No, her head and torso and arms simply disappeared, and Meg understood what was odd about Jenny Wren's appearance. Her hands were tiny, her arms were short, and indeed, Jenny Wren was all-over a smaller person than most, near the same height as nine-year-old Tobias. And she had come to disappear because she had jumped off whatever crate had lifted her to the height of the bar.

From under the bar a ruckus arose, and Jenny Wren re-appeared on her perch, carrying a plate of meat pie and a steaming mug of the blackest coffee.

Meg thought she would dissolve with joy at the sight of this meal, and her expression must have reflected her relief.

"Eat and drink, as the philosopher said." Jenny Wren patted Meg's hand again. "And don't fret a piece now. Miss Jenny Wren will take care of you." She moved away from Meg to the other end of the bar, where a one-eyed man was clamoring for another pint of porter.

"But—" Meg said too late. The meat pie was tempting, but more than hunger, Meg's curiosity gnawed at her. What could this woman tell her about séances?

The meat pie was entirely delicious, though the variety of meat was not entirely obvious. And the coffee, well, nothing surpassed a cup of thick coffee, Meg felt, to restore one's spirits.

In the ghosted mirror behind the bar, Meg found her own image and was shocked. Not at her bedraggled appearance—there was a bit of the wet-cat about her right now—but shocked by her presence here, in this tavern, among these conspirators. Her father would certainly be distraught if he could see her now, and terrified. Meg, though, was impressed. She was in this dangerous place, and her fear had not stopped her. She smiled and offered a little wink to herself.

In the background of the ghosted mirror, a dis-quieting movement broke through the crowd and smoke, and caught Meg's eye. She turned to look at it. Out of the dark recess of a far corner, a shadow seemed to be swirling, and swirling, seemed to coalesce into a figure, the figure of a man dressed in the colors of shadow. He was as thin as a lamp-post, with a long beard as thin as a smaller lamp-post. And he was staring right at Meg. Un-remarked by all, the man moved towards her, as if floating rather than walking. He did not take his eyes off her, nor did his lips stop moving.

Meg was transfixed. The man came to her, floating, and little by little, his words come to her, too, floating through the static cloud of pipe-smoke. Was this perhaps another spirit?

"Underground he lives," the man said. "Always underground, closer to hell that way, underground, that's where you'll find him, as close to hell as you'll ever be."

The man was upon Meg now, and she smelled his acrid, rotten breathing, and his words filled her head.

"Underground is hell, always so deep underground, so deep you can feel the devil's pulse."

He pointed a skinny, crooked finger at Meg, nearly touching her face with it. The nail on his finger was yellow and split in two.

"And you, you will find him there, won't you, you, you will seek him there, so close to hell."

Meg opened her mouth to scream. But her scream had no chance to materialize.

The shadow man screamed instead. Then screamed again, and bent and pulled away from Meg, and Jenny Wren was on this side of the bar, whaling at the man's shins with a short iron rod.

"Get away, Arthur. I'm telling you. Get away from the girl with your crazy palaver. Leave at once or you'll soon be as short as I am, I swear."

The shadow man turned and fled, though somewhat gimpishly. He was gone out of the door. Miss Jenny reached up and put a hand on Meg's knee.

"There, there, love, all safe. Don't let old Arthur trouble you. Comes in every day talking only about hell, which I'm sure he'll have a chance to visit soon. Harmless, though."

The Six Jolly Fellowship Porters burst into applause at this scene, but an applause Jenny Wren stifled with a loud whistle.

"The same for all of you. Back to your nefarious dealings, it's why you come here. And if anyone so much as winks at my young friend, it's knee-caps for all, and I'll charge a shilling for each knee I'm forced to cap."

There was a ripple of laughter, soon swallowed by the clouds of noise and smoke. No one, it was clear to Meg, went against Jenny Wren's wishes. Still shaken, Meg did have to laugh a little at these fearsome and "nefarious" conspirators, each of whom was clearly terrified of Miss Jenny Wren. Meg was safe, she felt, but where was Mr. Dickens?

Jenny Wren retreated behind the bar and poured another coffee for Meg, who held it with both hands.

The door of the Six Jolly Fellowship Porters blew open not a minute later, and Meg turned to see a workman enter.

He scanned the room, stopped his gaze on Meg, and came right for her. Meg pulled back against the wall, and

Jenny Wren reached for her knee-capper, but before trouble could be stirred once again, the workman spoke in a familiar voice.

"Meg," the voice said, breathless. "Thank goodness. I am so sorry. Are you all right? Tell me so."

Meg and Mr. Dickens embraced as they ought—like two old friends.

"Yes, yes, I am well," she said. "Though never so happy to see you. But your disguise—it's changed."

"Ah yes, these." He looked down at a grease-stained coat and trousers from under a grease-stained cap. The smell of fish rose to Meg. "A story for later. I had to make a barter. Let's just say that there's a brilliant-yellow fishmonger at large in London today. All to escape our pursuer, whom I'm certain we have lost. And you—"

"No," Miss Jenny Wren said, tapping the iron rod on the tin-topped bar. "You, sir. Who might you be?"

"All is well, Miss Wren," Meg said. "This is my uncle, Mr. Slaughter. At last."

"And you, madam?" Mr. Dickens said. "Have I found Miss Jenny Wren, the proprietor of this grand public house?"

"As I am Jenny Wren, and as I am the mistress of this house, then I would declare that you have found me."

"You are the proprietress?" Mr. Dickens asked again.

"And you are repetitive," Miss Jenny Wren said. "My back's bad and my legs are mis-formed, but I am the proprietress, and I am Jenny Wren."

"Then a word with you, madam?" Mr. Dickens said. He placed a tower of coins in front of her.

Jenny Wren swept the coins from the bar into her outstretched apron pocket.

"Delighted to have a word, sir," Jenny Wren said. "And more than one, for what you're paying. Ain't no place better for a word on the q.t. than the Porters. I always say so, and so do plenty more. Now, what word would it be today? Murder, perhaps, that's a good word. Revenge is also a good word, as is theft. Which word is it?"

"Séance," Meg broke in.

"Séance?" Miss Jenny snapped.

"Yes," Mr. Dickens said. "Séance. We wish to speak with the dead."

A wry smile crossed Jenny Wren's keen face.

"Why, good people," she said. "You are already speaking with the dead. There! Listen! That's the dead now, and this is what they're saying: You can't speak with us, the dead, because we are dead, and that is our last word on't. Ha!"

"You are a corker, Miss Wren," Mr. Dickens said. "A real corker."

"Ah, sir," Miss Wren said. "A corker you may call me. Or a storker or porker, or even lorker, but no matter what you call me, I will always be Miss Jenny Wren, and as long as I am Miss Jenny Wren, I will tell you, sir, that speaking with the dead is a futile pursuit. You see, the dead are so very dead, and it pains them so to speak."

Meg wished to tell Jenny Wren all about Dick Whittington, and how speaking for that young spirit seemed neither painful nor impossible. Whether the dead were able to speak was not the issue at hand.

"Miss Wren," Meg said. "Let us say that we wish to find only those who *appear* to speak with the dead."

"Ah, you speak and speak well, young lady," Miss Wren said, turning her full focus on her. "If it's the appearance of a thing you wish, let the appearance not deceive me."

"Yes," Mr. Dickens said. "My niece is correct. We seek only those who *promise* to speak with the dead."

"Then speak to me, who is most alive, and explain the whys of your search."

Meg watched Jenny Wren's face while Mr. Dickens spoke. Jenny Wren was clearly captivated by Mr. Dickens's words, but it was also clear that Miss Jenny Wren did not recognize the Great Man disguised or otherwise.

"You see," Mr. Dickens began. "My niece and I stumbled upon a séance in progress, and hidden as we were, were able to witness the séance and the preposterousness of it. We are searching for the men who perpetuated this fraud."

"If a fraud," Jenny Wren said, "why do you seek them? Was it your fortune bilked? You wish recompense?"

"No, not at all. From our vantage on that night, we spied a young man we both know and love, and we wish to return him to his home. We fear he may have been press-ganged."

Meg knew this last word. It was often in the papers. It was used to describe those, usually children, who had been stolen from their lives and pressed into the service of criminal gangs. If Orion had been press-ganged, it was clear why he had not escaped and returned—criminals held him. She shuddered to imagine what threats he lived under.

"Why did you not retrieve the young man on that night?" Jenny Wren asked.

"We were in no position to," Meg said. "We were on the roof and they were in the sky-parlor."

"Ho! Perhaps you are the dead, then. Skulking about nights and peering in windows."

Mr. Dickens waved away her objections.

"We fear," Mr. Dickens said, "that they know of our search. Which is why Meg was here under your gentle care. I was being followed, but have evaded them."

Jenny Wren's eyes glowed with an intense grey fire. She leaned over the bar, which caused Meg and Mr. Dickens to lean in, too. Jenny Wren again put her tiny hand on Meg's.

"There is only one gang," Jenny Wren whispered, "as foolish enough to attempt such a scam and hope for money from it. And then foolish enough to follow you. The Sampson Gang. Misters Ned and Niles Sampson."

Jenny Wren was looking only at Meg now.

"Stupid and vile, they are," Jenny Wren continued. "A

lovely combination, don't you think. They'll do anything for a bob and never do it well. And yes"—she looked up at Mr. Dickens—"I do recall a gossip that told of false séances as their specialty. This is the Six Jolly Fellowship Porters, after all. If it happens in London, it's heard of here."

"And where might I find them, do you know, Miss Wren?" Mr. Dickens deftly placed another pile of coins on the tin-topped bar.

Miss Jenny Wren swept the coins into the pocket of her apron.

"Just can't keep this place clean," she said, "never. But let me tell you. I cannot tell you where to find them. Months ago I barred their entry. Criminals a-plenty are welcome here, but fools are warned away. However, they are frequently seen, so I hear, near Billingsgate Market. Sam Weller's your man there. If I see all here, Sam Weller sees all at Billingsgate. Sam Weller the Boot."

Miss Wren pulled a single coin from her pocket and placed it on the tin-topped bar. Meg and Mr. Dickens stared at it numbly. Jenny Wren pushed the coin to Meg.

"Tell him," Jenny Wren said, "that you were sent—by a little bird."

"O," Meg said, and she picked up the coin. It was a tin coin, a coffee-house token, and it was stamped with a tiny bird, a wren.

"And no more?" Mr. Dickens said. "Simply we are sent by a little bird?"

"Does this bird ever speak more clearly, Miss Wren?" Meg asked, frustrated by such riddles. She had no choice but to trust the bar-keep's information, yet wished her to speed its delivery.

Mr. Dickens plunked down another stack of coins. He stared hard at Jenny Wren.

"Speak clear I will," she said, "and briefly. Sam Weller the Boot, he is your man. What you need to know, he can tell you. I am certain."

Mr. Dickens reached into his vest for another pile of coins.

"Enough now, sir. This little bird has run out of song. Now off with you both. I'm running a tavern here."

Meg felt at first, then saw more clearly, why Jenny Wren was suddenly wishing them to leave. Men were drifting away from their tables and gathering 'round the bar. While these men wore an air of nonchalance, it was clear to Meg that they were eaves-dropping. In the Six Jolly Fellowship Porters, a new conspiracy could not be ignored.

"I tell you, sir," Miss Jenny Wren said much too loudly. She was playing her part—the offended bar-keep. "I do not deal in such criminalities. Now take your daughter"—she winked at Meg—"and leave my house at once, or I'll summon the constable."

But unable to play the part to perfection, Miss Jenny Wren leaned over the tin-topped bar and gave Meg a brief but powerful kiss on the cheek.

Mr. Dickens led them to the door, but bade Meg wait inside. Next, the door opened again, opening onto another opened door, that of a Hansom cab.

"Quick, Meg," Mr. Dickens said. And the two of them bundled into the cab. "Cheapside, and waste no time, driver," Mr. Dickens called, banging the cab's roof.

Chapter VIII

The consolation of the father

AUNT JULIA PREPARED A LIGHT TEA, and the family gathered to listen to Meg and Mr. Dickens detail their dock-side adventures. Mr. Dickens did most of the talking, as was his wont, and Meg saw the wisdom in this. Her father was, by his nature, more apt to listen to Mr. Dickens. And he told them everything that had transpired.

In the cab on the way home, Meg had implored Mr. Dickens to not reveal they had been followed, nor reveal that Meg had been left alone in the Six Jolly Fellowship Porters. She was fearful that if her father knew of these real dangers he would call off the entire search for Orion—and they had only just begun!

However, Mr. Dickens politely but forcibly refused to keep any truth from Meg's father. He was correct, of course; her father had to know everything, and dishonesty could only hurt her cause. Still, Meg worried for her father's reaction. As Mr. Dickens recounted their adventures, Meg kept a wary eye on her father. She saw that he was pleased with the information that had been gathered, yet distressed at the manner in which it had been gathered.

"And that is where we are left, Campion," Mr. Dickens concluded. "We know some things, but not all, and what remains is another name—Sam Weller the Boot, of Billingsgate Market."

"And nothing more?"

"It is considerably more than we knew this morning. Micawber led us to Miss Jenny Wren, who leads us now to Sam Weller. That we have one name out of the countless names in London is a better beginning than the toss of a dart."

Meg could hold herself no longer. The riddles she'd encountered were driving her mad!

"Why does no one," Meg blurted, "simply tell us what they mean? Why do people speak in such roundabouts?"

"What do *you* mean, Meg?" Aunt Julia asked in a soothing tone.

Meg was pacing now, but quietly. "Mr. Micawber says this and that, and we have to guess at what he means. Miss Jenny Wren says this and that, and then that and this, and we guess at what *she* means. Mr. Micawber could say, 'Go to this tavern.' Miss Jenny Wren could say, 'Your answer is here,' and draw us a map. But no. Now we have Mr. Weller and another destination, and I hate to think what mumbo-jumbo he'll regale us with. Adults are all riddle-me-ree. Will they never talk straight?"

With some embarrassment, she realized that, in wishing to withhold certain "facts" from her father, she, too, wanted to speak less than clearly. Did no one ever speak the truth flat out?

"It's why I prefer typeface," Meg's father said. He sat forward and leaned on his knees. Meg recognized the tone in her father's voice; this was the voice he used to soothe her, no matter what riled her. "Type is solid and clear. Once you've set the type and printed the words, the meaning is there and obvious. People, people's talk, it's too slippery. It's all minnows in a pond."

"True," Mr. Dickens said. "People are afraid—of themselves, of one another. O they wish to speak the truth, I do believe that. But they know the truth can be brutal. So we concoct all these slippery words and habits of speech. The truth is in there, we all say, you just have to find it."

"Stupid people!" Meg folded her arms and fell into her chair. Mulberry rose from the hearth and moved to Meg's side. His message was clear: Everything would be all right.

"While this is a fascinating discussion," Aunt Julia said, "it gets us nowhere. Let us review the facts once more and assess our situation."

"We must go see Mr. Sam Weller the Boot," Meg said. "At Billingsgate Market. He is our next and only hope."

"No, Meg," her father said, and the silence that followed this utterance was profound.

Her father had spoken, had decided, and as was usual, it was expected that this was the end of the discussion. But there was nothing usual, to Meg's way of seeing, about this discussion. They were talking about finding her brother.

"Yes," she said. "We must. Why will you not allow it?"

"I have said no, and I will insist on that," her father said. He was sitting back again, retreating again. "It is far too dangerous a plan, a foolhardy plan. We do not know this Boot Weller. Billingsgate Market itself is a dangerous place, that's well-known. It is out of the question. You and Mr. Dickens have already risked too much."

"But, Father," Meg said. She softened her voice. Her father, she knew well, could often be persuaded by softness. "It will surely be safe in the day-light, with all business about. And Mr. Dickens—"

"Do not make me repeat myself, Meg." Her father pulled up on the arms of his chair as if he would wrestle them free. "It is an uncertain game you propose. You said it yourself, just now. It's all nonsense what these people say. We can be certain of nothing. I simply will not allow you to go."

Father and daughter stared at each other, hard and silent. The others in the room, people and dog and even the furniture, it seemed, looked away from their silent showdown. Everyone was pretending to have heard some stirring, scuttling noise in a dark corner.

Meg took a chance and broke the silence her father was trying to impose.

"But, Father—"

"Meg!" Her father nearly rose from his chair. "Speak no more on this. I have decided. I will not lose . . . one more minute on the subject. We must find a safer way to find your brother."

She was defeated; she conceded. For now. Her father was often stern, inflexible, especially in the immediate moment. But he could also relent, and rather gracefully, if with some gentle prodding from her.

It surprised Meg that her father had never caught on to her strategy. When she wanted something she suspected her father would deny, she would march right up to him, ask for her desire, and accept his refusal. Then some time later, she would ask again, only to receive another refusal, though a softer one. And she would ask again, and with each asking, her father's refusals grew softer until finally his will collapsed. She almost always got her way.

"Yes, sir," Meg said. She smiled inwardly.

"Perhaps there's something we've overlooked," Aunt Julia said. "What else can we do?"

Aunt Julia, as ever, was pulling everyone away from the conflict and back to the conference. And she'd given Meg, unwittingly, the opening she needed for her distraction. They would talk about something else, while her father slowly relented. A change of subject was needed.

"I've an idea," Meg said. "We can publish. Mr. Dickens and I stumbled on this today."

She took the broadside from her pocket and unfolded it

with care: BODY FOUND! Meg and Mr. Dickens told them about the signs, advertisements, notices they'd seen. Aunt Julia and her father listened, staring at the broadside; they seemed to be waiting for it to perform a circus trick.

"She's right," her father said to Aunt Julia. "This is something we can do, and do well, if I say so myself."

"Of course," Aunt Julia said. "If Orion can send a message to us, perhaps we can send one to him. If only to let him know he is missed."

"O, Father," Meg said, and she went to him and kissed his cheek. Her strategy was working as she'd hoped. "Thank you. Let's get started this minute."

"In the morning, Meg, in the morning." He patted her head, and she pulled away. "Such a project takes time."

Her father! Why was he so timid to act? She turned from him and stood by the fire. She wanted no one in the room to see the disappointment in her eyes. As hurt as she was, she knew she must bide her time.

All during this discussion, Tobias and Mulberry had been removed, as if speaking privately. Mulberry seemed quite content with their conversation, but then again, that was Mulberry's most favored expression, being a dog who was most often content with what was before him. But Tobias was growing more and more agitated. He kicked his feet against the floor, more and more rapidly, and he stabbed at the floor with his fingers.

"I've got it," he said of a sudden, prompting Mulberry to leap up. "We need to know *why*."

Meg growled, about to pounce on her younger brother, but he stopped her with a hand, as if he could sense her with eyes in the back of his head.

"No, Meg, listen," Tobias said. "We need to know *why* they kidnapped Orion. It's the one question we have not asked. We never asked *why* Orion. Maybe he had something someone wanted. If we only knew *why* they took him."

Meg shivered. She knew Tobias was right. In all the time she had imagined Orion's disappearance, she had not once imagined why it was Orion in particular who had gone missing or been kidnapped. As Dick Whittington knew too well, children disappeared every day in London—much too often. Meg read of these disappearances in newspapers, heard stories from the clucking gossips of her neighborhood, and of course, had read of such things in Mr. Dickens's own novels. It was as if London were simply too careless to hold on to its own, and had somehow misplaced them. Was there some large hole in London that swallowed children?

Tobias's notion—simple and perfect—opened her eyes. Maybe there was a particular reason Orion had been snatched. Perhaps whoever had taken him wanted only him. If only Meg could discover the reason.

Tobias was sitting up now, smiling and proud. He knew he was right, too.

"Huzzah, Master Tobias," Mr. Dickens said. "Spot on, my young friend. What a boy you have here, Campion. *Why? Why* did they take Orion? It's what I've been missing.

Yes, many children do disappear into London's underworld, but for many different reasons. And if whoever took him were following me, Orion must be worth something to them. *Why,* Campion, *why* did they take Orion?"

Meg's father turned away. Mr. Dickens stood above him, attempting to meet his eyes.

"Why did they take him, Campion? Think."

"Charles, please," Aunt Julia said. "It happens all the time—children disappear."

"Tobias is right," Meg said. "We never asked that question. After all, what harm could Orion do to anyone?"

"Aha!" Mr. Dickens spun on Meg. "A better question: What harm could he do *them*? That's the question. Campion, you may not know this—young men often keep secrets from those around them—but Orion had aspirations to be a reporter for the newspapers. We talked of it on occasion. Maybe he started his reporting career without informing us."

That was what Orion and Mr. Dickens spoke of, then, when Meg found them huddled in a corner over some notebook: reporting. If only he had told her, too.

"Perhaps he had discovered something," Aunt Julia said, "something someone wished to keep silent."

"A grand deduction, Julia," Mr. Dickens said, and he and Mulberry both leaped about a bit. "Think, everyone. What could Orion know?"

The room narrowed in Meg's vision. Now she saw only her father. There was something in his slow movements that drew all of her attention. He seemed to be rousing from a hundred-year's slumber—a great stone statue returning to its human form. During Orion's absence, her father had been a sleep-walker; he moved and spoke and was present, but only in the least way. Meg knew this was because his heart had been shattered—once again. He'd lost his wife and a new-born child, and now his oldest son. They had all lost much, but it had wounded her father most, and he navigated the world gingerly, as if afraid to open the wound again. But now he was rousing, and Meg saw, despite the rugged movements, some spark in him.

All eyes in the room fastened on her father, all mouths fell silent at the great effort it took him to rise. They watched him cross the room, throw back the curtain of his bed-chamber, and kneel by his bed. Meg thought for a moment that he might begin to pray. Instead he reached under his bed and withdrew a parcel, which he unwrapped slowly. He moved towards Mr. Dickens, holding a book before him. He held the book with both hands.

Meg recognized it at once—Orion's notebook. Orion was always scribbling in a notebook, one or another of them. He preferred a linen-bound notebook, with ruled paper to keep his sentences from spilling off the page, and he had obtained a selection of them in a rainbow of pastel colors. The one her father held now was peach-colored. He handed the notebook to Mr. Dickens, who sat down with it unopened in his lap.

At first a shout rose in Meg—how could her father have

hidden this, this notebook that might save Orion, bring him home? She wished to fly at him, to beat him with her fists—to wake him up!

But she saw she did not need to. Her father was stirring, and recrimination would help no one. After all, here was the notebook. And her father's face contained more than enough regret at that moment.

"I have been afraid of this, Charles." Meg's father was on the verge of tears, she saw. Tears that had been ages in coming. "Do not ask me why I have hidden it; I do not know myself. Fear is a fierce guardian of silence."

Meg moved to her father and put her hand on his shoulder. With great delicacy they smiled at each other.

Mr. Dickens opened the notebook. The first page was covered in ink. But the ink, to Meg's eyes, refused to line up in orderly letters and words. It was all scribbles, the tracks of a hundred small birds hopping about the page. Mr. Dickens flipped through the pages; each was filled with the scribbled tracks. Meg thought her eyes were failing.

"Lor-a-mussy! Why, it's shorthand!" Mr. Dickens said. "And if I know my shorthand, and I assure you I do, this is the Guerney Method. I should have this translated in no time."

"Shorthand?" Aunt Julia asked.

"Yes. A good reporter, I once told Orion, learns his shorthand first."

They huddled around Mr. Dickens while he translated the first page.

"'Saturday, 3 November. To Charlie's, half-day of fun, home again. Grilled capons for dinner. Exquisite. Sunday, 4 November. Frost on the panes this morning. Helped Aunt Julia bring in the summer plants. A clear blue bell of a day. Hazy orange sunset. Out walking at night with Charlie by the River.'"

Meg's heart most certainly did not leap. Part of her was overjoyed to hear Orion's words; she could almost hear his voice in Mr. Dickens's. But another part of her was crushed. While these were her brother's words, they revealed nothing, no secret, no signs of Orion's whereabouts.

"Campion," Mr. Dickens said, closing the book slowly. "I have some startling news. Your son appears to be an average young man who kept an average diary. But I know there is more here, much more. You have asked me not to inquire, but I must. Why did you hide this? You know it's shorthand, and you know you can't read it, but why hide it? Give me your intuition, so I may carry that into the notebook with me."

Meg's father walked to the hob and poured himself another coffee. He kept his back turned to them all. But even from this vantage, even through this silence, Meg sensed the change in her father's posture—his weariness was lifting, breaking off of him. Since Orion had disappeared, Meg had been sleepless, her father asleep. Now Meg was able to sleep again, and her father was stumbling from his slumber into the land of the waking. Meg wanted to throw herself at her father in joy. But she resisted.

Her father turned to face them, set down his tin cup with force.

"Orion," he said, "was up to something. In the months before he disappeared." He looked straight at Meg and offered her a thin smile only she could see. He went on.

"Orion was going out at night, late, often. By himself. Or so I thought. He thought no one knew, I suspect. But I'd hear him, after we were all asleep, or supposed to be. He'd slip out. Then he'd come back—I always woke up, that is a trait of parents—and he'd stay up for some time still, writing."

Meg's father paced a bit, stretching his arms high over his head. His sleep was continuing to thaw.

"I thought little of it. He's nearly a man, might as well be for all the work he does here. And so why shouldn't he go out on his own? I thought it all quite natural, and left him to it. But!"

On this last word, the room seemed too cramped for Meg's father. He paced about, uneasy. He went to the back door and opened it and stared out into the rainy afternoon. When he spoke again, he spoke very slowly, as if his fragile words might crash to the floor.

"But the moment he disappeared, I knew his night-trips were more than a boy's roaming. And I knew this notebook offered some connection. I have been afraid, Charles"—he looked right at Mr. Dickens—"to read that book for fear of finding my own failure inscribed there. I have been a fool."

Meg rushed to her father's side and held him. And so did, naturally, Aunt Julia. Tobias followed, holding on to

Meg, and Mulberry, too, circling them. The family gathered in a knot. And Meg almost laughed at them all, almost laughed at herself. Such a scene! It was, she saw, an illustration from one of Mr. Dickens's novels—all his novels were illustrated. The caption under this illustration would read "The consolation of the father." Nearly laughing, nearly weeping, she held on.

"Fine, Campion, very fine," Mr. Dickens said, standing and clutching the notebook. "That is a fine answer. And now we know. We must translate this. Until then, we are wandering in the darkness. The light of these pages is what we need."

Still surrounded by his family, Meg's father asked, "Will you do it, my friend? Will you?"

"I'd be honored," Mr. Dickens said.

Aunt Julia pushed away from Meg's father and straightened her dress and said, "We've much to do. I shall order a coffee-house dinner brought in."

But Mr. Dickens ruffled and gathered.

"It's near dark," he said. "Time for me to repair to my rooms. I'll begin to translate these tonight and return tomorrow when I've finished. With any luck, we'll know what to do next."

"And we shall create our broadside," Meg said. "It will be ready on your return."

Mr. Dickens stepped forward.

"Publish, Meg!" he said most theatrically. "You must

publish. The world must know, your brother must know, that we are looking to find him. Silence kills!"

And with that he clutched the notebook to his fish-monger's coat and fled the rooms into the rainy summer evening. But Meg hardly saw him go. In her mind, she was already designing the broadside.

Chapter IX

Draft—Copy—Compose—Chase—Galley—Again

It is generally accepted of reality that there are fields of endeavor suited to the male sex and fields of endeavor suited to the female sex. It is also assumed, generally, that what men will do women ought not to. Men, it is believed, may be statesmen or soldiers, bankers or bus-men, hod carriers, coal miners, ship's captains or crew, any variety, in fact, of gainful employment. Women, it is generally believed, may be wives and mothers.

Perhaps there will come a time—can we strain our minds to imagine a future one hundred, even two hundred years hence?—in which women and men will compete for the same positions of skill and adventure. But that time is not now. Now, today, 1862, in the year of our good Queen's Silver Jubilee, we assume that women will tend to the home, while men shoulder other duties.

But beware of thinking "generally." The world will often surprise you with its particulars.

Were there not women revolutionaries on the ramparts of Paris? Were there not women booksellers in medieval Italy? Are there not, today, women who write accomplished novels, though often under the guise of a masculine name? A quick tour of the world's history would offer us a million or more exceptions to what is generally accepted.

Take Meg's aunt Julia, for instance, who has ever been of a keen and inquisitive mind, most notably when it comes to the study of the Natural Sciences. All her life, Aunt Julia has devoted herself to the study of Botany, Geology, Mammology, Ichthyology, Ornithology, Entomology, Astronomy, Chemistry, and such. Yet, despite her inclinations *and* devoted study, she is not allowed to pursue her passion in a proper university. It is generally believed, despite evidence to the contrary, that the Natural Sciences are not the realm of the female mind. And so, refused from this avenue, Aunt Julia has continued her studies on her own.

Allow me another example, and a more pressing one, for it will lead us directly to Meg's doings on this quiet morning in the print-shop. Abby Letteri Pickel, Meg's mother, was one of the finest printers in all of London—how Meg hates the past-tense in that sentence, *was*. Like her father, her mother was born into a family of printers; each of the families—Letteri and Pickel—had been printers since before the Great Fire of 1666. Like Meg, her mother grew up in a print-shop, and printing was in her blood. And like Meg, her mother studied at home, educated *by* books and *in* the making of them.

Had it not been for printing, Meg often mused, there would be no Meg, nor Orion nor Tobias, for it was on an errand to Letteri's Fine Printing that Campion first met Abby. Meg, though not present on that day, has heard the tale so often, she sometimes believes she was. Campion, it seems, entered the print-shop all full of his nineteen-year-old bluster. Calling out to one of the apron-clad apprentices, "Boy, where is your master?" he was chagrined to find, instead of a lowly apprentice, the scowling blue eyes of Abby Letteri. This was how they met, and it is a memory Meg holds dear.

Campion, Meg's father, is known throughout London as a printer of excellent qualities. His work is meticulous, finely crafted, and always done on the best papers. But Abby Letteri may have been a superior printer. Her work shared all the traits of her husband's, but she was an inspired designer of printed matter. Meg used to watch, with fascination and admiration, as her mother took a customer's idea and turned it, with one quick sketch, into a piece of art. Her designs were elegant, balanced, and both clear and surprising. Meg and her father and her family and their companions in the London print-world considered her something of a genius. "Leonarda," Meg's father often called her.

It was with her mother in mind, then, that Meg woke on this morning and went down to the print-shop. She sat at the front counter, gazing at the BODY FOUND! broadside retrieved from yesterday's adventure, and tried to imagine her mother's spirit into hers. Staring at the broadside, however, she saw only her mother—her mother's straight black hair, tinseled with strands of silver; her small but powerful hands; her concentrated mouth; and most clearly, the sly sparkle of her mother's eyes behind thick spectacles.

However, no ideas came to Meg on this morning, and this would not do. She returned to the kitchen and made herself that necessary cup of coffee.

As she sipped her first sips, Meg fell deeper into her reverie, and her mother's voice arrived, too. "To *publish* is to make *public,* Meg. That is the meaning of the word. The reader must see and feel. No printed matter is for the printer's *expression*. The printer must *communicate*." How long had it been since Meg heard her mother's voice? But this thought roused no grief. Meg was thrilled to have her mother—if only in spirit, only in memory—in the print-shop this morning. And she was now able to see the BODY FOUND! broadside with greater clarity.

The entire top half of the broadside consisted of those two words—BODY FOUND!—set in the largest size of banner font. It was the size of typeface reserved for words like *War, Dead, Queen.*

Below that, in a much smaller type, were all the details:

where the body had been found, what it looked like, where to go to identify it, all signed with the ludicrous name, Detective Harold Organza. Whoever had created the broadside knew how to draw readers to it. The headline was astonishing.

A word crept into Meg's frenzied thinking—clarity. The printer of this broadside had used the simplest, clearest strokes. Nothing was obscure.

Then two new words leaped from Meg into the air—*Seeking Hunter!*

She dashed into the work-room. "I've got it!"

The entire family, Mulberry included, gathered around the work-table in the print-shop.

Meg pulled a broadside sheet from the scrap bin. The eleven-by-seventeen sheet of heavy paper had been smudged on one side with Tobias's thumb-print, and so was unusable. But paper was too valuable to ever throw away, and the scrap bin was a ready source of sketching paper.

The paper was laid out, and Meg's carpenter's pencil flew across it. At the top of the sheet she outlined the word SEEKING, and below that the word HUNTER. To this second line Meg added an exclamation point, to balance the number of characters, and then she shaded in the letters.

"Ah, yes," Meg's father said. "Bold, vivid." He measured the letters with a cloth rule. "I think we have that."

Below these huge words, Meg drew several horizontal

lines, indicating smaller type, where the body of the text would be.

"And here," Meg said, "we can leave a more detailed message for Orion."

"It's striking," her father said. He was standing away from the table, getting a farther look at the broadside. "And the message is a fine idea."

"But," Aunt Julia said, "the message cannot be too clear. If one of them—whoever they are, this Sampson Gang—if one of them should read it and discover it's for Orion, he may be in greater danger."

"True," Meg's father said. "It must be a message only Orion will understand, at the same time seeming a legitimate announcement."

Meg continued to shade the letters.

"Not necessarily," Meg said. "As long as Orion can read it, that's all that matters. The purpose of the message is to communicate with Orion, to let him know that we know he is still with us. If it's gobbledy-gook to the rest of the world, no harm. They'll simply move on to the next sign. London's too full of signs for anyone to bother with this one. They'll just shrug."

"Let's set a proof, then," her father said. "Meg and I will compose the headline. Julia, you work on the body of the text. Short, simple. Tobias, you—"

"No." Tobias stood perfectly still, his arms crossed. The print-shop was still, except for Mulberry, who now went to Tobias's side and sat tall next to him.

Meg waited. When Tobias got like this, waiting was all that mattered. He could be a most stubborn boy. And he would wait forever until he was heard.

"Have we missed something, Tobias?" Meg asked.

"Two things," he said, un-budged.

"And what might those be?" Aunt Julia asked with great earnestness.

"Thank you," he said. He stepped up to the sketch. "First: red ink. I know it costs more, but this needs red ink. So everyone can see."

"Absolutely," her father said. "Hang the cost. And second?"

"You've left off his mark," Tobias said. "Orion, the constellation. Without that, he might think it's just a hunter. It has to be even clearer."

Meg could instantly see it, the outline of Orion, nine stars in the shape of the Hunter.

Tobias turned over the broadside sketch and quickly tapped out the nine stars of Orion at the top of the sheet. Then he sketched in SEEKING HUNTER!, drew several lines for text, and at the bottom tapped out another outline of Orion.

This design offered less space for the text, but Meg saw that it wouldn't matter. The broadside was sharper now, and the two constellations were beacons. Tobias could not have been more perceptive. It was Orion's mark that had spoken to Meg at the Satis House, and so it should be Orion's mark that would return his communication.

Tobias stepped back, a huge smile across his face, all seriousness wiped away.

"That should do it," he said.

"O my," Meg's father said. "I'm afraid we have another printer in the family. 'Tis a pity."

Meg's father was always pretending to worry that his children would become printers. It was no kind of life, he always said. But his pride in his printer-children, even when he fretted, was evident.

Aunt Julia set herself up with a notebook and began to write the body of the text. Tobias was dispatched to count the supply of broadsheets and ready the press. Meg and her father went to the type-cases to sort the typeface and begin composing. Mulberry, left without a task, at first roamed from station to station, but, unable to help, settled at Aunt Julia's feet. His task, he seemed to decide, was to keep an eye on everyone.

Meg was charged with selecting the headline type and pulling the proper letters. There were eight different headline fonts, and Meg laid them out and studied them. Though the letters were backwards, Meg was used to looking at type this way. An experienced printer had to be able to read backwards, and sometimes upside down. Already she could see the printed page—in all its red-ink glory.

Her father was searching through the drawers of Odd

Sorts. These were marks and symbols that did not belong to a standard typeface, often ornamental pieces. Meg's father told her he was certain they had some star-shapes in the Odd Sorts—for the outline of the constellation.

Meg finally decided on an unnamed typeface that was plain and blocky. There were no flourishes on this type, no serifs. The lines of it were thick, nearly half an inch across for each leg of the *H*. This type did not whisper, it screamed, and what it screamed was, "Pay attention."

She chose two large composing sticks and set the letters in them. She tightened the composing sticks so the letters were flush and straight—compacted.

SEEKING
HUNTER!

She showed the composing sticks to her father. He carefully measured them, eyed them from far away, pored over them closely. He nodded his best nod, his unmistakable signal: perfect. Close was not good enough in printing; only perfection would do.

Her father had found stars in the Odd Sorts cases. There were a number of five-pointed stars, regular and symmetrical, each about one-quarter inch across. Then there were seven exploded stars, each with nine points of varying length; these were almost one-half inch across.

"These are beautiful," Meg said. "Let's use these. They're dynamic."

"They are lovely," her father said. "But we've only got seven. We'd need eighteen to make it work. We don't even have enough for *one* constellation."

Meg spread the dynamic stars in her hand.

"The belt," she said. "We'll use these for Orion's belt."

Meg knew that it was Orion's belt that made the constellation the most easily recognized. Out of all the stars, and the many combinations of them, there was only one straight line in the sky—the three evenly spaced stars of Orion's belt.

"Meg, Meg, Meg, O Margaret Julia Pickel!"

He laid the pieces out for the first constellation—three dynamic stars for the belt, the rest of the design in five-pointed stars.

Yes, Meg thought, I am quite clever, aren't I?

Without a word between them, they all set about their tasks. Aunt Julia was writing, and crossing out what she'd written, and writing again. Tobias was prepping the press. The print-shop was filled with the concentrated focus of activity.

Meg checked the spacing of her type again, then satisfied, for now, transferred the letters to the tray of the galley. Her father had taught her to hum as she lifted the letters, gently but firmly, from the composing stick. He'd told her that humming helped occupy her brain, so her hands wouldn't make a mistake. One wrong jolt and the letters would fly.

Once the letters were in the galley tray, Meg had to

reckon the leading. She had carefully measured the sketch and knew how much white space would be needed on the top and bottom and sides. The leading was lower than the raised typeface and would create only blank space on the page. When Meg was first learning to print, her mother had showed her that the white space in a design was as important as the visible elements. White space, what was absent, created the proper emphasis, drew the reader's eye to what was there.

Suddenly all the white space in Meg's life—the absence of her mother, the disappearance of her brother—filled her. Yes, absence was a powerful presence in everything. She shook off the absence, had to. Printing required full presence of mind. Distraction was costly. If she was going to communicate with her brother, she would need to forget him for the moment.

But before she could load the galley tray into the chase, which would hold the type securely in the press, she had to wait for her father to finish the two constellations. Working from his sketch, her father added leading and various stars directly into the galley tray. To check the true look of the backwards constellations, he put a piece of scratch paper over the design and pressed down, pushing on all the stars. When he flipped the paper over, Meg could see the indents of the stars in the paper.

But her father was not pleased. Orion's shoulders were too broad, he said. Working one constellation at a time, he removed the long strips of leading on either side of the shoulder stars, and replaced them with different lengths, both longer and shorter. Then he rubbed the paper over the type again and found he liked this version. Of course, changes might have to be made after they printed a "proof" of the broadside, but for now it looked good.

Meg and her father added one constellation to the top of the chase that held the headline. She placed the expandable metal quoins into the chase, and with rigorous turns of the quoin key, locked the top part of the chase tight. Even though there was no bottom to the chase's frame, the type would not fall out.

Tobias had prepped the press and stood by with a red-ink ink-ball. It was time for a first proof. Meg loaded the chase onto the press stone, and Tobias inked the type with the leather ink-ball. Meg lowered the tympan and its papers over the chase. The coffin was ready.

Meg's father pulled the printing bar, the machine gave an enormously satisfying clunk, and the entire coffin slid under the platen. The printing press groaned and squeaked, and Meg could almost hear the typeface impressing itself into the paper.

The coffin slid out from under the platen, and Meg lifted the tympan from the press stone.

Meg had always loved this moment, the paper pulled away from the typeface and the fresh, crisp ink, shiny and elegant. It was a lot of work getting a word into a piece of paper, but when it was finished, the word was no longer thin air, but embodied and undeniable. The word was now an idea become public; it was published. As her mother would say.

The proof was lovely. Orion's constellation looked perfect, and the headline—SEEKING HUNTER!—was bold and powerful.

Aunt Julia was ready with the text. She read it aloud.

> **Last winter our Hunter went missing, and since then, no other Hunter has filled our plane-tree table's feast. We are famished without our Hunter. While our Hunter has been spotted in the sky-parlor's dome, we still seek his return with the greatest Urgency. And we shall retrieve him.**
>
> **Signed,**
> **Mulberry T.D.**

The message was one Orion would surely understand. The reference to the Cheapside plane-tree would catch his interest, and Mulberry's signature would convince him. Orion would know he was sought after, know he was missed. Everyone else would be baffled.

While she had some doubts that the broadside was the magic charm that would return Orion to the family, Meg felt it crucial Orion know he was not alone, not forgotten. And besides, the more the family worked together on the broadside, the more her father seemed returned to his old self—the work was healing him. And the more he became his old self, the bolder he would be in the search for Orion. And the more likely he was to relent in forbidding Meg to go to Billingsgate. She only hoped that Mr. Dickens, in translating Orion's notebook, would bring news that would soften her father's resolve even further.

Her father called for more characters from the typecase, and Meg found them and handed them to him. For Aunt Julia's text they were using Bodoni Bold, a heavy, squat font that carried with it a certain grace. It was Orion's favorite typeface, too; always his first choice.

Meg's father began assembling a new chase, with all the elements included—constellation, headline, text, constellation. He tightened the last quoin and set the chase in the press. Tobias inked the constellations and headlines in red ink, the text in black, and Meg pulled the next proof—clunk!

The broadside was beautiful, or at least Meg thought so. It was loud and balanced—a perfect combination.

But Tobias was not convinced, and demanded another proof. He refused—as was his wont—to provide an explanation. He re-inked the headline in red and the text in black, but stopped there. He cleaned the type of the constellations and inked these—without a word to anyone—in bright blue ink. He loaded a sheet into the tympan and lowered it over the press stone.

"Pull," he demanded. Meg's father knew better than to resist.

The new broadside, with its bright blue belt of stars, was irresistible.

Tobias counted out the sheets of paper. They would start with one hundred copies.

The family got to their tasks: print, pull, ink; print, pull, ink.

Chapter X

The mysterious Mister B

IT TOOK ALL DAY to compose and print the broadsides. The Pickels were so busy with this task they'd forgotten to eat, and when they finished with the printing, they were famished.

Aunt Julia had gathered an early supper of cold ham and left-over potatoes, and the family were silently chomp-chomping when Mr. Dickens returned. No sooner had Mulberry inexplicably placed himself at attention by the back door, when the Great Man charged in without so much as a *tap-tap.* He was a member of the family now.

Meg wished to leap at him, beg him to tell her what he'd found in Orion's shorthand journal, but as was often the case with Mr. Dickens, a riveting distraction stopped her.

Leading Mr. Dickens into the rooms was a teetering tray of mugs and bottles suspended above a pair of cricket-thin legs. The teetering tray set itself upon the dining table to reveal a scruffy young boy. For all the commotion of his entrance, the boy was actually asleep in less than a second, right there on his feet. Not seeming to be asleep, but asleep actually. He stayed that way, snoring lightly and with all watching, until he heard the clink of the coin Mr. Dickens pulled from his waist-coat. The boy awoke with a start, snatched the coin, and fled.

Meg ran at Mr. Dickens.

"What have you found?" she cried.

"O, Meg, I've found plenty," he said. "But we must not enter such discussions on empty stomachs. I fear we've all worked too hard today. And it will take us some time to unravel this riddle. So time we must take. And supper, too."

The teetering tray of beverages was de-constructed and distributed. There was dark foamy porter for Aunt Julia, Meg's father, and Mr. Dickens, and for Meg and Tobias, ginger beer, a favorite treat of theirs but one they could rarely afford. And for Mulberry, a large bowl of stewed beef swimming in its own juices. Before Meg had her first taste of the tangy-sour ginger beer, the stewed beef had disappeared and its bowl was licked clean.

While they finished supper, all the talk was—to Meg's frustration—of the "nicety" variety. It was all she could do to hold herself, but she did, letting the niceties flow over her like so much water.

Mr. Dickens was just pushing himself away from the plate Aunt Julia had made for him, groaning with appreciation, when Tobias sprang up and sprinted down-stairs, whistling for Mulberry to follow. Meg had wanted to wait on the broadside and get right to Orion's journal, but Tobias, she knew, was as proud of the broadside as if it were his own creation. He had been most anxious to show it to Mr. Dickens, and Mr. Dickens would oblige. Patience, Meg counseled herself, patience.

When Tobias and Mulberry returned from the printshop, it was Mulberry who carried the broadside. Tobias had rolled it into a tube—as good a dog as he was, rolling broadsides was beyond his skill—and Mulberry held it gently in his teeth, dropping it into Mr. Dickens's lap. The broadside was in perfect condition, without a spot of drool, and for his delicate performance, Mulberry was offered the last chunk of cold ham.

Mr. Dickens admired the broadside no end, and even before he knew who had set it, was particularly admiring of the headline and its typeface. When Aunt Julia pointed out that it was all Meg in the headline, Mr. Dickens seemed to glow more brightly with admiration. Meg hid her blush under a long gulp of ginger beer.

Mr. Dickens wished to pay for the posting of the broadside, and Meg's father eventually conceded. Meg knew that her father's pride was uneasy with such a gift, and she also knew that any additional cost, at any time, might prove a hardship for her family. She watched her father struggle with this problem, but it wasn't until Aunt Julia spoke sharply to him—"Don't be ridiculous, Campion!"—that her father relented. He seemed relieved that the broadside would go up at Mr. Dickens's expense. Meg was relieved in her own manner, relieved that her father was relenting, that he was capable of relenting.

Mr. Dickens's reasoning was simple—he could afford it. Money, he claimed, was a burden as much as a benefit, and the sooner he was parted with it, the better for all concerned. "It's only a shame," he said, "more of humanity doesn't understand this simple notion. So much of humanity believes that the getting of money, and the keeping of that money, will improve their lives. Where it is almost always not so simple a formula. Just enough money, that's what benefits people."

All were agreed on the broadside, and the next morning a crew of boys from Wynken de Worde & Co. would arrive. Mr. Dickens often used this service to promote his magazines and books and performances. He would instruct them on "broad coverage," meaning the broadside was to be placed throughout London-Town, at its busiest points, and with some special emphasis on Thames-side.

Finally, it was time for Orion's story. Meg herself was impressed with her patience.

Mr. Dickens had spent the day translating Orion's shorthand. He was rusty at first, and found it frustrating at times. Orion used abbreviations for many names and places, but little by little, the squiggles leaped into the shapes of intelligible words. Mr. Dickens claimed to have enjoyed his task. It was, he said, like writing someone else's novel, and much easier for that.

The notebook, Mr. Dickens discovered, contained in its earliest pages whatever Orion saw and felt and heard on any regular day. Did Meg know, for instance, that her brother harbored a rather strong affection for a young dress-maker named Sarah Gates? Meg blushed at hearing this, as if on Orion's behalf. Orion had never said anything about this Sarah, who worked, if Meg was correct, at Trish Daly's Daily-wear on Cheapside. But she now remembered that whenever she and Orion walked past the dress-shop, her brother slowed his gait and occasionally offered a secret little wave. Of course.

Mr. Dickens opened the notebook and smoothed flat the first page with his hand. Everyone leaned closer around the dining table, eager for the tale to commence. Mr. Dickens drew back some.

"But first I have to ask about Charlie. Charlie may be our best hope in finding Orion. They were quite the chums, it seems, and he is certainly involved in this tale. Do you know Charlie, where to find him?"

They did not. No one had heard talk of a Charlie. Another secret Orion had been keeping. Meg understood it was only natural for Orion to be keeping his own counsel; she understood that the older one grew, the more one was likely to keep secrets from those one loved. Had she, in fact, ever told Orion about her feelings for the knife-grinder's son, a pencil-thin and wild blond boy whose name she did not know? Still, she could not help being angry with Orion at this moment. If he'd told anyone in the family about

Charlie, they might have already found Orion. Or if Orion had made his feelings for Miss Sarah Gates known to Miss Sarah Gates, Orion might be spending his time with her this evening. Meg would much prefer to lose her brother to a young girl's heart than to the vastness of London.

And why did Orion have to write in shorthand, that secret language? Plain English might have saved him months ago.

"There is much in this story," Mr. Dickens said, "that helps explain, or so I believe, Orion's rough departure. Listen close; help me to read it. It seems that last autumn . . ."

It's a wondrous thing, I hope you'll agree, to listen to Mr. Dickens spin a tale. But every story happens in at least two places—in the words of the storyteller, but also in the mind of the listener who receives the story. And who is to say which is more marvelous, the story told or the story heard?

I put this to you, dear reader: We have heard enough of Mr. Dickens, for the moment at least. Let us experience Orion's tale as perceived by our own Meg Pickel.

Orion's Tale
as heard by Meg

Autumn was coming on fiercely. The first bright, clear warm days of it gave way one morning to cold, blustery winds. The city felt skeletal, stripped to the bone of the summer that had embraced it for months. Orion loved such days; he could never resist walking out into them. So he invented an errand in the Leadenhall Market, and having convinced his father of its necessity, set off. It was on this day he met Charlie.

All that could be known of Charlie was his first name, the fact that Orion had met him by a food-cart at the market, and that the two young men became instantaneous friends.

Charlie, Charlie, Charlie—nothing but talk of Charlie for weeks. While there was no description of Charlie, Meg believed she could picture him—tall and thin, with an open face, green eyes that laughed most hours of the day, all topped by a mop of ginger curls. It did not matter that Meg had no basis for this image of her brother's best friend. All that mattered was that Meg had a bright enough picture of Charlie to be able to see her brother standing next to him.

Charlie and Orion found excuses as often as possible to get away from their families and spend time walking about London. This was their passion—walking about the City and absorbing every detail—the people, the buildings, the weather. Orion called their task "the Catalogue of the City."

Meg recalled that season, last autumn, when Orion was suddenly absent much of the time. He did his chores, he finished his studies, he helped their father in the print-shop, but he did all these things with great speed, hastening to get out the door to his "perambulations," as he called them. Meg remembered being jealous then, but oddly not-jealous at the same time. She missed her brother, did not like him being so often gone—missed his laughter and his silly hummed tunes. But Orion had been so excited last fall—his laughter that much louder, his hummed tunes that much sillier—that to watch him bolt out the door, towards who knows where, gave her great joy.

Then, on 17 November, everything changed—

And that, thought Meg, was where all stories started. One Day everything changed; One Day something happened that altered the course of life. It was on One Day that the ordinary world became extraordinary.

On 17 November, just as the sun was melting into the orange haze of the west, Orion and Charlie stumbled upon a kidnapping.

They had been traipsing about the construction sites of the new Blackfriar's Bridge, watching the furious hive of men working in the near-dark. They were watching this from atop a mound of brick and rocks, when Charlie nudged Orion in the ribs.

"Look," he cried. "Down there."

Orion turned and saw a knot of people at the entrance of a near-by lane. His senses sharpened in the lowering dusk; he heard the scuffle of shoes on stone and the hoarse murmurs of force and resistance, saw the circle of men close around two shivering boys. The boys—they were young, eight or nine—had been swept off the main thoroughfare and, surrounded, were about to be swept away from their lives.

Without a word between them, Charlie and Orion scrambled down the brick mound. If the boys were being press-ganged, and there was no doubt that they were, Orion and Charlie had to act fast.

"Stop! Police!" they yelled. Their only and best plan was to raise a ruckus. All about them, the people of London went about their business. Only Charlie and Orion seemed aware of the press-gang, while the rest of London turned a cowardly blind-eye. If Charlie and Orion could make enough noise, perhaps . . .

They were nearly upon the gang of men. Orion saw their ragged coats, the creased boots, soiled hats; he could not see the boys, who were hidden now by the members of the gang, as if they had been swallowed by a bear. Orion wrote that he and Charlie descended upon the men without foresight or fear. They knew, or at least felt, that they themselves were in no danger of being added to the press-gang. The kidnappers were too busily occupied with the younger boys.

How like Orion, Meg considered, to fly into a fray selflessly. She'd once seen him stand before a sway-backed dray-horse a man was beating with great cruelty. Orion placed himself between the horse and its master, un-flinching. The man was huge, and as angry as men come, but Orion's stubborn resistance eventually stilled his awful whipping. Her brother did not suffer cruelty.

Two of the gang turned on Charlie and Orion. In that moment Orion saw the eyes of one of the poor boys being abducted—only the eyes, his mouth covered by a man's gloved paw. Orion would never forget, he wrote, the fear in those eyes, never, not even after he was dead.

The world stopped still in that second, but soon sprang to life again. The two men who faced Charlie and Orion flipped open their torn and greasy coats and drew menacing truncheons. They stopped Orion and Charlie with the blunt ends of these dangerous clubs.

"Back off, lads," one of them said. "None of your business here, nothing to see. Shut your gobs and move on now. Or join us." And he laughed loudly at his partner, who laughed in return. This was another sight from that day Orion would never forget, the pink, laughing mouth of this hooligan and the fat caterpillar moustache that framed it.

Fat caterpillar moustache! Mr. Dickens looked

up at Meg when he recounted this. The man at the séance with the fat caterpillar moustache. Meg thrilled at the news.

Orion felt the truncheon heavy against his ribs. He stood motionless. Charlie growled and lurched forward, but the other kidnapper whacked him sharply with his truncheon, and Charlie fell onto his back. The kidnapper stood over Charlie, the truncheon planted firmly on the tip of Charlie's nose.

"Didn't you hear my friend here?" he whispered to Charlie. "He said there ain't nothing to see, and I can vouch for that. My friend here is a man of the highest honor—the *highest* honor—and if he says there ain't nothing to see, there ain't nothing to see. You don't want to be impugning my friend's honor. For if you do, I might have to impugn your skull. Understood?"

Charlie, his eyes angry slits, nodded grudgingly. Orion felt the truncheon in his own ribs again.

The description of this scene stunned Meg's heart. She knew Orion had survived the encounter, but the stark cruelty of these men, as expressed through her brother's words, made her see and feel—yes, *feel*. She *felt* the truncheon in her own ribs.

"A right honorable decision, my young friend," the kidnapper said. "Now off to your mam and pap."

The kidnapper rose and turned, but he swung around at the last moment and thwacked Charlie once, hard on the side of his leg. Orion heard the sickening thud of wood on flesh. Charlie cried out, clutching his thigh.

Meg's stomach lurched at this description.

The kidnappers swarmed the alley and surrounded the younger boys, and the suspicious knot fell in with the crush of oblivious London crowds.

Orion bent to Charlie and helped him stand. He was bruised and frightened, but otherwise all right. He wanted to race after the kidnappers, but Orion urged caution. They would watch until the kidnappers turned the next corner, then follow from a distance.

So they followed, from Orion's prudent distance, as the knot of kidnappers made their way through the streets of London. For the casual air about them, the kidnappers might have been going to a fair.

At last the kidnappers and their prey reached their destination, a freight-hold in the back ways of Billingsgate Market. The freight-doors were opened, and the two kidnapped boys were unceremoniously pitched in, followed by all but one of the gang. That last one sat on an overturned half-barrel, the lookout.

Billingsgate Market! Aha, Meg wanted to shout. It was where Miss Jenny Wren had urged them to visit and where her father forbade her to go. With each passing word of Orion's—as transcribed and re-told by Mr. Dickens—she felt herself drawing closer to her brother. And she found more and more evidence for urging her father to change his mind.

Charlie and Orion kept up their vigil from behind an abandoned dray-wagon, until nearly midnight. The only movement they detected was the nodding head of the look-out as it passed into slumber then jerked itself awake again.

Thus began their surveillance. For weeks they hung about Billingsgate Market, during the day and sometimes at night, but always together. They kept copious notes of the comings and goings of the gang of kidnappers. Nearly every day new boys were brought to the freight-doors, through which they disappeared. Orion and Charlie never saw any of the boys leave.

It was clear that these kidnapped boys were being press-ganged into some sort of work slavery. So Orion and Charlie began to ask questions in and around the Billingsgate Market, questions they hoped were innocent enough. If there was an illegal work-house being operated out of the lower holds of the market, with children toiling at thankless jobs for no wages but thin, watery gruel, someone would have seen evidence of it.

Charlie and Orion devised a plan of action. Knowing they were no match for the truncheons and brutality of the kidnappers, they decided they would tail the kidnappers until they were able to put all the pieces together—who was kidnapping, who was kidnapped, and most importantly, why. Then they would take their report to a newspaper and expose this criminal behavior. That was their best hope for rescuing the children. "The light of the truth," Orion wrote in his notebook, "will free them."

They kept up their surveillance, it seemed, until the day Orion disappeared. That day they had discovered a name. Orion was convinced the man who owned this name was behind the kidnappings. Mr. B was all Orion wrote in his notebook.

Meg returned in her mind to the night Orion disappeared, and she saw him, *Great Expectations* tucked under his arm and staring into the London night. She knew now what it was he had been thinking on that night. He had been thinking about the mysterious Mr. B.

And then Orion disappeared. The pages were once again white.

✦ ✦ ✦

"It seems," Mr. Dickens said, "that our Orion was already a reporter. And a fine and brave one at that."

"Maybe *B* is for Billingsgate," Tobias said. "The man who owns the market."

"O that it were so simple," Mr. Dickens said. "But good solid thinking, my boy."

If she weren't so tired, Meg might have snapped at Tobias, might even have tweaked his arm with a bee-sting. Lucky for Tobias, Meg had not even the splinter of wit anger requires. And he was just trying to help. They'd all run out of fresh ideas ages ago; at least Tobias was making an effort.

They had all—Mr. Dickens included—spent the last hour slumped in chairs around the hearth-fire. Even Mulberry, poor dog, sapped of all energy, was lying on his back in front of the fire.

The entire evening they had tried to figure which step was the next in their search for Orion. A round of fresh coffee for all—even for Tobias—had not helped. A stroll on the roof-garden, in the fresh after-rain breeze, had not helped. Writing down, again and again, everything they knew, had not helped. They were, to put a point on it, stuck.

It wasn't that Meg had no idea of how to proceed. She certainly did, and a very clear idea at that. She and Mr. Dickens would seek out Mr. Sam Weller the Boot, as instructed. And while there, they would also seek out the mysterious Mr. B and the freight-doors Orion mentioned in his notebook.

The time was now, Meg knew. She would ask her father—softly, softly—to allow her and Mr. Dickens to go to Billingsgate. Orion's journal had made the case for her.

"Father," Meg said, and she did believe she might have actually batted her eyelids. "Father, I know you have refused this once already, and I mean no impertinence, but listen to Orion's journal. Billingsgate Market is the place. We must go there."

But before her father could say anything, another obstacle showed its nasty teeth.

Mr. Dickens was sorry, he said, to inform Meg that he would be leaving London in the morning. He was obliged to "return from France." On the following day, Sunday, he was to offer one of his public performances, and in order to do this, he had to return to Dover on Saturday, so that he might get his papers duly stamped and "return from France." This was all quite silly, he knew, but he begged Meg's indulgence. On Monday, however, he would be delighted to accompany her to Billingsgate. If her father agreed.

Meg was shocked by her father's response; she had misjudged his softening.

Saturday or Monday or Guy Fawkes Day made no matter to Meg's father. No one, not even Mr. Dickens, was to go to Billingsgate Market. It was a dangerous place, and these were dangerous men, and Meg's father simply would not allow it. Not now; not ever: The discussion was closed. It was necessary, Meg's father tried to say with a voice of great calm, to imagine other actions that might be taken.

At that moment, Meg imagined, very clearly, another action she might take. It involved shaking her father by the shoulders until he came to his senses.

But she held her temper.

Relenting to her father's refusal, they all—Mulberry included—put their heads to thinking of other actions.

Perhaps the police again? Perhaps, but the police were often corrupted, paid by criminals to look, quite happily, the other way. And besides, hadn't Meg's family gone to the police before, only to be told that boys would be boys? There was this problem, too: What evidence did they hold?

What about Charlie? Maybe they could find Charlie. Looking for Charlie, however, might be as long a shot as looking for Orion. If they had been reporters together, maybe both had been press-ganged. And if Charlie was still at liberty, wouldn't he have come looking for Orion long ago? There wasn't a single clue in Orion's notebook that led to Charlie's address, not a thing about his family.

Every idea that arose sank again. They were all defeated.

There was only one idea, Meg knew, of any merit, and it was the one idea her father most adamantly refused. She had tried for hours to honor her father's refusal, to honor his position as her father, but she was giving up. If her father would not honor Orion, why should she honor him?

She stood and approached her father's chair. He looked like a rag doll that a child had played with much too often.

Pity clutched at Meg's heart—he seemed so forlorn. But pity would only reinforce his stubborn grief.

When she spoke, she spoke with great determination.

"Father," she said. She was shaking, she knew, but thought her nerves might not be visible. Mulberry sprang up, ears cocked forward.

"Father," she said. "I am going to Billingsgate Market tomorrow. With or without your permission."

Tobias actually gasped. Mulberry whimpered.

"You know how I feel about this. I cannot allow it," he said.

"I do not care if you allow it. I am going."

"Meg," Mr. Dickens said, "perhaps if you wait—"

"No, Charles," her father said. "This is our matter. I am shocked at you, Meg. If you refuse to obey, I will lock you up until—"

"Until when?" Meg stood her ground, stared intently into her father's eyes. "Until we are all dead? You have locked us up these six months now. And what? Nothing. We are still without Orion. How many more locks can you put on us? I *am* going."

All around, the room was silent; even the fire refrained from crackling.

Aunt Julia jumped into the middle of this silence.

"Then you go, Campion. Go with Meg; go by yourself; take all of us. Someone must go. If no one, then you. You go."

"But, Julia. How can I?" Her father was shaking. "Tobias;

you; the shop. How can I go there and be here, and how can I ever leave here? How can I let Meg go away from here? After . . ."

His shaking subsided; his voice died. Meg saw the terror in her father, and knew it for what it was. He did want Orion back, but at the cost of losing someone else? He was terrified.

Her father stood and faced her. They were nearly the same height now, Meg saw for the first time.

He kept opening his mouth to speak, but no words emerged. A minute crept by.

The same minute crept by again. Then Aunt Julia's voice, as quiet as the fog.

"If it were Orion in pursuit of Meg," she said, "I daresay you would allow him to go, Campion. And you and I know Meg is as brave and as clever as her brother. Perhaps more sensible, too. Let her go. She will return."

Her father turned to Aunt Julia, his face a gigantic plea for understanding. Aunt Julia smiled at him.

"Mulberry," Mr. Dickens said, and obedient Mulberry shot forward, prepared for any command. "She shall take Mulberry. It will be market hours, she'll be safe. I know our Meg, Campion."

Meg's father looked from Aunt Julia to Mr. Dickens and back again. All smiled at him.

"Father," Meg pleaded. "It's Orion. Our only Orion."

Her father looked to Tobias now, who was nodding with great vigor. Then he turned to Meg.

"Yes," he said, and Meg knew that her father's icy resolve had melted. It had been thicker than she had imagined. But now it was gone.

"Yes," he said. "Thank you."

And they embraced. Meg felt the violent shaking of a human heart—whether hers or her father's, it did not matter.

Chapter XI

To the hunt!

THERE WERE MANY MEGS in the mirror this morning. She had not expected that. Like most of us, Meg believed that a peek into the mirror would offer her a portrait of who she was, right then and there—a simple reflection. But she had not counted on the mirror's magical properties. In fact, she never knew of such properties until the moment she gazed into the mirror and found so many different people looking back.

It was a stroke of genius, Meg thought, the idea that she would dress like a boy today. That this was Meg's own idea did nothing to diminish the cleverness of it. After her father had agreed—at last!—to let her go to Billingsgate Market, Meg put forth the idea that dressing as a boy was a perfect disguise. Dressed as a boy, and accompanied by Mulberry, Meg was less likely to be harassed. She also believed her boy-disguise would put her father at greater ease.

Aunt Julia further refined the disguise by proposing that Meg appear occupied. Why couldn't she take some broadsides with her? A boy with a task moved more swiftly through the crowds; a boy with a task was expected somewhere. Tobias put it most succinctly, "You're going to be a sign sticker-upper."

Slipping out of her night-dress, Meg donned some old clothes of Orion's that were being saved for Tobias—breeches, buckle shoes, stockings, a torn and patched shirt, a brown waist coat with black glass buttons. Then she pinned her hair into a tight bun and hid it under a soft-billed cap, capturing a few stray strands and tucking them under. There—she was a boy!

This metamorphosis Meg registered first through sensation rather than sight. She felt her legs free and mobile in the breeches, her arms loosened from the constraint of a dress's pinched sleeves, her breathing eased from the fetters of a tight bodice. O and her feet, in the rugged, hard-soled, buckle shoes, ready to run and fly through London. She felt the changes in her body, and only after she felt them, did she see them in the mirror in Aunt Julia's chamber. Yes, she looked like a boy.

Orion, of course, how could she not be Orion, dressed as she was in his clothes? Not until this moment, though, did she recognize herself in her brother's face. How similar their noses were, a bit squarish. When Meg smiled at this thought, she saw how her nostrils flared a bit, exactly as Orion's did.

The portrait of Orion she carried in her heart was

growing more vivid with every passing day. In the months he'd been gone, that portrait of Orion had faded from her memory. Even the one photograph of him, taken only the year before and which she saw each morning above the hearth, had ceased to look like him, or anyone else. But since that first night, since the moment she stepped off her roof and went in search of him, her memories of Orion began to return, and with vigor. Not just the way he looked, but all about him. She carried these re-captured memories with her like a bag of shiny coins. And now, here he was, in her own face. He was coming closer and closer.

Then Tobias flashed into the mirror's reflection, his pointed chin so much like hers, with its little crinkle. When she laughed at this, the crinkle in her own chin became more pronounced, more like Tobias's, and her adoration of Tobias—even when he was a horrid little monkey—swept over her.

Aunt Julia, who had the same chin as she and Tobias did, suddenly stepped into the mirror. Meg wondered how many of her ancestors on her father's side had possessed this chin. Meg tried on a familiar gaze of her aunt's, that fully concentrated look she achieved when she was at her studies. Would Meg herself ever be able to appear so captivated by the world? She thought she caught a fleeting moment of her aunt's intelligence in her own visage.

And at this, her mother appeared in the mirror, all in Meg's eyes and high cheeks, and Meg stopped breathing for a moment. Her father often told Meg how much she resembled her mother and that this was a comfort to him. So Meg had always assumed she looked like her mother, but had not seen it herself until this morning. And she wondered if her mother's resemblance were truly a comfort to her father, or, instead, a source of grief. Losing Meg might be, for her father, like losing her mother all over again. She could not allow that to happen; she would stay cautious today.

As if to remind her, the fluid mirror transmogrified again, and there was her father. Did she resemble him at all? Undoubtedly, especially in her masculine outfit, but this resemblance was harder to describe. It might have been in the shape of the neck, or in the earlobes, and there was a definite similarity in the space above her lips. She couldn't say, it's in the eyes, couldn't say, it's in the mouth; no, the resemblance was everywhere.

Then she was Meg again, but younger, a girl still, before Orion's disappearance, and she laughed at this, the surprise of it, and in her laughter, returned to Meg, the Meg of today, who was both more troubled and excited than that younger Meg. She waited for this Meg to pass, to become some other version of herself—what might a future Meg look like?—but no change came. This was the one and true Meg—the Meg setting out to retrieve her brother.

She strapped on the canvas shoulder bag of rolled broadsides, checked once again for the brush and glue at the bottom of the bag, and the notebook and pencil there, and pulled her cap over her eyes. She was a boy now, a boy with a task.

✦ ✦ ✦

Torn between leaving without a word and upsetting her father, Meg stood at the front counter of the print-shop, rather close to the front door. If she called her good-bye from here, she might be able to exit without a last lecture. But before she was able to decide, her father, sensing as parents do the slightest movement of a child, called out, "Hold a minute, Meg, a last word."

Her father came to her, put his hands on her shoulders and gazed into her eyes—her mother's eyes. Meg saw her face in her father's, felt again the fear he must carry for her, and relaxed into his admonition. Mulberry stood near the front door of the print-shop, wagging and pacing.

"Meg, you are only to speak to Mr. Sam Weller. You are only to look about. Speak to no one else; do nothing foolish or heroic."

She offered more than required.

"I promise, Father. I'll only look today, only take notes. Sam Weller, I promise you, is my only contact. I will be very safe, and always make sure to be surrounded by the market crowds. Mulberry is with me."

He kissed the top of her head.

"You have the money Mr. Dickens gave you?"

Meg felt in her pocket for the pouch of coins Mr. Dickens had pressed on her.

"Yes, sir." She jangled the pouch.

"Take a cab, there and back. Don't dawdle. And . . ." His voice died.

"Yes?"

"Don't be late. Be careful."

He kissed her again on the head, then released her, but—

Ring-a-ring-a-ring! The bell over the front door chimed to life, and a customer entered. Meg started to leave, but her father put his hand on her shoulder. Mulberry pranced and whined softly. Exactly, Meg agreed, let us be off.

The customer was a woman. No surprise there; most of her father's customers were women. And a well-dressed woman, too. Again, no surprise, for a well-dressed woman was a wealthy woman, and these made up her father's clientele. The woman also seemed to be in an extreme hurry. All of her father's customers were always in a hurry. In a hurry to pick up their orders of calling cards, so they might drop them onto the silver trays in the homes of other well-dressed women, where they would then spend hours sipping tea and talking, Meg always imagined, of how busy their lives were.

"My good man," the woman said, "I've come to pick up my calling cards. And if you'd be so kind, I'm quite pressed for time. I ordered them via messenger."

"And you are, madam?"

"Why, I am Mrs. Bogle. Mrs. Charles Bogle. Please do hurry. I've a carriage."

While there was little in general to surprise Meg about this customer, there was one surprise, and a rather large one. Meg knew for a fact that this was not Mrs. Charles Bogle. The woman before her was Mrs. John Podsnap, the woman who had been at the center of the séance. It was this woman whose card she and Mr. Dickens had recovered from the Satis House sky-parlor. No matter what her calling card might say, Meg would recognize this woman anywhere. It was her head-dress that identified her. Meg had been struck by it that first night at Satis House, and found herself even more struck by it now. Surely no other woman in London would dare to wear such a thing.

To call this head-dress a hat would be a gross injustice to all hats. What the lady wore on her head seemed quite undecided; it could not choose whether it wanted to be a very small piece of architecture or a rather large piece of French pastry. It was a head-dress, Meg thought, of considerable ambition. Along with its ambition, and its height—which matched its ambition—were the golden ornaments that hung about it, hiding here and there in the massive structure like sparrows in a hedge. Meg recalled that at Satis House she'd thought of the hat as a Christmas tree, but hedge or Christmas tree made no matter, it was ornamental. One ornament was unlike another. There was a small key, a delicate lock, a fanciful heart, a prancing dog, a sleeping cat, a baby's rattle, a tiny star, and oddest of all, a railway engine. It was a charm hat, Meg saw, though far from charming. And there could be no other one like it.

But how came this woman and her ridiculous hat to the print-shop? And why did she go by two names?

Her politeness overcome by curiosity, Meg stared

openly at the woman. Mrs. Bogle—or Podsnap or Bogsnap or Pogle—offered a smile to Meg, but a small smile, the least she could afford. If her smile was money, it would have been a farthing, worthless.

Meg continued to stare. She was a boy now, and boys were not expected to be as polite as girls.

Meg's father returned from the work-room with a case of calling cards. He handed one of the cards to Mrs. Bogle, who examined it with the care a jeweler might give an heirloom pendant.

"I am quite satisfied, sir," she said, with an air of extreme self-satisfaction. "The workmanship is superb. The letters are fully drawn and in the proper order. The paper is obviously superior. It is a satisfying job, one fitting a lady who will distribute such a card—namely myself."

Meg snuck a peek at the cards. Indeed, they said MRS. CHARLES BOGLE. In full it read BOGLE MANOR, PARK LANE, HYDE PARK.

"Might you send the invoice to Mr. Bogle, good sir?" Another farthing-smile.

Meg was beyond staring now. She was, to put a word to it, gawping. Mr. Dickens had supposed, that night at Satis House, that Mrs. Podsnap was a grieving widow. And yet today she presented herself as Mrs. Bogle. It was a simple enough deduction; Mr. Podsnap, poor soul, had left Mrs. Podsnap a widow, and Mr. Bogle had married her. Hence, both Mrs. Podsnap and Mrs. Bogle, two names for one woman. This all seemed clear enough to Meg, with the exception of one query: If Mrs. Bogle was married again, what business did she have speaking with the spirit of the late Mr. Podsnap? All Meg could deduce from this line of thinking was, people were certainly odd.

"As you wish, madam," her father said in a hushed tone. Meg had often heard this tone in her father's voice. As wealthy as his clients were, he was continually battling with them for payment of the meagerest amounts.

"Good day, sir," Mrs. Bogle said, not so much straightening her hat as straightening herself under it. "And you, lad, if you'll take these to my carriage, there's a nice reward in it for you."

It took a fraction of a minute for Meg to realize that she was the "lad" in question. Meg tipped her boy's cap and picked up the box of calling cards. The box was no bigger than a tin of biscuits, and Meg was not at all clear why Mrs. Bogle was incapable of carrying such a trifle herself. Then Meg remembered the charm-laden head-dress Mrs. Bogle wobbled under, and understood that the least disturbance might bring both lady and head-dress crashing down.

Meg's father kissed her cheek, and she and Mulberry followed Mrs. Bogsnap into Tonson Lane, the door's bell clanging behind them.

At Cheapside, a carriage awaited, the finely liveried driver atop it a portrait of intense watchfulness, as though the carriage were already under way. The carriage itself was a marvel, and one of the newer marvels of the world. It was almost impossible to see the Brougham's six wheels and enormous size for the splendor of the deep plum sheen of its lacquer-work surface. Even in the dim summer haze-light, the carriage glowed.

The carriage door was already opened, and Mrs. Bogle contrived to get into the passenger compartment without upsetting either head-dress or carriage. Her pale, bejeweled hand patted the rich leather seat beside her. Apparently she was incapable, as of yet, of touching the box of cards in any manner. Meg wondered if Mrs. Bogle ever touched her own calling cards, or if there were some other "lad" whose role in life was that.

Meg dipped her head into the carriage and set the box of cards precisely where Mrs. Bogle indicated. From the dark corner of the carriage, a pale face emerged. It was a young woman, not much older than Meg, an attractive girl, with black hair severely pulled back. But such was her demeanor that one almost missed her attractiveness. The young woman had high shoulders and a low expression. She emerged from her corner as if peeking into the future, but as soon as the girl got a glimpse of that future, she retreated. The last detail Meg saw of her was a velvet choker around her thin neck. It struck Meg that the choker was very much like the collar of a dog.

Drawing back into the sunlight, Meg offered a feeble "Thank you, ma'am," her hand held out for its reward. Mrs. Bogle's pale, ring-laden hand flew out of the carriage, a coin pinched in her fingers. She dropped it into Meg's hand, and at that moment, the carriage darted into Cheapside, frightening several other carriages that already occupied the street.

The coin in her hand was a farthing. Worthless.

She pocketed the coin and pulled out her notebook, where she wrote "Mrs. Charles Bogle, Bogle Manor, Park Lane, Hyde Park."

Though Billingsgate Market could not yet be seen, Meg knew she'd arrived by the great tide of fish-stench that rolled over her.

A crowd was streaming into the main entrance of the Market. Meg insinuated herself into it and was carried along into the grand, high arcade. Rows and rows of fish-stalls filled the long hall, and the noise within was overpowering. Meg stopped at a nearby fish-stall and stared into the cold, gleaming eye of an enormous salmon. The sound-cloud that enveloped her now made its noises plain—the sound of humans cursing.

Billingsgate—that's what her father called the obscene language of London's streets. So renowned were the curses and threats of the fish-mongers here that all bad language was called Billingsgate. And now Meg knew why. She barely understood half the words that streamed past her, but what the sense could not tell her, the sound did—the rage of these words was scorching, and she suddenly felt quite vulnerable. To block it all out, Meg hummed and sang her favorite song—"I'm just a little girl, lost in the fog, me and my dog, won't some kind gentleman see me home."

Poor Mulberry! Assaulted by the odors and the noise, he seemed for a moment confused, his head rocking back and forth. But one mighty sneeze changed all that, and in quick order, he was on guard again.

When she crossed to the far end of the long arcade, Meg found several refreshment-stalls—coffee, tea, ales and porters, cigars and pipes, and of course, every type of fish, cooked in all ways imaginable. There were, as well, several booksellers. It was impossible to find a single space in London that did not have a bookseller crouching near-by. Perhaps, Meg often thought, London was not a real city, but merely an invention of those who had spent time reading it into existence.

The book-stall of K. Egan & Co., Bookseller and Stationery Services, drew Meg to it. The proprietor, a young woman of keen intelligence and wit, as made obvious by her charged gaze, smiled kindly at Meg. Meg returned the smile. In the loud and angry market, Meg found a comfort in the book-stall. She felt at home here.

K. Egan stocked new books and previously read books, cheap paperback serials and expensive leather-bound volumes much beyond Meg's ability to own.

Stacked at the far side of the stall on a flat table was *Great Expectations*, followed closely by a trail of Mr. Dickens's other novels. A lamp shone over the books, and painted around the lamp's globe was a silhouette parade of Mr. Dickens's most loved characters—Pip, David Copperfield, Mr. Pickwick, Peggoty, Oliver Twist, Tiny Tim, and the character all loved, for they loved to hate him, Ebenezer Scrooge. In a basket on the table were Mr. Dickens souvenirs—Pickwick pennants, Oliver Twist buttons, Tiny Tim ribbons.

"Do you favor Mr. Dickens?" K. Egan asked.

"O yes, ma'am," Meg said.

"Don't we all?" K. Egan said.

Meg's eyes were riveted on the final volume of *Great Expectations*. She prayed Orion had it in his possession still. She wanted him to have more than memories for amusement. She also still hoped, a little vainly she knew, that he would bring it back with him—so she could read it. This thought made her feel very small, but she could not help herself.

"Have you not read *Great Expectations*?" K. Egan said. "I think it's my favorite of all. We can only hope there will be new novels by Mr. Dickens."

"O there will be," Meg said, smiling to herself at the thought of the new novel Mr. Dickens claimed to have found near the Six Jolly Fellowship Porters. To think she had been there at the exact moment of his inspiration!

K. Egan picked up the third volume of *Great Expectations* and stroked the cover. She handed it to Meg. Like all good booksellers, K. Egan knew the irresistible lure of a book once it's put in a reader's hands. Books were purchased, K. Egan knew, as much with the hands as with the mind.

Meg stroked the violet-and-gold binding. She felt the

pouch of coins in her pocket. Would it be so awful to use Mr. Dickens's own money to purchase the final volume?

"Would I be able to purchase volume three alone?" Meg looked up with hopeful eyes.

"I'm sorry, young man. I must not break up the set. You understand. What good is the first part of a rousing tale without its rousing conclusion?"

Meg handed over the book, quite relieved.

"Thank you, ma'am," Meg said, and without thinking, offered a little curtsy. A girl's curtsy.

K. Egan offered a puzzled smile and returned to alphabetizing her stock.

Meg wandered among the other book-stalls, pretending to gaze at their wares, but sneaking glances about the Market for Sam Weller the Boot. In the dim corner of the food-court, a white hat bobbed about, seemingly unconnected to the head that bore it. Meg focused on the hat, and the market's dimness pulled aside like a theater curtain to reveal a figure seated on a boot-polisher's stool. Boots and shoes crowded around him, as if their wearers had suddenly disappeared. This was the only Boot here, so Meg snapped her fingers for Mulberry's attention, and together they approached the white hat.

"Pray, sir," Meg asked with her best politeness, "are you the gentleman they call Sam Weller?"

The Boot stood and stretched, and laughed most heartily.

"Aye, young man," he said. "Sam Weller I am. But as to 'gentleman,' well, like the banker said to the pick-pocket, 'You don't know me very well, now do ye?' "

"Why no, sir, not yet I don't."

Sam Weller was, without a doubt, jolly in all his countenances. His white hat, old as it was, was a cheerful hat nonetheless, tilted to one side like a drunken balladeer. His waist-coat was coarse-striped, but his black calico shirt-sleeves relieved it of its coarseness, as did its blue glass buttons. And to make a final point about the jolly nature of this man, around his neck hung a bright red kerchief. Taking all this in, Meg conceded to the man's jolly air, and she smiled at him.

"My dear boy," Sam Weller said. "Don't be afraid. For all my talk I am still Sam Weller, and Sam Weller is here to assist you. Is it a shine you need?"

Meg looked down at her brother's old shoes. No polish could help their cracked leather.

"I've come for your confidence, sir," Meg said. She was trying to use her lowest register of voice. Did she sound like a boy? "A little bird has sent me."

"Ah," Sam Weller said. "Miss Jenny Wren. That name to me is like the question the traveler utters upon seeing his manse, 'Are we home then?' But tell me, so I may trust in you. How big is Miss Jenny Wren? Show me with your hand."

Meg placed her hand at her waist. Mulberry, attentive dog, moved under it, expecting a pat.

"Yes, it's true," Sam Weller said. "She is small of

stature—poor creature. But also how big is she? In what other ways?"

Meg pondered this question. Then she threw her arms wide, wider than all of Billingsgate; for such a tiny figure, Miss Jenny Wren was huge in spirit. And then Meg drew from the pocket of her brother's breeches the wren-impressed coin Jenny Wren had given her. She handed it to Sam Weller, who examined it, then returned it to Meg.

Sam Weller snapped his fingers.

"That she is. As big as all the world, she is, and twice as smart, and believe it or not, five times as wise. And so no poor creature is she. It's true, then, that you are Miss Jenny Wren's friend if you see past her arms and legs and aching back. 'What,' my boy, 'brings you here?' as the well did say when the run-down horse approached it."

For one moment Meg considered playing her cards close to her chest, but Sam Weller's smile overwhelmed her caution. Meg knew a real smile from the farthing-smiles of most of London. She looked to Mulberry for his assessment; he agreed that Sam Weller could be trusted.

She reconstructed for Sam Weller the links in the chain that had brought her here. First, her brother's disappearance, then the long months of waiting, the Satis House sky-parlor, the séance and the Sampson Gang, Mr. Micawber, Miss Jenny Wren, and of course, Orion's notebook and the mysterious Mr. B. It was an odd and lengthy chain, she said, but it seemed to her to lead in one direction, and one only: Orion had been kidnapped by the Sampson Gang.

Meg paused for a breath. Had so much happened in the space of mere days?

Though his smile continued, the timbre in Sam Weller's voice grew suddenly somber.

"Sit, boy, sit," he said. And of course, Mulberry sat—good dog! Sam Weller turned over a bucket for Meg. "Now, let us continue smiling and talking, as did the cat after he had swallowed the master's canary. And I will tell you what."

Sam Weller picked up a crumpled, lifeless boot, spit on it several times, and began to brush it.

"The Sampson Gang is near, aye, and a work-house they do operate. Them who run it think it is well hidden below floors of Billingsgate. That is, it is right below our feet. So well hidden, do they imagine it, that what they call a work-house is more a prison. And because the men who run it do believe it is so well hidden, why, everyone in London knows of it."

He propped the boot on a stump and began to black it.

"As to your mysterious Mr. B, I cannot help you there. But it 'seems a natural slope,' once you find the Sampson Gang, as the river said to the ocean."

He stropped the boot to a shine with a rag that had once been white.

"But I cannot take you to this vile work-house, as I am Sam Weller, and Sam Weller is not welcome. You see, when those who belong to that work-house see Sam Weller a-coming, it might as well be the fox into the hen-house, for 'Alarm, alarm,' is all they say."

He started in on the boot's partner.

"But you, you're a smart lad, and unknown, and if it's your brother you seek, you must seek him. Here is what you do."

Meg listened intently. The idea was clear. She—or *he*, in this case, as Sam Weller seemed to believe—would walk out the east end of the market, then turning left, and left once again, should come to the first set of doors on that wall. But under no charge should he—*she*—enter those doors. Near to the doors, however, was a window casement, always open. If Meg, unobserved, could obtain the window and enter it, she would be in the work-house, but on a ledge high above the work-house floor, and all hidden by wooden crates. From there she could observe and perhaps pick out her brother.

"Can you do it, d'you think, my boy? Caution, though. Once in, you are on your own. Sam Weller'll never hear your distress. Can you?"

Her father had sworn her to observe today. Therefore, it seemed logical to Meg that entering the work-house, at Sam Weller's urging, was a form of observation. What possible danger could there be in that?

The first doorway was where Sam Weller said it would be, and the minute she saw it, Meg knew it was the doorway Orion and Charlie had seen the night of the first kidnapping. She froze for a moment, but Mulberry yipped at her and recalled her to her purpose.

She unpacked her glue-pot and brush, and unrolled a broadside, posting it over an older broadside for a closed theatrical. To the right of the doors, she glued another broadside, this over an advertisement for a brand of ready-made shirt collars.

Just as she was sticking the broadside to the brick, she spied—startled, breathing sharply—the smudged chalk outline of Orion the Hunter. As she'd seen it on the floor of the Satis House sky-parlor. It had rained a gusher two days before, and yet here was the vibrant white chalk, intact and dry. Orion had been here, and since the rain.

A huge bubble rose up in Meg's chest and threatened to burst her into smithereens. Or she would weep. Or she would faint.

She knew what her father had insisted on, that she was only to look, no more. No heroics, he'd said, by which he meant no danger, and this building suddenly smelled of danger. She knew that if she entered the work-house, she would be trespassing against her father's wishes. But could she simply turn now and go home, when Orion might be only feet away from her, separated by mere bricks? Could she go in? Could she refrain from going in?

She was here to observe, she promised, and she decided that to observe *properly,* she would have to trespass. That seemed the only logical conclusion. Even if she knew she was lying to herself, and breaking her promise.

Nearly sunken into the ground was the window

casement Sam Weller had spoken of. There was no glass, no iron grating—it was open, as promised.

Meg moved to the window, pretending to work at her broadsides and glue-pot and brush. Mulberry poked his snoot in her way, obviously anxious. Meg gently took his snoot, gazed into his eyes, and spoke to him calmly.

"Mulberry. Stay." He whimpered. "You must. Stay. If someone comes close, raise your alarm."

Mulberry quieted and lay down, glancing at Meg with an uneasy expression. She kissed him, then rolled onto her side, and slipped into the open window.

Chapter XII

In which porcelain is transformed into iron

MEG LANDED WITH A THUMP on a brick ledge high above the basement floor. A wall of wooden crates hid her from view, and hid the view from her, it must be pointed out. She lay still, wondering if her entrance had betrayed her. Nothing. She waited again. Nothing, no alarms, only the steady clang of metal striking metal, a chorus of enormous mechanical birds. She sat up and peered over the edge of the top-most crate.

The basement of the Billingsgate Market was a long, low cavern of stone and brick, as dingy and desperate as the catacombs of St. Paul's Cathedral. But no dead lived here, only a sort of living-dead. For at table after table were hundreds of dead-eyed but still alive children.

There were boys *and* girls here, and Meg's brain was shocked at this fact. When she had thought before of all the disappeared childen of London, she always imagined boys, and boys alone. In an instant the reality of the picture became clear to her. If grown-ups were heartless enough to enslave children, why not girls, too? Enslave one child, enslave them all. Meg took a deep breath.

Each child—girl or boy, it did not matter: children—was ragged in rags, filthy in soot, haunted by no-expression, worked at the same task. Hammers raised and struck iron; hammers raised and struck iron; hammers raised and struck iron.

Meg was so in the thrall of the scene that she lost, for a moment, all sense of her mission. She forgot that she might be in danger, and forgot, worst of all, to look out for Orion. But the sharp prick of a splinter, where her hand ran across a wooden crate, awakened her. She removed the splinter with her teeth.

There was no Orion here, no children at all close to his age. None of these dead-living children were older than Tobias. Two thuds of grief, then, pounded her chest. First, that there was no Orion, and second, that these young children were kept in such an infernal place and tied to such hellish activity. This was a horrible world she'd invaded. She'd read of work-houses, in the papers and in the novels of Mr. Dickens. These accounts of children forced into degrading labor always filled her with horror, as is only natural. But to see such a place with her own two eyes; well, Meg now knew the true meaning of horror.

On a raised platform at one end of the hall, a round and red-faced man in a cocked hat and woolen coat presided over the work-house. The man held a hook-topped staff, and with this staff he beat out the time to which the living-dead worked. Each time he beat the rhythm, the golden embroidery on the man's coat shimmered briefly. Though his expression was dull, the man seemed proud of the order of his world.

There were two other grown men in the work-house, both in greasy great-coats. They flitted about from table to table, and child to child, and at each child they moved to, they each cracked a wooden rod on some part of that child—a back, a shoulder, a hand, a noggin. These random beatings were precisely that, random. The two men offered their beatings under no direction, without any system, and to no obvious purpose. The men seemed to offer the beatings simply because they were able to.

The children who suffered these beatings must truly have been the living-dead; not one of them offered a yelp or a groan. Or perhaps they did yelp and groan, but their protests were killed by the awful cold of the place that now settled into Meg's bones. Today, London was stifling hot, but its under-world was arctic. Meg took a fit of shivers—whether from the bone-chill of the place or the dead-alive children, she was not sure, nor did it matter.

Meg thought she ought to weep, but tears seemed inadequate. The scene before her was eternal, with no beginning and no end—these children had always been here in this work-house, and would remain so forever. How could tears change that?

"Mr. Bumble," one of the overseers cried out. He had grabbed a boy by the collar of his shirt, yanked him out of his place at the long tables, and was dragging him towards the man with the staff. "Mr. Bumble, Mr. Bumble."

Mr. Bumble's staff stopped its pounding rhythm, and the work-house's hammers grew quiet.

"Yes, Mr. Sampson," Mr. Bumble said. "Is there a problem?"

Sampson! Horrible as this place was, it was the place Meg sought. She had found at least one of the Sampson Gang. And Mr. Bumble, too. Bumble with a B.

This Sampson turned to face the long tables, speaking more to the living-dead children than to Mr. Bumble. Meg recognized the fat caterpillar moustache at once—the man she'd seen at Satis House, the man her brother had described in his notebook.

The boy trembled before Mr. Bumble. Mr. Sampson cuffed him on the ear—because he was able to.

"O yes, Mr. Bumble," Mr. Sampson said, speaking to the children. "Mr. Wag Eddgelington, nine years old, of this establishment, has been kind enough to point out a grave error to his esteemed masters. It seems that young Wag here is tired. He was wondering if he might have a bit more rest."

"Rest?" Mr. Bumble cried. "You want rest, Mr. Eddgelington?"

"Yes, sir, please, sir," the boy said, with more strength than Meg thought the dead-living could muster.

"Thank you, Mr. Eddgelington," Mr. Bumble said. "For pointing out the great deficiency of our work-house."

Here the boy straightened up, as did most of the other members of the living-dead.

"We must keep you from fatigue, then, Mr. Eddgelington. The only known cure for fatigue, my young man, is more work. Do you see the sense in that?"

The trembling boy trembled more.

"Mr. Sampson," Mr. Bumble called. "Please see that our friend here is given the largest hammer we have." He held up a hammer whose head was twice as large as that of the others. "Back to work, you curs!"

Mr. Bumble pounded out a quick-step rhythm, and the hammers flew to iron. The boy was returned to his table, where he struggled to strike with a hammer he could scarcely lift. Mr. Sampson cuffed the boy's ear again—because he could—and set off in search of another victim. The work-house returned to its hellish clanging.

Meg wrote feverishly in her notebook, attempting to capture all she saw, and by capturing it, make some sense of it. But how, Meg wondered, did one make sense of something that should not exist at all?

There was a strange task a-foot in the work-house. Runners ferried bucket-loads of iron pieces to each table. A child seated at that table picked up one piece of iron, dropped it into a wooden docket, then poised a rod of some sort over the iron piece. The hammer swung down on the rod, pushing it into the iron. The iron was removed from the docket and set aside, where it was collected by the runners and their buckets.

The scene was so indecipherable that Meg would have to get closer to find the reason behind it.

There was a narrow gap between the ledge on which Meg had perched and the wall of wooden crates that hid her from view. She eased herself into this gap, her fingers gripping the ledge, and then let go, landing softly on the basement floor.

This passage ran the entire length of the work-house, and Meg inched herself along it, towards where Mr. Bumble stood fiercely beating the time. It was a risk, she knew, to move towards him, but that was where the crates were being un-packed, and as it turned out, re-packed. Holding her breath, she sidled that way, careful of the noise she might make, wary that she might nudge the wall of crates and send them tumbling like a giant-child's blocks.

Each of the crates had pasted on it an elaborate label type-set in a fanciful Gothic script. The design entranced Meg as she scooted along, and she wondered why so much pride had been exerted on a label that was only an indicator, she assumed, of the crate's origin and destination. At first she was so struck by the design of the labels that she overlooked the words on them.

Fortunately, the power of typeface, no matter how elaborate, will eventually force the reader to make sense of symbol, and one word from the many packing labels she had passed blossomed in Meg's consciousness: Bogle.

She stopped short and touched the label of one of the packing crates, but with a little too much force. The stack of crates wavered. Meg held her breath. The crates did not fall. She read the label.

Bill of Lading:

From: Bogle Kiln-fired Manufactory
Prinsengracht
Amsterdam

To: Bogle's Porcelain Emporium
c/o Tellson's Bank Forwarding

Contents: Bogle's Enchanted Chinese Tea Sets

Bogle!

Mrs. Bogle, who was also Mrs. Podsnap, had been at the séance at Satis House, and as fate would have it, was also in the print-shop this morning. Was the Bogle on the crate the Mr. Bogle of the Mrs. Bogle who wore a silly Christmas tree of a hat? Could there be more than one Bogle in London? Surely there was a connection. Meg knew that this was the work-house Orion and Charlie had been spying on, and Orion had pointed to a mysterious Mr. B, who seemed to be intimately connected with the work-house. And now, in the work-house, the name of Bogle again. And, too, the man with the caterpillar moustache from the séance! So many connections—too many.

There was also Mr. Bumble to consider—was he the mysterious Mr. B? He hardly seemed mysterious. And Orion's notebook pointed to the man *behind* the work-house. Mr. Bumble was surely *inside* it. She had no proof, but her instincts told her that Mr. Bumble was no mysterious Mr. B.

Thank heavens for her notebook. Mr. Dickens was wise in his insistence on the notebook, for it allowed her to put down her thoughts, and once her thoughts were safely there, etched into the paper's memory, she could turn her attentions to other matters. Nothing would be lost.

Into her notebook she copied as faithfully as possible the names and addresses on the crate's label, and what she could make of the connections between the names Bogle and Orion. And Mr. Bumble, too, for thoroughness.

Done recording, she inched along again and made her way to the end of the narrow passage, where the crates were being un- and re-packed. Here the stacks were shorter, so Meg dropped to her knees and crawled. She peered around the last safe corner of the crates.

Labels often lie, that is a given on this earth, and that was certainly the case here. What were being removed from the freshly opened crates were not Enchanted China Tea Sets at all. In fact, it might be said that what emerged from the wooden crates were the opposite of Enchanted China Tea Sets, being that what emerged from the crates were capable of turning Enchanted China Tea Sets into piles of porcelain rubble—large iron bolts, each about two inches

long and one inch thick, mounds and mounds of heavy iron bolts. Nary a tea set in sight. What magic crates these were—to transform porcelain into iron!

Meg peeked deeper into the warehouse.

The bolts were taken to the tables, where the children, living or dead or in between, stamped each with a punch and a hammer, and the bolts were then re-gathered, replaced into the crates, and those crates re-sealed. Not a sliver of porcelain.

But why? Meg recognized the punches the living-dead held above the bolts, which they slammed with hammers into the heads of the bolts. They looked like long pieces of type, the punches did. She had watched a silversmith friend of her father's punch his maker's mark into silver bowls, candlesticks, cups. The children were, whether they knew it or not, placing their marks on these squat pegs of iron.

One of the bolts had fallen from a crate, but several feet away, where Meg might be vulnerable to discovery. Yet now was no time for shrinking, and Meg knew it. The pounding of Mr. Bumble's staff, and the pounding echoes of the hammers on punches on bolts filled the air. She stretched out and grabbed the bolt, retrieved it. Unseen.

Meg inched herself back along the narrow corridor between crates and wall until she could stand safely again. She examined the bolt and found on its dome letters that would not reveal themselves to her until much later—MR. The mysterious *MR* B? But no time for that now, Meg.

If the work-house was too much of a cacophony for

anyone to notice Meg's hand reaching out for a bolt behind an opened crate, it was not so much of a cacophony that no one could fail to notice the stacks of crates that tumbled outwards from the wall. Those crates on which Meg leaned while examining the bolt—forgetting the caution required—were empty, and they tumbled. And there stood Meg, examining a bolt while the entire contents of the warehouse examined her.

"It's a boy!" Mr. Bumble shouted. "Boy! Boy! Boy! You, Sampson, you, get that boy!"

They were all closing on her, Mr. Bumble and the two Sampsons, and Meg had yet to consider her options. Considered, then, she concluded that the only way out was the way she'd come in. And as if to ratify that thought, Mulberry, fine dog, began barking at her from the window casement.

There are some who say that every down-turn in fortune brings with it a surprising up-turn—the proverbial silver lining. This theory has not yet been proven, and is open to considerable debate, but on this day, a silver lining did appear. The crates that had tumbled, along with exposing Meg, provided her now with a neat stairway up which to run. And up which she did run, headed to the window casement.

Behind her Mr. Bumble ran—if you could call it running—and below her the Sampsons, Mr. and Mr., slapped at her legs. But Meg was too fast and reached the window and slid out of it at the precise moment that Mr.

Bumble's intimidating staff brushed the last of her heels to leave the work-house.

Mulberry barked once at Meg, telling her in his own way to run as fast and far as she could. Then he turned his attention to the window casement, barking and snapping, attempting to tell Mr. Bumble and the Sampsons that they should return to their positions, they were not wanted on this voyage. Mr. Bumble and the two Sampsons apparently did not speak fluent Mulberry, and they would each have glowing red reminders of this fact on their hands and arms for several weeks. In short—to quote Mr. Micawber—Mulberry bit them.

When Meg reached the far end of Billingsgate Market, she turned and whistled for Mulberry, who, proficient in all languages, understood her immediately: We must be off. And they were.

Meg often used to come to the Iron Bridge—Southwark Bridge it's named but Iron Bridge it's called—for the relief of it, for being away from the boisterous streets. Being here, alone above the broad Thames, was as close to being in the countryside as Meg had ever come. No buildings here encroached upon her—all was broad sky and the mirror of that sky in the flowing river. London's spires and domes and sky-seeking roof-tops seemed only a wondrous dream.

And the wind, O the wind, blowing in from the sea, O the wind refreshed her mind and her soul. This bridge was often her refuge. Often? Not as often as she'd like, for the threepenny toll was not often found in her pockets. She would manage, in some fashion, she promised herself, to re-pay Mr. Dickens for the loan from his leather pouch.

She dropped three penny pieces onto the toll plate, and she and Mulberry strolled onto the bridge, staying close to the railings to avoid the carriage traffic. She stopped one moment behind a gas-lamp, and scanned the crowd for her pursuers. No one chased her. She had lost them. Cutting and dodging through the dock-side's narrow streets, and with Mulberry leading the way, there was no hope for Mr. Bumble and the Sampsons.

Walking along in the thick river of pedestrians, they stuck to the eastern rail of the bridge. Mulberry's twitching nose poked at the air. Time above the river, with all the river's mingling smells and steady breeze, must be for a dog, Meg considered, like reading a novel in five minutes, the story of so many scents in such a brief time.

Beyond London Bridge the great ships stretched, docked and under way, like a forest of leaf-less trees, their masts spindly in the hazy light. An unaccountable fear overcame her there. Was Orion, at this very moment, outbound on one of those three-masters, was he bound for the far world, was he kidnapped aboard? Had Mr. B shipped him suddenly away? No, he must still be here. She'd seen Orion's fresh mark, seen today a man who'd seen him lately. She must continue to believe he was in London.

Halfway across the bridge, she and Mulberry chose one of the recessed benches, an oddly empty one, and sat quietly for some time. A boy and his dog, Meg thought. No one passing knew anything about her, not even that she was a girl, and there was comfort in this, and security, too.

Her body was in repose, but her mind was a-buzz, racing through the events of the rather confusing day. She took out her notebook and reviewed her notes. A neat triangle formed, one that seemed unavoidable. Orion to Mrs. Bogle, Mrs. Bogle to Bogle's Enchanted China Tea Sets. Bogle—the name haunted her. It all came back to the name of Bogle. But her mind could go no further at the moment. All the pieces were gathered—in her mind and her notebook—and that was sufficient for now. She could not wait for Mr. Dickens to return from France. She had such news to share.

Directly across the bridge from her, on the mirroring bench, a girl not much older than Meg sat all alone. She was petite and pale under a dainty bonnet, and wrapped around her was a woolen shawl the color of mourning. And the girl did seem to be in mourning, though for what or whom, Meg had no idea. Her eyes were puffed from tears, her countenance weary. She was indulging her emotions, cradling them softly the way her shawl cradled her from the wind and the traffic and all of London.

"She might be me," Meg said to the Thames breeze. A week before, Meg understood, she herself was still cradling her grief for Orion, as she had cradled it for six months. It had comforted her to indulge herself. But now, since that night on the roof of Satis House, since she'd earnestly undertaken the hunt for her brother, she could no longer allow herself to weep and mourn. A black shawl and a wistful gaze would not bring him back. Action was imperative. Yes, she might have been that girl once, but she was not her now and would never be again. Keep moving, that was her commandment.

Meg stood and hailed a passing cab. Mulberry leaped in, and they were off. Surely Mr. Dickens would want her to make haste.

Chapter XIII

What is revealed; what is concealed

ONCE AGAIN BEFORE THE MIRROR. Except that on this morning, the mirror refused to show the many Megs that had recently inhabited it. Today, Sunday, it showed only one, the clear and plain reflection of an indivisible Meg. She saw and understood the reflection in her aunt's bedchamber mirror—there was no denying its reality—but she was uncertain how to feel about the Meg who stared into her eyes. This Meg was a liar.

She brushed her tangled hair, tugging hard at her scalp, tilting her head to one side, then the other, and examining her reflection. There was the mouth that had spoken falsely to her father. There were the eyes that had darted away from her aunt's questions. There was the Meg who had feigned sleepiness. There was the Meg who had lied to those she loved most.

It made no difference what she looked like on the outside; on the inside she was who she was.

When she had returned from Billingsgate Market, her family were all waiting for her, her father obviously relieved to have her home, hugging her to him with great ferocity. It was when she felt her father's arms around her, and in his grasp felt how fearful he'd been for her, that she knew she would have to lie to him. If her father knew what had transpired at the work-house, if he knew that Mr. Bumble's staff had brushed her shoe, if he knew that the Sampson Gang had nearly captured her and that only Mulberry's heroics had stopped them, if he knew any or all of this, then Orion would be lost forever. Her father would simply put a halt to it, as he almost had before.

Gathered around the dining table, Meg told her family what true parts of her adventure were necessary. Yes, she'd found Sam Weller the Boot, and yes, he'd directed her to a basement work-house. She had seen the children, the living-dead children, at their work, but no, there'd been no Orion. The children were all much younger. But she had seen Orion's mark, his fresh mark, and it was plain he had been there recently. This was the best news of all. Her family, as was only natural, rejoiced.

And the mysterious bolt, stamped with the letters *M* and *R*, she showed them that, and they puzzled over it, but were unable to crack its code. And her notes of what she'd read on the crates' labels, these she showed them, too, and all were convinced that Mr. Bogle and the mysterious Mr.

B had to be related, if not one and the same. She told them, too, about the woman who'd come to the shop that morning, Mrs. Podsnap, who appeared to be Mrs. Bogle. All were delighted with what Meg had discovered, but that delight was only made possible by her lie.

Meg did not even hint that she had put herself in danger. Instead, she told them that she had witnessed all she'd seen from a perfectly placed crack in a wall, and that she had found the crates and this one bolt left heedlessly in a trash heap. She had been fortunate, she said.

"Fortunate, indeed, Meg," Aunt Julia asked more than said, and her aunt's suspicious gaze raked Meg's countenance.

"Fortunate, yes," Meg answered, her eyes darting from her aunt and settling on the bolt, which sat in the middle of the table. "And this bolt is most fortunate, too, for it may be our best clue."

Her aunt relented, though suspicion clouded her face still. They all proceeded to discuss the bolt, endlessly it seemed, and what it could possibly mean, how it might lead them to Orion. They talked until enough time had passed and Meg felt she could reasonably begin to feign sleep. She yawned and stretched and rubbed her eyes, until everyone, including Tobias, insisted on her retiring for the night. And so, while the sky still held its last vestige of evening, Meg readied herself for bed.

"One last thing, Meg," her father said. "This arrived today, from Mr. Dickens. We shall see him tomorrow, as promised. Perhaps he can help us unravel the mystery of Mr. Bogle's bolts."

Meg unfolded the crisp note.

> To La Famille Pickel,
>
> Have returned this morn from France. Carriage to meet you all at 11:00 sharp. Lunch at Hanover Sq. Rooms, to be followed anon by a public performance of a literary work, both performance and literary work the invention of your humble servant,
>
> Mr. Charles Dickens

"Yes," Aunt Julia said. "Mr. Dickens may help us. And a good night's sleep, too. Yes, a good night's sleep"—here Aunt Julia looked too closely, too warily at Meg—"a good night's sleep might help us all."

But Meg did not sleep. Not at first. Not for a very long time, truth be told. She lay in her bed, her head a-flame with the events of the day, all she wished to report to Mr. Dickens, dreams of Orion's return, and the thudding realization that she had lied, and quite easily, to her family. To her father.

Do not, however, mistake Meg for some perfect child who had never ever told a lie. She had, as all children, and—*ahem*—adults, had, too. In the past, she had, and with some frequency, protested that she had not done what she indeed had, or had claimed to have done what she indeed had not. These lies, our commoner lies, seemed miniscule, though, compared to the lie she had told her father that evening. The lie she had told her father—that she had not been in danger—was a lie that, when found out, would break his heart. She had lied to him about the one thing he would most wish her to speak of truthfully.

But it was impossible now to turn back on that lie. Too much was at stake. It was no longer just Orion who had to be saved. She vowed to herself, twisting in her bed and waiting for sleep, that she would save the work-house children, too. No child, she knew, should ever be made into a member of the living-dead.

Only after she swore to herself that one day, when the world was made whole again, she would tell her father the truth of the Billingsgate adventure, was she able to fall asleep. And that moment, dear reader, came long after the midnight bells.

Whether Meg approved of herself as a liar was of no concern the next morning. So she brushed her hair with several vigorous strokes, and let it stay down and loosened, the portrait of a perfectly innocent and honest young woman.

When Meg rose to dress, a quick excitement flushed her—she was going to one of Mr. Dickens's legendary performances. All the world loved his performances, but while Meg knew of them, knew Mr. Dickens as a friend and as the writer of her favorite books, she had never once dared imagine she would be in his audience. She had to look her best.

It did not take her long to choose the dress she would wear—she owned only four dresses. And of those four, only one would suffice for today. This was her finest dress, which meant that she wore it twice a year, on Christmas Day and Easter. Petite corn-flowers covered a field of pale yellow cotton. It was a summer's day of a dress, and certainly the most extravagant piece of clothing she'd ever owned, as evidenced by the lace on the hem, neckline, and cuffs. It was a beautiful dress, she loved it, and while she would never share this secret with anyone, believed it made her look very, very mature.

But since Meg had worn it last Easter, and the Christmas before, this meant the dress was at least six months old. It also meant that the dress, though purchased originally to be large for her, was now one hair from being too small.

Normally Meg would have worn her best and fullest petticoats, but today she allowed her thinnest summer one. After she had slipped on the dress, she called in Aunt Julia to help with the buttons, and her aunt frowned at once over the dress's fit. They decided together that the two last buttons on the back would be left undone—there was no choice about this, they would not close. Aunt Julia sewed the third button shut above its hole, so the remainder of the buttons would not pop off. This improvisation was covered up by Aunt Julia's favorite spring shawl, whose lemony yellow shade complemented the dress.

To complete her outfit, Meg slung over her wrist a delicate draw-string purse that had belonged to her mother. The purse was velvet, deep crimson, and didn't match her outfit in the slightest, but it was one of Meg's prized possessions, and today was a rare opportunity to show it off. Into this Meg placed the iron bolt she'd retrieved from the workhouse, and as a matter of course, her notebook and pencils.

She stole one last glance at herself in the mirror: a girl again. She nearly believed her own lie.

It wasn't until she was installed in the Green Room at Hanover Square that Meg was able to forget the constriction of her clothes. In fact, she thought the dress's cotton might actually be stretching a bit now. She was able to breathe. When Mr. Dickens offered to take her shawl, however, she claimed a chill.

Mr. Dickens was delighted to see them all, and he seemed refreshed as well. Meg, for her part, felt she hadn't seen him in months, though it had only been one day—so much had transpired.

The day's arrangements conspired to soften Meg's anxiety. With her father's permission—granted gladly—Aunt Julia and Tobias and Campion would dine in the Hanover Square Rooms, from where they would follow the reading. There would be enough time for the luncheon guests to stroll the neighborhood before the performance began, promptly at three. Meg—again with her father's kind permission—was invited to dine with Mr. Dickens in the Green Room, just behind the stage.

The Green Room was the waiting area for performers before their arrival onstage, a long-standing theatrical tradition. And it was Mr. Dickens's own tradition to dine with one good friend, and only one, before a performance. It kept him occupied and softened his nerves, which he claimed were ferocious. Besides, didn't he and Meg have some catching up? Meg rejoiced at this arrangement.

One quick panic jolted her—would she also lie to Mr. Dickens? No, she decided on the spot. She would tell him everything. She had to tell someone everything, or she felt she might explode.

The Green Room was, as advertised, green. The walls were painted a pale green, the color of spring's first apple-tree leaves, and the furniture was also green, settees and sofas in shades of dark emerald. Even the small dining table and chairs, though wooden, were painted green, a slightly alarming shade of some Italian olives. Mr. Dickens explained that the name Green Room derived from Shakespeare's time, when the waiting area for actors was filled with potted plants. It was believed, back then, that plants gave off "vapors" that were beneficial to the voices of the actors. Though for all Mr. Dickens knew, this might be a myth, nonetheless, it was a myth he enjoyed contemplating.

Alas, Meg saw that the only green plant in this Green Room was a rather sickly potted ivy.

A silver cart was wheeled in by a man dressed all in white. His face said nothing, his body said nothing, and he himself said nothing. He removed a silver lid from the tray, revealing the lunch's bounty, and without saying a word, tiptoed from the Green Room.

"Coffee, I believe?" Mr. Dickens asked, and he poured them each a cup. Meg tried very hard to keep her pinky finger extended when she drank, though she couldn't remember why this was considered proper.

Mr. Dickens ate only toast, he said, before a reading. Anything heavier made him logy. A reading of this kind, he told Meg, was an enormous effort for him, though he loved the doing of it. He was as nervous before a reading as a fox before a pack of hounds, but the nervousness was mandatory. He had to spring to life when onstage. A large meal would bring him no advantage. But he had insisted on a feast for his companion, and Meg was to help herself.

She could only nibble at the enormous offering of oysters, strawberries, salmon, cold roast beef, potatoes swimming in a bubbling cheese sauce, chilled asparagus, a plate of many cheeses, and several other dishes she was unable to identify. It wasn't merely the over-abundance of the luncheon that defeated her appetite, it was that she had so much to talk about—all that crowded her head.

"So, Meg," he said. "Tell me about yesterday. Your face when I first saw it telegraphed a great urgency. I take it there's news."

Meg pushed aside her little plate and leaned over the table.

"O yes, sir," she said. "Grand news."

"Meg?" Mr. Dickens asked, and when she looked at him, she saw his open, welcoming face—as easy to read as the face of a town-hall clock. His was the face of a true friend. When she first arrived at Hanover Square, she was certain of telling him the truth. But as much as it pained her, she knew that she must continue to lie.

If she told Mr. Dickens everything, she would have to ask him to be a part of her lie. She would have to ask him to lie to her father. This was too large a burden to place on a friend. For now, it was best to shoulder her woes alone.

So she told her friend only what she had told her family, laying down the facts like the cards in a game of whist. She drew the connections, as she saw them. Mr. Dickens, for his part, listened with great intensity, only stopping her now and then for clarification. She ended her re-counting with the mysterious Mr. B, Mr. Bogle, and the strange discovery that Mrs. Podsnap was also called Mrs. Bogle. All trails led, it seemed, to one destination.

"Bogle," Mr. Dickens said slowly. "Bogle. Bogle. Bogle." He spoke solemnly, as if he were uttering a genie's name and trying to coax him from a lamp.

"Yes?" Meg asked.

"It seems I know that name," he said. "But I can't place it. Never mind. It'll come to me. Now, about this bolt."

Meg, who had been fingering the iron bolt all morning, pulled it from her draw-string purse and placed it on the table.

Mr. Dickens stared at it a good long while, as if examining it under a jeweler's loupe. Meg had seen this concentration in him before, how his entire focus could gather around one small object or topic. People often said someone had a "penetrating gaze"; this was true of Mr. Dickens at such moments. It was also said that at such moments an observer could "see the gears turning" in someone's thoughts, and this was also true of Mr. Dickens now. His face projected every observation and every deduction.

He picked up the bolt, turning it slowly between his thumb and forefinger. He turned the bolt's rounded cap towards him.

"Why the stamp? Those letters *M* and *R*?" Meg asked. "I can't imagine any purpose to those suffering children forced to sit stamping all day. I keep thinking these bolts would be stamped at the manufactory."

Again, the workings of Mr. Dickens's mind showed on his face.

"That may be it, Meg," he said. "The question of the day. Why were they *not* marked by the factory? Let me see, let me see, let me see."

He re-placed the bolt on the table.

"If I have un-stamped bolts I can sell for cheaper than I

can sell bolts stamped with an *M* and an *R,* I might want to do that. And if I can en-slave children to stamp them for me, why then I just might. I can save a penny here and a penny there, by counterfeit, and that's an entire trunk of money I can save—one penny at a time. And all it costs me is the pain of an impoverished child and a maggoty potato to keep it alive. Do you see?"

Meg thought she saw.

"So," she said, trying out the words slowly, "Mr. Bogle wants people to believe these bolts are not what they seem. He wants people to believe these are MR bolts when they are no such thing."

"Concisely."

"And he'll make more money that way? By selling them as bolts that should have *M* and *R* stamped on them?"

"Precisely."

"And he doesn't give a fig for these children?"

"He cares for them, but only because they do tasks which he himself would never do."

"And he does this all for money?" Meg asked.

"Only for money," he said.

"Is Mr. Bogle a rich man already?"

"Undoubtedly. Undoubtedly very rich."

Meg's face, if she'd a looking-glass in which to see it, showed the gears of her brain's machinations.

"Money makes people cruel, doesn't it?" Meg asked. "It can make them behave very badly."

"Often," he said. "For some, the getting of money is the

only love they have. And it makes them miserable, as romantic love makes others miserable."

"Will there ever be enough money for such people?"

"Not for the likes of Mr. Bogle, I'm afraid. Which is why we must stop him, before his misery becomes the misery of yet others."

Meg pounded the little green table with her fist, and all the silverware jangled.

"Mr. Dickens," she said, and folded her hands in her lap, hoping this would signal that her outburst was not directed at him. "You have been so kind, so generous, and yet I have one more favor to ask of you."

"Tell me."

"We must not save only Orion, you see. Promise me that we will . . . What I mean to say is, will you help me save the other children? All of them. The living-dead children. If anyone can do it, you can."

"You need not ask me that," he said. "I have already vowed as such. And I know that you have, too. If we are to save one child, we must save them all. There is no other choice."

Meg nodded and allowed a tightened smile. It was all the gratitude she could offer, lest she burst into agonized sobs.

She picked up the bolt and examined it.

"What does this bolt signify, with its *M* and *R*?" she asked. She knew her eyes were full of tears, but she kept on. "Where does it point? O if only Dick Whittington and his ghost-cat would appear. Couldn't he, by his supernature, provide all the answers to this army of questions?"

"The time of spirits is over," Mr. Dickens said. "You must understand that, Meg. There are no magical answers to the problem of your brother."

"But it would be so much easier," she said, and truly believed. In an instant of frustration, she wanted it all to be over, to have the world restored to how it should be.

"It would be simpler, yes," Mr. Dickens said. "Perhaps more entertaining. But don't confuse books with life. If you and I were characters in some cheap and bad novel—no novel that I would ever write—then a ghost or spirit would appear and solve all our problems. But this is not a novel, Meg, this is real life. The only life. No phantom can help us now. Yes, we are haunted, you and I, but only by the living. It is all on us, Meg, to solve this riddle. And so, we go forward, as we have been doing."

"But, Mr. Dickens—"

"You must be your own hero, Meg."

She knew that Mr. Dickens spoke the truth. Spirits could change nothing, but she could be her own hero. No, she *must* be her own hero, if only for Orion's sake. And with this new understanding, her frustration vanished.

"Let us go straight to Mr. Bogle then," she said.

"I don't believe Mr. Bogle will entertain us so gladly just yet. But there's a name other than Bogle we might consider. What is the name of that bank, the one on the label?"

Meg opened her notebook.

"'Tellson's,'" she read.

"Perhaps tomorrow you and I shall pay a visit to Tellson's Bank. What say you?"

Meg nodded and smiled. She piled her plate high with strawberries and went at them with a voracious hunger. It had been years—before her mother's death—since she'd eaten a strawberry.

Chapter XIV

The artist steps out on the high-wire

THE SOFT-LEATHER VALISE held several volumes of Mr. Dickens's most famous novels. Meg thumbed through them, each so familiar to her—*The Pickwick Papers, A Christmas Carol, David Copperfield, Oliver Twist, Little Dorrit, The Old Curiosity Shop, A Tale of Two Cities,* and of course, *Great Expectations.* O how Meg wished to dive into that! A bran' new book is a beautiful thing, all promise and fresh pages, the neatly squared spine, the brisk sense of a journey beginning. But a well-worn book also has its pleasures, the soft caress and give of the paper's edges, the comfort, like an old shawl, of an oft-read story. Not only were Mr. Dickens's own copies of his novels softened and worn, they bore his quill marks, too, in the margins and between the lines. "Weep," read one note, "shudder," said another. "Emote," "strike lectern," "gasp!" These were his prompt-books, the directions and cues that guided him through his public performances.

The newspapers wrote frequently of Mr. Dickens's performances—here and abroad—and the reports were never less than intriguing. According to most, Mr. Dickens had invented a new art form—the author reading, with great theatricality, from his own works. Now, of course, many authors tried to ride Mr. Dickens's coat-tails, and such readings were more common. But no one, the papers reiterated, could touch an audience like Mr. Dickens. He was an actor of some skill, but as the writer of his scripts, he brought a powerful authority to the drama of his readings. No one, the papers said over and over, could bring an audience to its knees the way Mr. Dickens could. Members of his audiences—mostly women, though sometimes men—fainted at his performances. Those who fainted were frequently described as "overcome." Meg believed these accounts, though she also believed that more women than men fainted simply because women's clothing, especially among the wealthy, prevented one from breathing as Nature had intended.

"I thought, Meg," Mr. Dickens said, "that I would read some of my standards today. From *Oliver Twist,* 'More, please,' and the Ghost of Christmas Past, from *Carol*. But today I would like to add a scene from *Little Dorrit*. Where Little Dorrit refuses Arthur upon Southwark Bridge. In your honor, of course. She is, I think, the favorite of many young women."

He smiled and waited, but Meg found she could raise no excitement. She merely nodded, looked at the table, and mumbled a brief thank-you.

"What is it, Meg?" he asked. "Do you not approve? Are you no reader of my books? Your father tells me—"

"O, sir, please," she said, still looking down. "I am your most devoted reader. Why, I think we've read everything, me and my family."

"What then, Meg?" Mr. Dickens reached across the table and put his hand in the spot where Meg's gaze fell. She could not help but look up at him.

"Meg. We have shared too much for you to hide from me now. Is it *Little Dorrit*? That name seems to have soured you."

"Yes," she said. "But it is Little Dorrit the girl, rather than the book."

"You do not like her?"

"Sir, please, you must—"

"Meg," he interrupted. "Please, it is I, your friend. Tell me. I have certainly heard worse about all of my works than you could possibly tell me today. Please."

"It's not so much . . ." she said, but did not know how to continue.

First she had lied to her friend, Mr. Dickens, and now she was asked to tell the Great Man of London an unflattering truth. Yet he seemed so eager to hear her opinion. She would like to lie again, if only to spare his feelings. But she could find no reason to lie now. When she'd lied to him about Billingsgate, much had been at stake—her father's trust, Orion's return. On this matter, the opinion of a novel, there was no real reason to lie. She wondered if a difficult truth could make up for a necessary lie.

"It's not that I don't like Little Dorrit, Mr. Dickens. I like her in all the ways I am meant to like her. She is dutiful, and even-tempered, and thoughtful, and possesses a kind heart."

"But?"

"She is nothing but all those very good things. I like her well enough, but I would never want to be her. She does not suspect she could be her own hero. She waits for others to be that for her."

Mr. Dickens sat back and scratched one ear. His thinking was not visible on his face. He seemed ambushed, surprised, though not unpleasantly so. He sat forward.

"Thank you, Meg," he said. "No one is ever that candid with me, at least not face-to-face. Bold of you, and necessary. And correct. If I had known you before I wrote that book, if I had known how brave a girl could be, which you have proven to me, well, *Little Dorrit* might have been—a much better book."

Meg blushed, as she would have to.

"So, my stalwart companion, what would you rather hear?"

"*Pickwick,* sir, if you please. Anything from *Pickwick*. We could all use a good laugh, I should think."

"Indeed. *Pickwick* it is. Now, go to your father and family. I must rehearse a bit. The show begins anon."

With that he stood and bowed.

"And thank you, Meg. You honor me with your friendship."

The grand hall of the Hanover Square Rooms was empty. The audience, including Meg's family, had lunched here while Meg and Mr. Dickens were in the Green Room. They were all now, she was told, strolling the grounds of Hanover Square itself, "taking the air."

Meg was ushered to her family's table, which was near the very edge of the raised stage. The manager of the Hanover Square Rooms, a Mr. Lumchuck Hickle, held a chair for Meg and waited for her to sit. It took her a moment to comprehend that Mr. Hickle was holding the chair for her, but she did, and she sat, and Mr. Hickle eased the chair under her and scooted both Meg and chair to the edge of the table. She would kindly, at Mr. Hickle's insistence, wait here. The rest would return shortly.

It all seemed a bit much, this ceremony, Meg thought, especially since the large concert room was empty save Mr. Hickle and herself. When she had realized he was holding the chair for her, she'd thought it ridiculous. She was perfectly capable of sitting down by herself; she'd never missed a chair's seat in all her life—except those few Orion had pulled out from under her, an older brother's prank. But Mr. Hickle was silently adamant, and so Meg had dropped into the red velvet chair.

Then she grew embarrassed at herself. Here she was in

an elegant hall, and she was behaving like a girl when she might be adopting the air of a lady. As Mr. Hickle walked away, his sharp heels tapping out time on the polished parquet floor, Meg sat up straight in her chair, folded her hands primly in her lap, and stretched her neck to its fullest. She was attempting to appear as regal as the glittering, candle-lit chandelier that hung from the room's high dome.

She held this pose for several seconds.

"Ha!" The laugh burst out of her and echoed about the room. Meg put her head on the linen table-cloth and stifled the remaining bits of laughter that wished to join their escaped fellow. From far away, one might have believed she was sobbing, but no, she was laughing—if only to herself. When the last "Ha!" died in her breast, she looked up, teary-eyed and relieved.

Who was she kidding? She was not a lady, she was a girl, and an alien girl in this milieu. She knew who she was, and more importantly, who she wasn't. The joy in this discovery was that she could stop pretending to be a lady and act as a girl. And that meant snooping around.

She peeked under the thick white table-cloth and discovered ornate legs on the table. She wandered the edges of the room, touching the gilt scroll on the high wainscoting, stroking the flocked roses of the busy wall-paper, and dared to dab her finger to the surface of a framed painting of cows and dogs in a meadow. This painting was far larger than the entire wall of her room at home, and while Meg loved both dogs and cows, and thought this a fine depiction of them, she wondered why such a pastoral subject was chosen for such an urbane place.

Tiny wine-glasses had been set at each place, and in the center of every table, crystal decanters of Sherry and Port stood like sentinels. Meg knew the reddish brown liquids in the decanters were Sherry and Port because etched silver medallions saying so hung from chains around their necks. Meg dipped a pinky into one and tasted it, then into the other and tasted that. Both were something like wine—she was allowed a thimble full of wine at Christmas—but sweeter, smellier. On the whole, she thought, she preferred the Sherry, though her favorite beverage, ginger beer, was far and away more pleasing.

Meg was about to dip another pinky into a decanter when she heard the clack and slip of shoes in the vestibule—the audience was returning from their stroll. She hied to her place and awaited her family. Soon they joined her, and the Hanover Square's main room filled with noise and spectacle.

Meg tried hard to pay attention to her family's talk of lunch—Tobias apparently ate fifteen oysters, and there was some concern at this fact—but it was hard to listen when there was so much to see. And what there was to see today was fashion.

The men, it must be said, were all dressed very nicely. But they were dressed all alike. Every man wore a black suit over a white shirt and a white waist-coat, and all their ties were black. It was as if, Meg thought, all the men in the world had decided fashion was too difficult a prospect for them, and one night had voted to simplify the matter by choosing one outfit—the black suit.

But the women, O the women, they had held no such election. No one woman wore the same dress as another, and the variety of colors was remarkable, though each dress was primarily bell-shaped in the skirts, thanks to the cage-crinoline hoops underneath. It was as if Meg had entered a tropical aviary where each species of parrot from each of the world's jungles had been gathered. Meg's world—Tonson Lane off Cheapside—was a world of sparrows and pigeons, all greys and blacks and browns, but here the parrots shone in all possible shades—peach, lavender, pumpkin-orange, azuline-blue, tangerine, copper, fuchsia, daffodil. As if to stress the comparison to the birds of the tropics, a woman one table over from Meg's waved a large fan over herself, a fan of iridescent fowl feathers in shining black and green, all surmounted by an actual hummingbird, dead and stuffed, its red throat shining. Meg wondered if, under the power of the feathered fan, the woman might actually take flight from the table and head south to equatorial climes.

And the hats! The men, decorously, had left their hats—each one black—in the vestibule's cloak-room. The women, however, retained their hats. Like the dresses, there was an infinite variety of hats, and like Mrs. Bogle's—or Podsnap's—each hat was more like architecture than fashion. The room, when looked at only for its hats, was a city of hat-buildings, each created by a slightly mad architect.

There was a Roman Coliseum of a hat, complete with arches and crumbling ruins; a domed St. Paul's of a hat, replete with tiny spires; a hat of Taj Mahal proportions and all in white; even a Parliament of a hat, squarish and officious and filled with a hundred windows. And there, in a private box near to the stage, was the unmistakable hat of Mrs. Bogle, its gold charms dangling like a pharaoh's treasure on a Christmas tree.

Next to Mrs. Bogle was the pale girl who had so timorously emerged from the dark of the carriage. The black choker she wore that first day still held her in check. Surely this was Miss Bogle—or Miss Podsnap. Whatever the name.

Mrs. Bogsnap sat to the left of Miss Pogle, and to their right sat—dressed in the blackest of all black suits—the husband and father of his two companions, respectively. But make no mistake about his name, for Meg knew that this was Mr. Bogle. He looked like a Bogle. Leave all Podsnaps out of it, his stern countenance seemed to say. This man was Bogle through and through.

Meg stared at him, willing him, daring him, to look her way. Was this the mysterious Mr. B of Orion's notebook? Was this the man behind the men who supervised the infernal work-house below Billingsgate Market? More than anything, Meg wanted to meet Mr. Bogle's eyes, see what might be seen there, and show him the anger in her own. She wanted to frighten him. But Mr. Bogle simply stared at his own hands; he would look at no one, it seemed.

The lights in the domed room were dimmed. Only the

chandelier's candles glowed. The lime-lights at the front of the stage sprung to life, a brilliant but sickly green-white. A theater-hush fell.

Mr. Dickens strode alone across the stage. Polite applause began at his first appearance, but by the time he reached the lectern, the applause had swelled to a voluminous roar—the public hungered for the voice of their master. Mr. Dickens, unlike every other man assembled, including Meg's father, did not wear black. His suit was a muted grey, thinly striped with paler grey, and the waistcoat was not white but pearlescent with pale spots of color. However it was not the suit that one noticed about Mr. Dickens—it was something keener that struck one. His eyes blazed in the lime-light, and his face carried the charged possibility of every emotion in it. Mr. Dickens was alive.

He held up a hand to silence the applause, and the room obliged him. He placed three prompt-books on the lectern's slanted surface, opened one, looked up.

"Good friends," he said, and his voice carried across the stuffy room. "Welcome to our afternoon's indulgence. Allow me, your humble servant, to present three divertissements for your delectation. The first of which you may recognize. Follow me, then, to a time not so long ago, when our hero, Mr. Ebenezer Scrooge, is visited in his dismal chambers by a Spirit—the Ghost of Christmas Past."

Once the thunderous applause abated, Mr. Dickens

read out, "When Scrooge awoke, it was so dark that, looking out of bed, he could scarcely distinguish the transparent windows from the opaque walls of his chamber."

While he read, Mr. Dickens gestured and moved about, and at times it was apparent that he had little need of his prompt-book. But Meg hardly noticed him on the stage, hardly took notice of his presence at all, and so saw nothing of the great changes that overtook his person when he switched from character to character, how he became each character he read.

No, Meg herself was not present in the Hanover Square Rooms. Rather, she was in Scrooge's chamber, at Scrooge's boyhood school, at Fezziwig's grand ball, and the voices she heard did not emanate from Mr. Dickens, but from the very characters themselves who stood, more solid than spirit, in front of her. She was entranced—she had entered another world.

At the moment when Belle returns young Scrooge's engagement ring, leaving Scrooge to his love of money, Meg could no longer hold back her tears. She wept, along with most of the Hanover Square Rooms, wept copiously, wept for all the young Scrooge had lost, and how that loss would shape his wretched life. Meg's father was weeping, as was Aunt Julia, and even Tobias. Mulberry, too, she thought, would be weeping if he were here.

There was only one person in the audience not moved by the reading, and that, not unexpectedly, was Mr. Bogle.

While his wife and daughter sobbed into their finely embroidered hand-kerchiefs, Mr. Bogle, dry-eyed and stone-faced, pulled his watch from his waist-coat and checked the time. He had other places to be, it appeared, than in an imaginary past.

Oliver Twist's adventures in the work-house followed *A Christmas Carol,* and Meg could not help but compare the work-house there with the work-house she'd seen the day before. She much preferred, she thought, Oliver's work-house to the real one. An imagined horror was a tolerable one, at least.

When *Oliver Twist* was finished, Mr. Dickens spoke at some length.

"Ladies and gentlemen, I beg your pardon. Now comes the last of today's entertainments"—a flock of noes rose from the dark room—"and some explanation is necessary. It is always a risky venture for an artist to perform in public. The artist always goes off into the performance as if hovering over a void—like a tight-rope walker over the abyss. There is always the chance—or so the artist believes—that he may plummet to his death upon one slight mis-step."

Mr. Dickens moved from behind the lectern and stood at the very edge of the stage, half in darkness, half in limelight.

"Today, just now, I should like to set out on an unusually perilous attempt. And I must. I am going to read for you now a section of a story I have never before read aloud, and which I was only asked to read a mere hour ago."

He looked directly at Meg, smiling.

"You will forgive, I pray, any stumbles. But I must risk this, you see. And why? For that person who requested this of me is one to whom I owe a good deal, and so safety cannot be accounted."

He turned and walked to and fro on the stage—shadow and light, shadow and light.

"Without this person, I would be a haunted and hollow man. When we first met, I had no direction, no sense of where to turn. But since our meeting—and our many adventures—I have found myself among the living again, and know without one sliver of a doubt what a life is for. I am no longer a haunted man."

Mr. Dickens returned to the lectern and opened a novel.

"I shall not risk the embarrassment such a proclamation might bring, so allow me, kind gentlefolk, to refer to my savior by a false name. My lasting thanks, then, to Hunter's Hunter, for whom I shall now read from *The Pickwick Papers*."

Her father's hand found Meg's and squeezed it. Applause obliterated the room for a long moment.

The reading was of that famous passage where Mrs. Bardell mistakes Pickwick's words for a marriage proposal and throws herself into his arms. Everyone laughed, knowing the outcome, with the exception of one person. And that person was, you may be certain, Mr. Bogle of the box and the wife and the daughter and the incessantly checked pocket-watch.

When Mr. Dickens was finished, the audience applauded and cried bravo and called for more, but Mr. Dickens, after a long bow, retreated from the stage and did not return. The gas-lights were re-illuminated, and the crowd began to disperse.

It had been arranged that Meg and her family were to meet Mr. Dickens in the Green Room afterwards, but Meg took off at a clip. She passed through the crowd, weaving through the brightly colored women and the dull men into the day-light.

Ahead of her the Bogles were already getting into their fine Brougham carriage, Mr. Bogle checking his watch one last time.

Meg was calling, "Wait, wait," though she had no sense of what she would say to any of the Bogles had they waited. She was merely afraid of losing sight of them.

Too late. The plum-colored door closed, and the gleaming carriage took off at a brisk pace, westward, into the slowly falling sun of the suddenly hazy summer Sunday.

Chapter XV

The underground city

SUNDAY, THE DAY OF LEISURE. The shops of London are all closed, as are the manufactories, the banks, and every other means of commerce and labor. Sunday is the respite from the week's toil.

Yet you would be hard-pressed to know that London was at leisure today, what with all the people and carriages out and about, and all the attendant commotion. London, you see, pursues its day of leisure with the same vigor it pursues its days of commerce and labor. And this is quite vigorously, indeed.

Mr. Dickens had arranged yet another treat for the Pickel family—a Sunday carriage ride. When he'd announced this, in the Green Room after his performance, Meg had envisioned a stately clip-clop stroll down a green and empty tree-lined way, the loudest noise a quiet breeze ruffling her hair. And then when the carriage pulled up to the Hanover Square Rooms, Meg's vision of an idyllic world was only multiplied. The carriage was a Barouche, a cloud-silver Barouche, open-topped and elegant, pulled by two sleek white horses and guided by a driver in pearl-grey livery.

Meg had never seen anything like it. It was impossible, on first sight, not to imagine that this was the solitary cloud-carriage in London, and that it would carry Meg and company through the unimpeded sky-streets of sky-London.

While Meg's dream was a pleasant one, it was, alas, a dream. The carriage in which she and her family and Mr. Dickens rode might have been the only cloud-silver carriage in all of London on this Sunday, but it was far from the only carriage.

Assisted by the liveried driver, Meg was handed into the carriage, followed by Aunt Julia, who was followed by Meg's father and Mr. Dickens. Tobias—*O lucky boy,* Meg thought—was allowed to sit next to the driver on the high banquette. Meg settled herself into the cloud-silver upholstery and waited for a soft breeze to caress her.

The driver snapped his reins, called, "Hup, Ed'dard, hup, Dora," and the carriage creaked and clocked, moved forward, and began to sail over the street's smooth pavvy. Then the carriage thudded to a stop.

Meg opened her eyes. The streets all around the Hanover Square Rooms were jammed with carriages—Hansoms,

Phaetons, Victorias, Broughams. No one carriage could move; each waited for each.

This was just like her search for Orion, Meg realized. What had seemed so simple at the outset was beset at every turn by too many other people. Each time she navigated her course towards Orion, some road-block stopped her. And after that road-block, setting out again at best speed, another road-block. Stop-and-start. How Meg wished London were a city devoid of all but herself and Orion. Then she could walk the empty streets, crying out, *Orion, Orion, ollie-ollie-oxen-free, come home, it is safe*.

Slowly the carriage made its way out of Hanover Square and into broad Regent Street. The shade of the Regent Street buildings fell over the carriage, and this softened Meg's mood and re-called her to the conversation that filled the carriage.

"Yes, Charles," Aunt Julia was saying, "it was delightful. I thought *Pickwick* an inspired choice."

"Perhaps your funniest bit ever," Meg's father said. "And to think that Meg chose it for you."

"An inspired choice," Mr. Dickens said. "My thanks go out to you, Meg. I think that in the future I—"

But Meg, as much as she'd enjoyed the performance, did not wish to speak of it at the moment. If her journey to Orion was going to be all stop-and-start, then best to get on with it, best to start stopping-and-starting right now.

"I saw Mr. Bogle," she said. "He was at the Hanover

Square Rooms today. In a private box, with Mrs. Bogle and the daughter. He seemed a very impatient man."

Mr. Dickens leaned forward.

"Are you certain?"

"I am certain it was Mrs. Bogle's hat," she said. "And it is an unmistakable hat. If it was her hat, then she was under it."

"And if she was under it," Mr. Dickens said, "then Mr. Bogle was next to it."

Meg nodded emphatically.

"But are we certain," Meg's father said, "that this is the Mr. Bogle we seek? London is, after all, a rather large city."

"Ah, yes," Mr. Dickens said. "But like all large cities, it is also a small town. Stand on one corner for a day, and you are bound to meet everyone you know."

"But," Aunt Julia said with emphasis, "we still do not know if this Mr. Bogle is our mysterious Mr. B."

"Your aunt—" her father started, but Meg stopped him.

"It must be him," she said, and verily rose from the plush upholstery. "Follow the chain. We know that Orion and Charlie were watching Billingsgate Market, and that's where we found Bogle's bolts, which we know from the crates and their labels. Mr. Bogle *is* the mysterious Mr. B. We all know that. Or at least we think we do."

For a moment the carriage was silent; only the creak of a thousand carriage wheels was heard.

"She is right," her father said. "We cannot let our minor doubts intrude. We must act as if Bogle were B."

"If only," Aunt Julia said, "we knew what the initials *M* and *R* represented. Then we might have further proof of Bogle's involvement. I keep thinking . . ."

"I had hoped," Mr. Dickens said, "that our little ride might provide us all some respite from our tiring search. But I can see there will be no rest for any of us until Orion—and poor Charlie—have been returned. I fear my performance has left me peckish. If we are to think well, our bellies must be quiet. Driver, stop here! *Un petit qouter!*"

Tobias was dispatched to a cafe, returning with coffees and biscuits and cheese for all. Mr. Dickens had paid extra for the tin mugs and the tray, and our party would dine as they rode. Like a queen, Meg thought, such luxury.

"Driver," Mr. Dickens called. "To Birdcage Walk."

The Birdcage Walk was a marvel of such renown that Meg had assumed it could not exist. Yet here it was, surrounding her, and there was no mistaking the reality of the place, for all the squawking and calling of the very real birds attested to it. The carriage clopped along the southern edge of St. James Park under a tunnel of vast trees, and hung from these trees were hundreds of enormous birdcages. In the cages were parrots and toucans and macaws, as well as pelicans and albatross, hawks and eagles, and finches and lovebirds and sparrows. Every species in the world, Meg imagined. The stately train of carriages moved haltingly down the Walk, and the people eyed the marvelous birds, while the birds, heads tilted, warily eyed the people.

Regarding these marvelous creatures, Meg could not help but think of the brightly frocked women at the Hanover Square Rooms. Birds and women both were lovely in their finery, but both women and birds seemed suited to cages. Whether to protect them or to keep them, Meg was uncertain.

In the distance, through the trees of the Birdcage Walk, the glittering surface of a lake appeared, and Meg watched swans and geese and ducks a-light there and take off again. These were ordinary birds, not exotic in the least, and Meg was certain she would rather be a common duck. The birds in the cages were beautiful, but what good to be a bird if you could not fly?

Mr. Dickens and Meg's father were talking, head-bent, about Bogle's bolts, and what they might mean. Tobias, who had turned around on the driver's banquette to face them, had joined in, too, chatting away, offering ideas for the meaning of the initials stamped on Bogle's bolts. As befitting Tobias, most of the ideas were rather silly, but inspired. Only Aunt Julia was strangely quiet.

"Master Regiment," Tobias said. "Or Minute Recovery. O I know, Malaprop Ruminant."

"Tobias, please," Meg said. "Be serious."

"Let him speak, Meg," Mr. Dickens said. "He's the only one with further ideas. He may just hit on it."

Tobias stuck out his tongue at Meg, and she had to laugh at him.

"Aha," Tobias said. "I have it. Malicious Redwall. It's the perfect name for a mouse king, don't you think?"

"Mouse king?" Meg said. "Tobias, we are not—"

Aunt Julia spoke out, loudly, clearly, and with her most imperial authority.

"Metropolitan Railway," she said.

Even the birds silenced at this announcement, as if comprehending the importance of it.

"Metropolitan Railway?" Meg's father asked.

"Absolutely!" Mr. Dickens said. "Julia Spragg, you've hit on it. Driver—"

"Charles," Meg's father said. "How can we—"

"Campion," Aunt Julia said. "We cannot. But it is our best hope. Think on it. The Metropolitan Railway is tearing through London these days; there's been no project like it since the Crystal Palace. What other *M* and *R* could need so many bolts stamped *M* and *R*?"

"Yes," Meg said. "That is it. I just know it." And truth be told, she felt a little dull that she had not thought of it before. Her mind had been so much on Orion and the one little corner of London where her brother was hidden that she'd forgotten to see all of London.

Meg read of the railway project nearly every day in the papers. The Metropolitan Railway was now digging the first of many tunnels and laying track, and generally causing an enormous disruption, all with the end of putting railcars underground in long tubes. No one was certain such a feat could be accomplished, and no one was certain that the people of London desired such a thing. But the project went forward, as if the Railway were a creature with its own volition. No city anywhere, it was reported, had ever undertaken such a gargantuan project. Men and materials were flooding into the capital. Why not these bolts? *M* and *R*: Metropolitan Railway.

"Yes," her father said, his face lighting up. "Yes, yes," and he added no buts.

"Driver," Mr. Dickens called. "Marylebone Road near Park Crescent. The railway trench there. And please, if you will, speed this plow."

A flock of ducks exploded from the lake and flew off into the lowering afternoon.

As they moved north, towards Park Crescent, the Sunday traffic eased, and the steady clip-clop of the horses, Ed'dard and Dora, quickened to an actual clippity-cloppity.

Meg was watching Tobias, where he sat face-forward again on the driver's banquette, and she wished that she might be more like him, always pleased by whatever came next. Tobias never doubted that he would have a good time. When they were setting out for the Metropolitan Railway trench, and doubts still fluttered about the carriage, Tobias had calmed everyone by pointing out that at least they were going to see the railway under construction, and wouldn't that be interesting and useful in itself. So, he continued, if they found anything at all helpful, that would be like pudding after dinner. All agreed amiably with Tobias's observation; the word *pudding* alone put everyone in a cheerful frame.

They were approaching Park Crescent now—Meg saw the vast slope of Regent's Park fanned out ahead—when Tobias began acting rather oddly, even for a younger brother. His head tilted to the sky, and it swayed from side to side. His head would come to rest for a minute—held still, in focus—then begin to nose about again. That was it, Meg thought, he was nosing about, sniffing for something. And she was just putting together in her head the words *He is acting like a dog, like Mulberry,* when Tobias cried out.

"O I do wish Mulberry were here with us," he said, turning to face them. "Mulberry would love this."

The scent Tobias had been chasing arrived in Meg's nose. It was a fresh scent, clean and deep, a cold, mineral scent. It smelled of—of—*sniff, sniff* . . . earth. This was the rich smell of earth freshly turned.

"There it is!" Tobias yelled, standing up and pointing. The driver eased him down.

Where Marylebone Road met Park Crescent, a great gash in the earth appeared, hundreds of yards long. A low fence surrounded the gash, but given the length and width and depth of this trench, the fence seemed Lilliputian, feeble. The earth-scent exhaled in a great cloud from the trench.

"Ho, Ed'dard; ho, Dora," the driver whispered, tugging the reins.

The carriage stopped hard by the trench. The citizens

of London, all at their vigorous leisure, passed on either side of it, ignoring it as if embarrassed by an earth that was neither covered nor manicured—a naked earth.

Only Meg and her family stopped. The entire party climbed down and gazed west into the enormous trench of the Railway construction. Tobias, as if feeling the lack of Mulberry's presence, seemed to take the dog's place and was jumping about, from one side to the other, unable to keep still.

"Driver, good man," Mr. Dickens called. "Your lantern, please."

As a group, and without a word, they set off. The low fence did not hinder the view. Marylebone Road had been stripped of its pavvy, and beneath it lay the sinew and bone of London—rock and soil and the scaffolding to keep the future tunnel from collapsing. The trench here was as wide as Marylebone itself, wide enough, Meg thought, for twelve Tonson Lanes.

At one end of the site, west in the direction of Paddington, to where the tunnel was eventually destined, the trench ended in a wall of shored-up earth. At the opposite end of the trench, hundreds of yards behind them, in the direction of King's Cross, from where the tunnel was coming, stood the open and completed section.

They gazed down into the earth—tools, machines, support beams, a chaos of rubble. It was such a spectacle, and of such scope, Meg almost doubted this was the work of men. Perhaps London's giants, Gog and Magog, had come to life and this was the ghastly garden they tilled. There were no workmen today, it being Sunday and London too seething with leisure, and this added an aura of myth to the scene—the work of giants.

"Cut and cover," Aunt Julia said with her voice of authority. Aunt Julia was uncommonly wise about the world and its workings, and Meg had learned long ago to pay close attention when she spoke so. "That's what they call this method. Quite simple. They build the tunnel one section at a time, around a quarter-mile long. They tear open the street—cut it, if you will—build that portion of the tunnel, then cover it up again, replacing the street. Then move on to the next section."

"Ingenious," Mr. Dickens said. He pulled out his notebook and began to scribble, but now he wrote with a carpenter's pencil, which delighted Meg. "Go on," he said to Aunt Julia.

"Yes, it's quite efficient. It allows them to follow the roads, but leaves homes and shops undisturbed. And it allows them to shut down only bits of each street. And if there's a problem with any section, they can easily return to it. Look, Meg."

Aunt Julia was leaned down next to her. Meg followed the gestures of her hands. "They cut down to a certain level, perhaps a hundred feet or so. Then they put up Brunel's scaffolding, which allows them to build the tunnel within it, and from outside it as well. They build the iron skeleton of the tunnel around the scaffold, then cover that with masonry, and fill in the trench. You see the tunnel's mouth there? It goes all the way to King's Cross. You could walk it. And in two years, an underground train will take you all the way. In mere minutes."

There were so many cities within London, and everywhere she turned these days, Meg kept finding more. She knew of the streets, and of course, the city of roof-tops. Once, when she'd seen a hot-air balloon, she had imagined a London that floated among the clouds. And now this, an entire London underground.

Mr. Dickens and Meg's father were conferring, pointing and sketching. Meg was peppering Aunt Julia with questions. Little huddles of curiosity. But to these little huddles came a faint voice, far away—Tobias.

"Come on, everyone. Hurry. You must come see."

Tobias, un-remarked by all, had slipped over the low fence and was yards away, waving back, and headed towards the tunnel's open mouth. You see, while most of mankind, especially the wisest among us, will intuitively shy away from perilous places, a boy of nine years old will, because he is unable to resist the allure, be drawn to any tunnel, trench, or hole in the ground. It is in the nature of nine-year-old boys, and that nature will be obeyed.

"Tobias!" Meg's father called. Tobias immediately halted, for it is also in a nine-year-old boy's nature to respond to a parent's voice—thank heavens! Tobias quivered there on the spot where he stopped, pulled oppositely and equally by his two natures: adventure and obedience.

Meg stared at her father. Would he call Tobias back? Say it unsafe to venture forward? She prayed he would not. Her father had come a far way in throwing off his caution, in showing his courage again, and she despaired that he would retreat once more.

"Tobias! Do not move another inch!" her father called. Meg's heart slipped, but only for a moment. "You will wait for the rest of us, you hear. I won't have you going in there alone."

Caution *and* courage, Meg thought.

Mr. Dickens lit the carriage's lantern. Aunt Julia, in a most un-lady-like manner, hoisted her skirts and fairly leaped over the fence. Meg started to do the same, but her father stopped her. He made a cradle of his arms, into which he scooped Meg, and eased her over the fence.

In that moment of suspension, Meg had a realization. It had been years since her father had lifted and held her like that, and she felt herself in his arms now as so much larger, so much older. She wondered if her father also felt this difference, the weightiness of her, and she imagined that, yes, of course, he must also have felt the changes.

Mr. Dickens scrambled over the fence, and our little pack moved towards the tunnel's mouth.

The sun hung low, and in the deep trench, shadows loomed over everything. A chill breeze blew from the tunnel's mouth.

They huddled together—as is only natural—and descended into the tunnel. The meager flame of the candle-lantern threw light but created new shadows, too.

They inched into the tunnel, their movement inhibited by wooden crates of building materials. But once in, and adjusted to the funereal aspect of the place, they felt freer to move about.

While the others inspected the scaffolding and the workers' tools and rubbish, Meg went as far into the tunnel as light allowed. From there she stared into a black abyss.

Tomorrow, she knew, this trench and tunnel would be over-run with workmen, men toiling in the dark, chased down here like rats. And she imagined, then, all of underground London filled with workers, and knew that not all of these workers were men. Some were boys, some girls. She remembered the living-dead children in the workhouse, boys and girls, and the dank, dark cellar in which they were compelled to toil.

Suddenly, all of underground London was, to her mind, filled with children and laborers, all scuttling across the dark tunnel floor, rats all, and she wondered if this were the fate of London. The living-dead would toil underground, in darkness, while on the surface, another London, bright and shining, would go on its merry way. She shuddered and saw Orion here, filthy and exhausted and under-fed, and working his way farther and farther from the sun and the air and the pleasures of the world above. She must find him before he was tunneled into oblivion.

And then Meg remembered the shadow man at the Six Jolly Fellowship Porters, the one Jenny had called Arthur. What had he said? "Underground he lives—closer to hell that way." A chill swept through Meg. Here she stood at the mouth of the underground. Was it the mouth of hell, too? Had the shadow man been speaking of Orion, or was he merely insane?

"Meg!" Mr. Dickens called. "Quick. Come see."

She ran to him. He pointed to a spot on the tunnel's iron skeleton. He raised his lantern to it. "See. *M* and *R*. It is our bolt. We were absolutely correct. There is an undeniable connection between Bogle and this Railway."

Everyone gathered around; each was inspecting a different bolt. Each bolt bore the *M* and *R* impression.

But it wasn't right, the bolt. This was not the same bolt. The difference was slight, Meg knew, though she couldn't quite put her finger on the skewed detail. What was it? She took the lantern from Mr. Dickens and examined, first, the bolt already in place, and next, the bolt she took from her purse.

"The typeface!" she said, smiling at Mr. Dickens. "The typeface is different."

Since Mr. Dickens had not been in Meg's thoughts, as we have been, he was somewhat cambozzled by Meg's assertion. And so he said what is only natural to say, and polite.

"Excuse me?" he said.

"Look," Meg said. "Our bolt has no serifs. It's a *sans serif* typeface. The bolt in the scaffold, it has serifs."

The letters on the bolts from the work-house were plain, like bent tubing. But the letters from the bolt already in the tunnel had small amendments to them, like the typeface of a printed document. The two bolts were clearly different.

"What does it mean, Charles?" her father asked.

"What it means, Campion, is that the work-house bolts are counterfeit. What it means is, Mr. Bogle!"

Meg was on the verge of laughing, but had no chance, for at the next moment, lantern beams swept over our little party, and a deep voice rang out through the trench.

"What's all this, then?" asked one of the two policemen who bore down on them.

Chapter XVI

The city unveils itself again

WHILE IT MAY BE an unjust fact that the presence of a celebrity can ease a difficult situation, it is nonetheless a fact. And a fortuitous fact on this Sunday evening for Meg and her family. The policemen, both of them, recognized the Great Man at once, and having recognized Charles Dickens, refused to hear any explanation—reasonable or otherwise—for the appearance of this family in a Metropolitan Railway trench on a Sunday evening. Meg was certain that if it weren't for the presence of the famous Mr. Dickens, the Pickels' Sunday evening would have been considerably more complicated.

But there is a price to pay for every advantage. The payment on this night was a slight one, nearly weightless on the scale of payments. With the signing of two autographs—both officers claimed they had children desirous of them—Mr. Dickens purchased liberty for our little search party.

"With the author's good wishes, Chas. Dickens," he wrote, in pencil, on sheets torn from his reporter's notebook. Underneath each signature was a serpentine flourish larger than all the words.

The police, handsomely paid, they felt, escorted our party to the Barouche and sent them on their way. The police—one very tall and very round, the other very small in all ways—seemed delighted as they waved good-bye to Mr. Dickens and the Pickels. For a moment, Meg felt herself like a celebrity.

It was near twilight now, the vaulted sky shading to lavender.

"Adventure," Mr. Dickens said in his storyteller's voice, "gives me an appetite. Let us have a late supper, shall we, and there discuss our discoveries and what's to follow."

Appetite, that was the best word to describe Mr. Dickens. Except for the delicate snack of toast before his reading, Mr. Dickens was continually feeding his endless appetite. Meg knew it was not simply food he craved. Mr. Dickens had an appetite for the world. He had seemed to Meg, that night on the roof-top of Satis House, somewhat gaunt, somewhat starved. But since then, since the search for Orion had begun, Mr. Dickens was always hungry for what came next. And his appetite was contagious. Meg was famished.

"We've not much at home, Charles," Aunt Julia said. "But I'm sure we can scrape together something. Monsieur Sept-Onze might open the Chandlery for us."

"Forbid, Julia. This calls for a robust dinner, a restaurant dinner. And as my celebrity has kept us all out of jail, so shall my industry pay for supper."

"Charles," Meg's father said. "It is Sunday. No place is opened for business."

"O, Campion," Mr. Dickens said. "There are places in this world where it is never Sunday, realms where doors never shut and lamps are never extinguished. Driver!"

With that, the Barouche jolted forward and picked up speed, headed east again, into the narrower streets of London Town proper.

The carriage was a maelstrom of conversation. All were intent on the Marylebone trench, the counterfeit bolts, the rescue of Orion.

Meg, however, though continuing to speak and nod when expected, fell out of the conversation. A vivid portrait of her brother had come to her in an instant, Orion humming a silly tune and coming in the front door of the printshop, carrying the third volume of *Great Expectations* and a rather daft smile. This image did not dispirit Meg, far from it, and she fell into an ease she'd not felt in months, able to relax, at last, and enjoy the green and gold and purple of the London evening that swept by her. It was easier to enjoy the evening knowing that Orion might soon be found.

They were headed Cheapside-way, at least in general, Meg assumed, but half an hour into their journey, the familiar landmarks of London disappeared. They were near the river—the rank smell and slight breeze confirmed their location—but otherwise she had lost her bearings. Was there yet another London she did not know?

Unexpectedly, dead ahead on the narrow, winding street the carriage slipped through, a red glow appeared. It took Meg a moment to make sense of the glow—a string of red lanterns in the shape of Christmas bulbs. The lanterns hung over the entrance to—to what? Was it another tunnel, a gang-plank to some fantastical ship? No, an alley, a bye-street. And into and out of this entrance streamed currents of curious figures, all bathed in the red glow.

The carriage stopped at the entrance of the lantern-festooned alley, and the party climbed down. They stood under the paper lanterns—were those Chinese characters that decorated them?—and stared into the teeming alley. Here, on a Sunday night, while London prepared reluctantly for sleep, this strange street overflowed with life—stalls, shops; runners, walkers; odors, sounds, sights.

"Ladies and gentlemen," Mr. Dickens said with a sweep of his hand. "I give you Singapore. Please allow me to be your guide."

He crooked his arm, and Meg tucked her hand into his elbow. Meg's father offered his arm to Aunt Julia, and off the foursome strolled. Tobias ran ahead, skipping from one side of the alley to the next, from one open-sided shop to the next, saying only, "Look at this, look at this."

As they made their way into the narrow, curved alley, they were stared at as much as they stared. The familiar is as exotic to the exotic, as the exotic is to the familiar. The shop-keepers and patrons of Singapore found this ordinary-looking family to be quite unusual.

Mr. Dickens narrated.

"I've wanted to bring you here since that first night on the Satis House roof. I knew that as a fellow insomniac, as a fellow night-wanderer, you, Meg, would appreciate Singapore as do I. It was made for the likes of you and me. While the rest of the world sleeps, a few of us stay wide-awake to its unseen possibilities.

"I have been a patron of London and its wonders for half a century now. It is a place that fascinates simply because it does not end—a riddle without a solution. A city cannot be bounded by fortified walls, nor by a surveyor's plans. A city is a living thing, always growing, never the same one day as the next. Just when you imagine you have discovered every one of its qualities—*voilà!*—entire new vistas blossom before you.

"When I left my home at Gad's Hill and traveled to France, which is to say, when I arrived alone and sleepless in London this season, I knew nothing of Singapore, indeed, had never heard of it. Imagine that! Me, your very own Charles Dickens, the Great Man of London, the man who some say invented all of London, I would know nothing of this place? It seemed impossible.

"And that is what haunted me, you know. I had forgotten the impossible. I was no longer looking for the stories I might tell; I thought I had told them all. And the same with you, Meg, if I may be so presumptuous. You had stopped imagining a city in which Orion still existed. You saw only the London where there was no Orion, until you allowed yourself to be carried out onto the roof-tops."

To one side of Meg a man in a conical hat chopped off the heads of roasted ducks. To the other side of the narrow way, gleaming ivory sculptures crowded a stall where a man in a turban stared blankly into space. Overhead a golden monkey chattered and screamed, leaping from pillar to post.

"I had never imagined Singapore," Mr. Dickens went on, "and yet, here it is. As I walked deeper and deeper into my nights, I stumbled upon it. A haunting can lead to wondrous possibilities. This street is less than a quarter-mile, and yet I've not come to the end of it."

A man in a saffron-colored robe held a blue gem to a gas-light; a sailor with a wooden leg nodded at it appreciatively. Two women in embroidered gypsy blouses made round pieces of flat bread on a stone. Glass tanks of purple, green, yellow, and red fish, their flowing tails like cursive penmanship, floated above a stall of ornate sea-shells. It was difficult for Meg to train her gaze on any one spot before a new amazement distracted her.

"I don't understand," Meg said. "This place is astounding, but where did it come from?"

"That is the glory of Singapore," Mr. Dickens said. "It comes from all over the world. Every time England went out into the world in her ships—to China, India, the Americas, Australia—the world came back to England. It's never a one-way journey. Singapore is the seed of what the world will bring to England. Perhaps that is the moral of this tale. One cannot explore the world without being changed by the world."

A fat snake sat lumpily around the neck of a befeathered man who seemed to be asleep.

"But why 'Singapore,' then, if it's all the world?" Meg asked.

"Because that is what I choose to call it, and I choose to call it Singapore because of this establishment right here."

Mr. Dickens stopped and turned to Aunt Julia and Meg's father. Tobias tore himself away from a terrarium of bearded lizards.

"Lee Ho Fook's, ladies and gentlemen," Mr. Dickens said with yet another theatrical flourish. "Mr. Fook is a chef of incomparable abilities. He arrived, from Singapore, aboard a haggard and leaking ship twenty years prior, and so appalled was he at life a-sea, that he never set foot on a ship again. It was then, at least that's his claim, that what I call Singapore was born. Who's to say if the story is true? No matter. We do not come to Lee Ho Fook's for his stories, but for his food. And it will be my extreme pleasure to introduce you to the greatest of all Oriental mysteries—chopsticks."

They entered a narrow doorway that was concealed by a soft cotton banner, and were greeted by a slender man in a blue silk jacket.

"Mr. Dickens," the man said, bowing deeply. "My dear friend. As always, a pleasure."

Mr. Dickens bowed, then introduced all in the party to Mr. Fook. They were then seated at a table on an open verandah that hung out over the water. Meg had reckoned they were close to the Thames, but not close enough to abut it. Still, here was calm water, lapping and flashing in the glow of a thousand lanterns. Was this the Thames or some hidden canal, some impossible bay? Small ships and large boats littered the water's surface, like leaves upon a pond. Maybe it was the glow from the lanterns that hid the sky, but Meg was unable to see any of it from here.

Mr. Fook and Mr. Dickens huddled close. Mr. Dickens swept his hand across the table, circularly, and Mr. Fook stepped back and smiled. Then he evaporated. Or that is how his leave-taking struck Meg, a puff of disappearing smoke.

"Chopsticks," Mr. Dickens said, "make our clumsy forks and knives seem barbaric, don't you think?" He held two slender wooden sticks in one hand, pinched gently between his fingers. "Chopsticks are elegant *and* precise."

He reached over and tweaked Tobias's nose with the long sticks. He handed a pair to each of the party, who each proceeded to fumble them. Only Tobias achieved mastery. Within minutes he was able to pluck a lost crumb no bigger than a pin-head from the rough, wooden table. Meg would find she was able to eat with chopsticks, though without the precision and elegance Mr. Dickens had promised.

For hours, it seemed, food arrived at the table, Mr. Fook landing one dish while taking up the previous one. Meg had never known such food—at first it was so unusual it confused her, but by the time the second set of dumplings arrived, she was already craving what she had yet to taste.

A soup with the tang of sweetness in it. Dumplings, delicate and stuffed with meats and vegetables. Vegetables steamed but otherwise unfamiliar. Soft buns filled with pork shreds, and filled, too, with shrimp. Quail eggs. Squid, if you can imagine, delicately fried. Crackling, fatty pieces of duck. Pots of fragrant tea.

Meg knew that she would never be able to remember all that they ate, but she knew at the same time that she would never stop wanting to taste new dishes. Cold mutton, as they often ate at home, never seemed colder. Her tongue was newly alive.

Everyone ate as if eating for the first time.

Newly refreshed by their unending meal, they turned their talk to Orion again.

Meg revealed to her father that she and Mr. Dickens wished to pay a visit to Tellson's Bank the next day.

"But why Tellson's?" her father asked. "What have they to tell us?"

"We need proof of what we only believe," Meg said.

"Hard evidence," Mr. Dickens said. "The name Tellson's Bank was on the labels, we know that, and so we go there. We have the clear sense that these bolts of Bogle are counterfeit, but we need better proof. A piece of paper, perhaps, something undeniable. Tellson's may just have that piece of paper, whatever it might be."

"Because then," Meg said, "we'll be able to approach Mr. Bogle directly."

"Ah," her father said, and once again, Meg expected him to offer a rebuttal, a considered excuse for failing to act. But he offered no such thing. When he spoke again, Meg knew that her father's fear had been completely extinguished. Meg knew now that there was only going forward, and that her father was joined to that expedition. Her heart leapt. And she knew all of this because when her father spoke again, what he said was, "I see, I see. Without evidence, we have no power over Mr. Bogle. But if we can prove—prove!—that his bolts are counterfeit, we're no longer nosy Nellies. With proof of that crime, we are a threat to him."

"Indeed, Campion," Mr. Dickens said, and he reached over and squeezed his old friend's shoulder.

"But where is Orion?" Aunt Julia asked. "How does this help us find him?"

"We don't know yet," Meg said. "But we do know that Mr. Bogle knows."

"It's the power of our threat, Julia," Mr. Dickens said. "Mr. Bogle, confronted, may tip his hand, or he may throw all his cards in the air. Nothing quite unsettles a person of secrets like the light of day."

"Then we must hurry," Aunt Julia said, nodding with great force.

All agreed: They must move fast. All agreed: They were closing in on Orion. All agreed: Tomorrow, Meg and Mr. Dickens would fly to Tellson's Bank first thing.

It was near midnight when they left Singapore, and as they creaked through the streets towards Cheapside, the last Sunday bells rang out, and the London sky erupted with chimes. Monday was here; the day of leisure had exhausted itself.

The leaden circles dissolved into air. Time was upon them, Meg knew.

Chapter XVII

In which business is conducted in a place that is all business

"TELLSON'S BANK, DRIVER," Mr. Dickens called when they were settled in the Hansom cab. "Fleet Street at Temple Bar."

Mr. Dickens paged through his notes. He had drawn a quiet around him, like a cape, and with Meg desirous of quiet as well, both occupants of this rather tattered Hansom cab tucked into themselves. Meg peered at the overwhelming city through the cab's small window.

Orion, as usual, was at the center of her thoughts this morning, but he was no longer alone there. She had observed too much else in the course of her journey to see only Orion anymore. One of her thoughts was: Could men be so greedy as to kidnap children for the sake of a few pence or shillings or pounds? Her thoughts answered, Yes. Another thought: Was it possible for all London, by which she meant all of England, by which she meant all of the world, to allow such men and the kidnappings and the work-houses? Again her thoughts answered, Yes. Was it possible to redeem Orion and bring him home and restore the life she'd known before?

To this last question, her thoughts had a more complex answer. Yes, her thoughts seemed to say, Orion could be—*would* be—returned. But, her thoughts went on, would that be enough? Knowing what she knew? No, her thoughts said clearly, that would not be enough. No, it would not be enough unless Meg did all that she could to redeem, as well, the children she'd seen in the work-house, the children she'd imagined in the tunnels. Yes, Orion was to be saved, but no, it would not suffice. Meg must do what she could to save them.

The Hansom skittered to a halt at Tellson's Bank, Fleet Street near the Temple Bar.

"Arrivées, Meg," Mr. Dickens said, and he helped her down.

Since the moment it had been decided that they would go to Tellson's, Meg had imagined walking into the bank—a vast marble staircase, framed on either side by classically vast pillars. In her imagination she could nearly read the gilt letters on the whistle-clean glass doors, and she prepared herself to be blinded by the gleam of Tellson's interior.

Alas, Tellson's was no gleaming temple. It was, at first glance, a narrow, barely perceived door of dark and most certainly un-polished wood, above which a dark and more un-polished sign declared Tellson's presence. As if to indicate its stubborn refusal to be noticed, the door of Tellson's refused to open. The bank seemed to say, *O no, we are not here, and we certainly have no money, and if we did have money, there would be no way for you to extract it.*

But the idiotic door did give way at last, with a weak rattle in its voice, and Meg and Mr. Dickens stumbled down two odd steps into a miserable little shop. Tall bankers' counters declared themselves dully, and at these counters, several very old men thumbed and rummaged through piles of paper. No one looked up when Meg and Mr. Dickens entered.

The only two windows, both on the Fleet Street side of the bank, offered little illumination. While high up on the bank's walls, the windows were actually set at street level, the bank being a basement of sorts. Because of the feet and the carriage wheels that went past, the windows were spattered with mud and ageless grime, and made an already-dark place that much darker. By the feeble light of these windows, one very old bank teller examined a parchment check, which rattled in his grasp like the last leaf of an autumnal tree.

Meg wondered if the old men who worked here were home to the bank, or was the bank home to them. Perhaps the old men and the rattling dead leaves of paper they perused and signed, perhaps these had been here first and the bank constructed around them. It was hard to say which might be older.

There was only one spot of brightness in this dismal

place, and that was the fiery red hair of a red-faced young man who sat all alone at a desk in a corner. He wore a vivid costume of blue with red piping, all of which accented his great red-ness overall. It was plain to Meg that the red-man was new to Tellson's. With some horror, she realized he would probably be kept here until his red-ness, his vitality began to fade, until he was as old and papery as the other men who made up Tellson's Bank. He might be here, she gasped, for as long a time as thirty years or more, a thought that deeply saddened Meg.

It was to the red-man Mr. Dickens directed them. The papers on his desk, though the red-man moved them with his own hands, seemed to fly about of their own volition, a spouting fountain of paper.

Meg read the name-plate on the desk as Mr. Dickens pronounced it.

"Mr. Burge Bloze, I assume," Mr. Dickens said loudly. "And how do we find you this morning, Mr. Bloze?"

Mr. Bloze looked up.

"Shattered, sir, you find me quite shattered, I'm sorry to report."

"Shattered, sir?" Mr. Dickens inquired.

"Indeed. Both shattered and shattering."

"But why, good Mr. Bloze?"

"O ho ho, a good question, but a better answer," Mr. Bloze said. He stopped the rain of paper on his desk and looked up with a bear cub's grin. "You would think, would you not, that among all these papers, I would most certainly find one sheet of paper. But there are too many sheets for only one."

"Sir," Meg said. "Here is one here, and here another, and so on. Perhaps if you left them still, you would find one."

"Clever, miss, clever, I can see you are a clever child. One yes—many are, after all, only one multiplied. But not *the* one, I'm afraid. And I'm afraid that without *the* one piece of paper, the whole lot of them are useless." And he went back, without a glance, to producing a shuffling shower of paper.

"Mr. Bloze," Mr. Dickens said. "We are sorry to imperil your task, but we come on urgent business. We come about Mr. Bogle."

The shower of paper ceased. Only the sound of the creeping age of Tellson's Bank and its employees could be heard. Mr. Burge Bloze leaned back in his chair, his thumbs hooked into his red waist-coat's pockets.

"O ho ho," he verily sang. "The name of Bogle . . ." and he fell into a practical reverie. But it was a short-lived reverie, at that, and he immediately snapped forward again.

"Mr. Lorry!" Mr. Bloze bellowed. "They've come about the name of Bogle." Mr. Bloze's desk erupted into a veritable Mount Vesuvius of paper, through which he could hardly be seen.

Meg was distracted by a series of business-like footfalls approaching. She turned. The man she saw before her was in a perfect harmony with the sound of his foot-falls:

all business. He was not near as old as Tellson's or its other employees. Might he still have a chance to escape it?

"Mr. Jarvis Lorry, sir, at your service," he said with a great accounting. "And you might be?"

Mr. Dickens shook the man's hand. "I might be Napoleon Bonaparte," Mr. Dickens said, and Meg had to suppress a giggle. "But I am not. I am, I'm afraid, one Mr. Charles Dickens."

"Welcome, sir. And may I ask your line of business, sir?"

"You may. I am a novelist."

Mr. Lorry looked quite stunned; Mr. Dickens likewise.

Meg, for her part, was not stunned, merely surprised. Was it possible that any Londoner did not know the name Mr. Charles Dickens? It was possible, she knew, for the look on Mr. Lorry's face told her so. Perhaps too much business had occupied his life.

"I write novels," Mr. Dickens said, by way of explanation.

"And these novels which you write—they are good business?"

"Chiefly, no. More art than business."

"Then I do not know them. I am, you see, a man of business. But you do have business today?"

"Indeed. I am come to inquire about Mr. Bogle."

Here Mr. Lorry stopped, as did, again, it seemed to Meg, all the business of Tellson's Bank.

"Ah, the name of Bogle." Mr. Lorry sighed when he said this, but an unexpected twinkle brightened his eyes. "The name of Bogle. And what is the nature of your business with the name of Bogle?"

"I wish to inquire into the nature of *his* business," Mr. Dickens said. "Especially as it pertains to Mr. Bogle's Porcelain Emporium."

"Perhaps, sir, your business is to produce a novel regarding Mr. Bogle and his Porcelain Emporium?"

"Let us say yes."

"Well, then, sir, that qualifies as business, as novels are your business, and as a man of business, I must offer assistance. What would you know?"

Meg could see clearly the clock-work of Mr. Dickens's mind turning in its gears. In planning their excursion to the bank, Mr. Dickens had insisted, and Meg agreed, that it was odd a Porcelain Emporium should accept deliveries of iron bolts. This was what the labels on the work-house crates stated. But if there were no bolts in the Porcelain Emporium, then that would be proof enough that Mr. Bogle's bolts were truly counterfeit. In short—at Tellson's they hoped to find that Mr. Bogle was, without a doubt, up to no good, and to do that, they must locate Mr. Bogle's Porcelain Emporium.

"I am in need of visiting his Porcelain Emporium. For business, that is."

"Burge Bloze!" Mr. Lorry called. "Fetch me the job-lot of Bogle papers, if you will."

Mr. Bloze rose and scurried into another dark corner

of Tellson's, returning with a loose ream of foolscap in various sizes and colors and shapes. Mr. Bloze carefully held the papers, both a secretary and a secretary—that is, both man and furniture—while Mr. Lorry riffled the papers, finally selecting and withdrawing one.

"Aha," Mr. Lorry said, dismissing Mr. Bloze with a half-wave. "Here we have it. Mr. Bogle, you well know, is a valued customer of Tellson's, and I'll say no more on that. Don't ask me to say more of his character." With this last, Mr. Lorry gazed sternly at Mr. Dickens and Meg. "Here it is. If your business is with Mr. Bogle, allow me to offer this—Mr. Bogle's Porcelain Emporium, in Penny Lane, near Portsmith, but not on it, mind you. *Near* but not *on,* take note. I have no fancy on whether your business with Mr. Bogle is pleasant—or otherwise. I'm simply a man of business, and if your business is with the name of Bogle—so be it. Your answer, sir."

"With great thanks, Mr. Lorry," Mr. Dickens said.

"Now, if you'll excuse me, other business calls."

"Pardon me, Mr. Lorry, sir," Meg said. "But one more matter of business, if you will."

A sudden question had come to her mind. There was a matter concerning the name of Bogle about which she was ravenously curious.

"A matter of business? Then yes."

"Is Mr. Bogle a married man?" Meg asked.

"And how is that business?"

"Marriage is, is it not," Meg asked, "a matter of

business? In marriage, the fortunes of two become the fortunes of one, and that is certainly a matter of business."

"Point well taken, miss. Yes, then, as a matter of business—and business only, mind you, nothing of affection—Mr. Bogle has recently married. To a widow, one Mrs. Podsnap and her one daughter—all for the business of it. If you follow my business meaning."

"Yes, sir, thank you, sir," Meg said.

There it was. Mrs. Podsnap, from the séance, was definitely Mrs. Bogle, and if that was the case, it was Mr. Bogle, *the* Mr. Bogle, Meg had seen at the Hanover Square Rooms. Perhaps Mr. Bogle himself had arranged the séance for his wife. The connections grew tighter and tighter: Orion to Mrs. Podsnap to Mrs. Bogle to Mr. Bogle.

"And thank you both," Mr. Lorry said. "For offering this unexpected piece of business today." He took Mr. Dickens's hand firmly and did not let go before earnestly gazing into his eyes and saying with great force, "And may your business with the name of Bogle be most profitable for everyone."

Had he winked at Mr. Dickens?

No matter, they were leaving Tellson's Bank, stepping out of the life of business and into the business of life again.

A carriage was called for. But before Meg could climb into it, she stopped in wonderment and stared across Fleet Street. Immobile one moment, she burst out of her immobility and dashed across Fleet Street, perilously avoiding the herds of carriages that swarmed around her. Mr. Dickens, still immobile, called after her, but she would not stop. That is, until she came to the broadside pasted over an un-used window—SEEKING HUNTER! Here she stopped gratefully and read the words scribbled on it in pencil—"O alive at large continue search a friend C."

C as in Charlie, Meg realized. Charlie had seen their broadside; Orion was alive still, and getting closer by the minute. *It must be so,* Meg whispered to herself.

Chapter XVIII

What is no longer there;
what has been there all along

THE SUMMER DAY was darkening now, thickening into a deep pudding of black and ominous hue—a storm approached.

"That's a grand sign, Meg," Mr. Dickens said. "Charlie, dear Charlie—whoever he may be—has seen the broadside, and so Orion must still be here in London. For now. We must hasten all."

"Yes, yes," was all that Meg seemed capable of uttering. Her mind was too full of Charlie's scribbled message for any rational speech to escape. Mr. Dickens continued to speak, but Meg was too insensible to hear him. He spoke of bolts and shops and Bogles, though he may have spoken of Xanadu and California for all that.

Meg scarcely registered that the promised storm broke over them. A swift, bucket-full rain pelted London.

From Fleet Street they ventured into Clement's Inn,

and from there into narrower and narrower ways—though Meg saw nothing of any of this—until the carriage rolled to a stop in Portsmith Street.

"Driver, what ho?" Mr. Dickens called.

" 'Tis it, sir, ain't it?" bellowed the driver.

"Penny Lane?" Mr. Dickens asked.

"No, sir, kindly sir. Portsmith, off which you claim is a Penny Lane."

"But no Penny Lane?"

"I know no Penny Lane, sir, not yet at least, and if there is a Penny Lane, off Portsmith, as you called it, sir, then this is Portsmith off of which you will likely find it."

"Confound you, sir, it rains, and with great force. Does it not?"

"Indeed, sir," came the dis-embodied voice of the driver. "It rains, to be sure. As they are likely to say—it is coming down. Which I suggest is to be preferred over it going up."

Meg was roused from her Orion-dream by the bellowing of the driver and the bellowing of Mr. Dickens. It was raining. And Mr. Dickens seemed most vexed.

"And what do you suggest that we do then?"

"Get wet," called the driver.

Mr. Dickens was just pumping himself up for a good, long bellow when Meg stopped him.

"It is only water, sir," she said. "We have seen worse."

Mr. Dickens laughed, his bellow softening to a burble of amusement.

"Very well, driver," he said. "We shall take your sound counsel. Get wet, it is."

He hopped out of the carriage, flipped several coins, one at a time, to the driver, put his head back, hand on hat, as if to taste the rain.

Both hands on the doorway of the small carriage, Meg jumped directly into a quick-gathered puddle, splashing a thick spray of street muck onto Mr. Dickens, up to his knees. She'd intended no such gesture, but there it was, and it was quite disarming to both of them. To be exceedingly clear—they laughed.

"You see, good sir," Meg finally said, "it is, after all, only water."

The carriage wheeled off, a shower of mud rising from its spoked, wooden wheels.

They scurried to the narrow eaves of a near-by public-house, while the sudden squall continued to pelt. No lane was obvious off Portsmith, but Meg espied a narrow opening, from which a young boy escorted his younger sister. Perhaps that was Penny Lane; she pulled Mr. Dickens along. Just as they reached the narrow entrance, the rain abruptly ceased and the skies broke blue directly above them. And as the sky opened up, so did Penny Lane.

The entrance was narrow, no doubt of that, but the street itself—cobblestones glistening from the fresh shower—was broader than might be imagined. Shop-fronts and house-tops glistened, too, all fresh a-showered, as if the lane were bran' new. All the people were coming and going in this freshness. Meg and Mr. Dickens strolled Penny Lane, searching for their destination.

Ahead of them, a man in a severe black suit was chased along by a pack of children who were imitating his ungainly walk. Meg could easily imagine the circumstance. The man was a banker—how she knew this she only guessed from his awkward stride—and the children, upon seeing him, had begged for his spare coins. But because the man was a banker, he refused to part with a single coin, especially a coin that might be spent on something so trivial as a child's pleasure—where was the profit in that? Refused, the children had no choice but to follow and bother him. How did Meg recognize such a scenario? She had often done the same herself—when she was still a child. Children, she knew—no longer a child herself, she accounted—would have their revenge one way or another.

The banker clutched his valise and trotted as fast as his stork-ish legs could carry him. The children followed, hooting, stork-legged, too, until the banker swerved into a barber's and took a seat to wait for a trim. The children pasted themselves to the barber's window and stuck out their tongues and continued their taunting. The banker pretended not to notice, as did the barber.

Drawn so, Meg could not help but notice the interior of the barber-shop, and was so struck by what she saw there that she halted Mr. Dickens's progress. Above the smoky mirrors and around the walls were photographs of men's heads, each man freshly shaved and trimmed. In the corner of the small but clean shop, a large camera apparatus stood ready. The sign above it read EVERY HEAD I'VE HAD THE PLEASURE TO KNOW.

Meg and Mr. Dickens both smiled and shrugged; they had never seen the likes of such a place.

All the people came and went in Penny Lane. It was full of fish-shops, and a bookseller's, too, and a Chandler's, and one small Curiosity shop that displayed relics of bygone times and places. A seller of finger-pies—steak, kidney, and steak-and-kidney—rolled his cart along and rang his bell and called out his wares. A nurse selling poppies on a tray—"For her majesty's veterans," she said—approached, and Mr. Dickens bought one for himself and one for Meg. He pinned his to his coat's lapel; she tucked hers behind her ear.

Continuing on their way, they passed the open carriage-gate of the Lennon and McCartney Private Fire Insurance Company. Here four young men in brilliant suits and silvered helmets polished the brass machinery of their steam fire-engine. They joked about, flipping wet rags at one another, singing all the while, in delicious harmonies, a song about one Mr. Kite. Meg could only wonder why they had taken up the profession of fire-men.

Up and down Penny Lane all the people came and went, from shop to shop.

At last our heroes came to the end of Penny Lane, where it opened onto dreary Drury Lane and its falling-down houses and bleak windows. There was no Porcelain Emporium on Penny Lane. They had peered into every shop-window, but nothing fit their needs.

"What does it mean, Mr. Dickens," Meg asked, "that we do not find it?"

"Unclear, Meg. It may mean that our Mr. Bogle is a counterfeit. Or it may mean that Mr. Tellson is wrong in his directions. Or it may mean we have been sent on a wild-goose chase. No matter which, it is inconclusive."

"I don't understand."

"You see," Mr. Dickens said. "If we could find this Porcelain Emporium, and see for certain that it is such, and not a home for railway parts, then we would have uncovered at least that lie—proof of that lie. But with nothing, the lie is merely our conjecture. We need to see what is not there. But without what is not there, we have nothing."

Penny Lane glistened under the coat of sudden rain that had cleansed it, and the spark and charm of sunlight illuminated every shop. Meg looked back down the lane, and in the new brightness of the afternoon, she saw on the window of one shop what she might not otherwise have seen.

On the window of one shop were clearly painted the words CURIOSITY DEALER, but she had seen that in passing the first time, and it was not this sign that now drew her. Behind these words were older words, faint now, barely traceable, but in this new light visible. She distinctly made out the letter *P*.

Meg took off for the Curiosity Dealer, plashing on the cobblestones. Mr. Dickens followed.

She pressed her face close to the window, not looking *through* the window but *at* it. Her fingers felt along the rippled glass, following the forms of the letters that had once been painted there, and whose shapes still remained in a ghostly out-line. Mr. Dickens saw at once what business she was conducting.

"Bogle's Porcelain Emporium," he read. "Meg, you lovely quibbling, you perceptive wonder. It's right there. Hard to see, but you saw it. You looked hard enough to see what is not there, and there it is."

"It's the sunshine, sir," Meg said. "See the letters. This is our Porcelain Emporium. And right there, Mr. Bogle's own name."

"True enough," he said. "Mr. Bogle seems a man fascinated by his own name."

"But if so fascinated by his own name," Meg said, "why has he removed it from this window?"

"If we know Mr. Bogle, or at least his kind, then don't we imagine that he's removed his name from here for a very good reason. My guess is that he wants the world to *not* see it here. Mr. Bogle does not seem prone to mistakes."

Now they peered *through* the glass of the window.

Taking in the dusty, dim light of the interior, Meg began to ascertain some of the scattered articles in the shop. A suit of armor, as if guarding its castle, stood in one corner, and around it rusty swords and helmets gathered. There were fantastic carvings—in china and wood and iron and ivory—of mythical creatures and odd religious figures. Tapestries and strange furniture abounded. Though not a single piece of porcelain, save one chipped and faded tea set.

"This is it," Mr. Dickens said, "or I am a goose. This is our once-existing, non-existing Bogle's Porcelain Emporium. It is what we have come looking for, and blessedly, it is not here at all."

From the dimness of the shop, the out-line of two figures became apparent. One was a haggard old man, grey of hair and stooped, looking as old as the treasures he stocked. The other was a girl, Meg's age, a pretty girl wrapped in a black shawl. The girl at first did not see Meg, and she coughed hoarsely into a handkerchief Meg saw was spotted with blood; her entire body was wracked with effort and pain. The girl, recovered, looked up at Meg and offered a weary wave and pallid smile. Meg was utterly saddened by this sight, and came near to tears. She wanted to go to the girl, to hold and comfort her. Meg feared, unconsciously, that the shop-girl was not long for this earth.

Mr. Dickens pulled her back with his voice.

"Quick, Meg. Lunch. We must plan our next steps. We know what we need to."

With one last glance and a little wave of her own, Meg bid a final adieu to the sickly girl in the black shawl.

✦ ✦ ✦

The sadness that had rushed through Meg when she saw the pale and obviously ill girl in the old Curiosity shop left her for a moment. It was almost impossible, she knew, to wallow in such sentiments when Mr. Dickens was on the move. It wasn't that Mr. Dickens was oblivious to such emotions, far from it. She sometimes believed he felt the most deeply of all; in fact, Meg had seen him take note of the pretty, but withered, girl in the shop, and was certain that a tide of sadness had engulfed him at that moment. No—he did feel, and felt deeply, and sincerely. He felt both joy and despair, in the equal measures that life meted out.

It was simply that Mr. Dickens would not wallow, would not allow the emotion of one moment to keep him from the next, especially when the next moment might help alleviate the suffering he was only too aware of. She imagined Mr. Dickens as a vast ship upon the seas, all sails raised and coursing forward through uncharted and hazardous waters. He was all forward motion, all intrepidity.

So she and Mr. Dickens coursed ahead and found themselves—after yet another brief carriage ride—in Kingsway, at the hoped-to-be elegant Pelican Coffee-house.

When the young red-haired waitress arrived, even she was surprised at the speed with which Mr. Dickens chose his dishes, and more surprised, she seemed, by the number and variety of them.

In moments, their plates arrived.

Meg, starving, grazed her grilled pork and roasted

potatoes. Mr. Dickens, as ever, seemed intent on running through his meal, as if he were reading a thrilling novel and could not wait to get to the final page. Mulligatawny soup, salmon in lobster sauce, pigeon and peas, four different cheeses, and the obligatory plate of oysters.

They sat in the front window and watched the Kingsway traffic go by. Mr. Dickens sat with his back to the window, the better to ignore the stares of those who might recognize the Great Man.

The new set of facts before them, Meg was trying to find the proper order.

"I understand," she said, "why Mr. Bogle cheats on the bolts—he's greedy and wishes to spend less money as to make more of it. But I'm mystified as to his ruse. Why all the work involved with false labels on crates and directing them to an address that does not exist? Why doesn't he simply ship the bolts and do without the rest."

"Paperwork, Meg," Mr. Dickens said. He set down his knife and fork, and pushed away from the table. "It's all about paperwork. London, you see, is a monster voracious for paper. Surely you've noticed. Everywhere we go, mounds of paper, armloads of paper, snow-falls of paper. Without paper, it's as if London itself doesn't exist. Mr. Bogle is a man shrewd enough to know this. If he is to fool the world with his counterfeit bolts, he needs the paperwork to fool the world completely."

"As when you are in France?" Meg asked.

"Once again, Meg, nothing escapes you."

Mr. Dickens called for coffee and sorbet for both of them—lemon sorbet.

"Take Mulberry, for instance," he continued. "He is a fine dog, an exceptional dog, you and I would both agree. Without papers to prove this, he is merely a dog. However, if I were to produce a file of papers attesting to the fact that he is blue in color, which he is certainly not, and that he is capable of both flight and human speech, which he is also not, and"—he raised an authoritative finger—"if those papers were dutifully signed and stamped and otherwise made to appear official, then London, the business of London, that is, would have to accept, and willingly, that Mulberry was a blue flying dog who could afterwards detail his journey for us. If it exists on paper in London, it therefore exists. And Mr. Bogle knows that. My guess is that this phony paperwork is only for the customs and the tax man. It's all a lie."

The coffees were slid onto the table before them. Meg was so anxious for the sorbet she could already smell the sour tang of it.

"Allow me, sir," Meg said, stirring lumps of sugar into her thick coffee. "Mr. Bogle, our mysterious Mr. B, directs these labels to be made, so that the readers of these labels will believe the crates are filled with porcelain rather than iron, and that said porcelain will be deposited in a Porcelain Emporium rather than in a work-house at Billingsgate Market. If one believes the words, one believes the lie."

"Yes, Meg, you've nailed it down. Words, as you well

know, may expose the world as it truly is. Or they may be used to paint a world that never was nor will be. Words reveal and conceal, and sometimes both."

"Both?" Meg asked.

"Consider your broadside," he said. "Devilishly clever. It conceals from Orion's captors a message that is exceedingly clear to your brother."

Finally the sorbet arrived. As has been recently observed, our expectation of a thing often exceeds the thing itself, but not so with this sorbet. Meg had never once stood in a grove of lemon trees, but she knew that the taste of this sorbet must be equivalent to that. Leaving all words aside for a moment, she closed her eyes and fell into the sheer joy of sensation.

The rain was tremendous again, and falling falling falling—harshly, drearily, without thunder or lightning—and Meg and Mr. Dickens continued to reckon what would be their next step. All the while Meg stared out the window at the traffic of Kingsway, watched the people come and go, sipping her coffee.

Her attention narrowed to a small spot, across the broad avenue, under the dripping eaves of Coutt's Bank. There stood a boy and a girl, the boy Meg's age, the girl Tobias's, an inverted image of herself and her younger brother. They might have been, this brother and sister, the same two children she'd seen coming out of Penny Lane. Or they might be every child at large in London. They were only two, but they represented many.

The boy's clothes were rags—not much else could be said of them. His face was streaked with grime, his hair disheveled, his eyes showed no light. He held out one plaintive hand, begging for the smallest farthing. The little girl wore a dress, which, it was obvious, she had worn for-ever. And while it did little good to keep the rain from soaking her, she had nonetheless wrapped a once-blue shawl over her head. She held on to her brother's hand with one of hers, and with the other beseeched passers-by for any small coin they could spare. Looking closer, Meg saw that they both shivered, even though the rain was tepid. They looked as if they would never be warm again, nor had they ever been.

Meg recalled all such children. Everywhere in her life, everywhere in London, everywhere in the world, children stood on streets, shivering, and begged only to stay alive. Even in her quiet Tonson Lane, the children there were left to fend for themselves. Most did not attend school, and so had no future other than more begging, and most certainly had no home like Meg's, where a future was given to them through books, through learning, through the examples of her father, Aunt Julia, Meg's long-passed mother. Instead the children were sent into the streets all alone, or pressed into work-houses, even more alone there.

She gazed up and down Kingsway. At a far corner was another sister and brother, but the brother was too tired to stand, and so sat in a puddle while he begged to stay alive. And beyond them, an older sister clutched an infant child, begging for herself and the babe. And beyond, three boys of varying heights, perhaps brothers or perhaps only brothers of common circumstance, stood huddled with great expectations of a meager hand-out, stood waiting for some bright future to burst open.

All of London swarmed around these children, ignorant of them, conducting the business of London. As usual.

Meg interrupted Mr. Dickens, heedless of what he had been saying.

"Mr. Dickens. You have promised me that we shall save the work-house children, and I trust in you. But how shall we save them? What shall we do? It seems impossible that we should save them all."

He set down his coffee.

"We shall publish, my dear," he said. "We shall use the power of the words that reveal to expose this travesty. We shall publish. *All the Year Round*."

Meg knew these last words. This was Mr. Dickens's own monthly magazine. It was read by all of London. And a magazine, Meg knew, was so much quicker than a novel. A novel might take years to write; a magazine was now. And now was what these children needed.

"We shall tell their story?" she asked.

"And it shall set them free."

The rain, at last, was relenting. If for a moment.

Chapter XIX

Another carriage! And another!

PLANS, MAPS, STRATEGIES—of which there were many flying about that day and night and the next day—all are well and good and necessary. But there comes a time in every tale when discussions of plans and maps and strategies only impede one from entering the fray of the final chase. So, instead of plans, let our focus be carriages. This is London, you see, and carriages transport us to our actions.

A carriage was taken by Meg and Mr. Dickens from the Pelican Coffee-house to Tonson Lane, and after much planning and mapping and eating and all the rest a life requires, Mr. Dickens was dispatched in another carriage to strategic venues, and from these to his rooms at . . . well, wherever it was he kept his rooms. Meg was still uncertain as to where Mr. Dickens stayed when he was "not in France."

The next morning, Mr. Dickens climbed into yet another carriage, thence back to Cheapside, where he and Meg entered another carriage, which tore in the direction of Park Lane, Hyde Park, far to the west.

Can you not hear the velocity and urgency of all these carriages? The drivers' snapping reins and barked commands, the creaking leather, the squeaking springs, the thundering wheels, the horses' clips and clops and snorted breaths. The chase is on!

There will be yet other, even more urgent carriages, but the one with which we are most concerned on this page is that which, this soot-choked morning, deposits Meg and Mr. Dickens in Park Lane, adjacent to Hyde Park, and directly in front of Bogle Manor. They knew they had arrived at their destination because of the highly polished plaque that proclaimed the name of Bogle.

Meg was dressed in a rose-colored silk dress, the likes and quality of which she had never worn. It was, in fact, not a true and fine silk dress, but a theatrical imposture of one, borrowed by Mr. Dickens from a friend of dramatic employment. Mr. Dickens, dressed in theatrical garb as well, was all the eccentric character, in pale linen trousers covered neatly by a pink-and-grey silk waist-coat, over which rode an embroidered long-coat in alternating stripes of forest and jade green. His hair and moustache and beard were dyed coal-black. He and Meg were masquerading as wealthy and newly arrived Londoners.

Their plan on this morning, as they had devised last night, was to infiltrate the Bogle house-hold. Rather than attack the Bogles head-on, they would approach them softly. "More flies with honey, Meg," Mr. Dickens had said.

As was agreed, then, Meg and Mr. Dickens, posing as a father and daughter, would attempt to flatter their way into the confidence of the Bogle house-hold. If confronted with his crimes, Mr. Bogle might flee, and they did not wish that. Rather, they hoped that Mr. Bogle would not be home at all, and by endearing themselves to Mrs. Bogle and her daughter, they might discover information that would lead to an awareness of Mr. Bogle's business, and from that, an awareness of Orion's whereabouts.

Meg and Mr. Dickens a-lighted from the carriage and stood before Bogle Manor. Mr. Dickens, of course, had stood before such mansions, and had, it is well-known, been in many of them. Also well-known was that he had lived in such enormous houses. It is of little import to see this view through his eyes—all he is thinking is, where is the front door?

But Meg, Meg is new to such places, and so through her eyes such a place is best seen. A Londoner through and through, Meg has passed many a mansion in her time, in the heart of London-Town. Sunday, traveling by carriage with her family and Mr. Dickens—*Was that only two days before?*—they had passed scores of these enormous homes. But seen from the distance of the carriage, they were less true buildings of stone and brick, and more like pictorial postcards of faraway lands.

Here, on this broad, tree-lined street, the verdant expanse of Hyde Park at her back, the houses un-crowded in their neat rows and surrounded by the vast greenery of their suburban yards, Meg stopped and stood and saw.

Her first thought: Bogle Manor was out of scale, even for colossal London. What stood before her was not so much a human construction but a feature of some fairy-tale realm. All that was needed to complete the scene was an echoing *fee-fi-fo-fum*.

And following anon, what Meg thought was: bran' new, spick-and-span new. The sparkle on the windows, the sheen on the marble columns, the fine-honed edges of the stucco ornaments, all attested to the fact that yesterday this mansion might not have been here. The style of Bogle Manor, Meg knew from her reading, was what might be called Palladian, a style that spoke of Italy during its Renaissance. Bogle Manor was historical but without history. Bran' new.

Then she saw deeper into the house—without entering it—and imagined room upon room, and a small sorrow filled her breast. In all this big and bran' new house only three inhabitants, Mr. and Mrs. and Miss Bogle. How would they ever fill this house with *home*? How would they ever infuse the enormous rooms with sufficient life? She thought of her own home, the ramshackle print-shop and the crowded, curtained rooms above, and she was desirous of being back there in its coze and comfort. Bogle Manor was impressive, but aloof.

As they walked up the broad drive, Meg's gaze shifted to the carriage that rested idle and horseless. It was the same plum-colored Brougham she'd seen in Cheapside and at Hanover Square. The carriage was magical, a magnificent fairy-tale bed fit for a princess. But the princess Meg had seen in this carriage, Miss Podsnap-Bogle, seemed anything but enchanted.

Finally they stood on the ship's-deck of a porch, and Mr. Dickens tugged at the ornate bell-pull. The Manor's hollow rooms clanged with brass chimes.

Before these chimes dissolved into air, the vast oaken front door swung wide, with a *whoosh* rather than a *creak*. A house-maid, dressed in pale grey under a white apron, her hair stuffed unwillingly under a small white hat, stood before them. She held a silver tray the size of a tea-cup saucer. The maid curtsied and spoke. "Good day, sir," she said, her eyes downcast. "May I ask who is calling, sir?" She nudged the tray towards Mr. Dickens.

Mr. Dickens bowed deeply—Meg saw at the back of his neck a spot of greying, un-dyed hair—and pulled a card from his waist-coat.

"Mr. Furie Bights, miss," he said, in an oddly booming voice. "At your service, if you please. I call upon the esteemed Mrs. Bogle by way of introducing an old and dear friend of her late husband, namely myself."

"One moment, sir, but please step in," the maid said in a voice that had died long ago. "I'll see if Mrs. Bogle is in."

Meg and Mr. Dickens stepped into the hall, from which

rose a pair of grand, curved stairways. The door gently shut behind them, unprompted by human hands.

The entrance-hall was cold and bright and bran' new, of course, and in its scope, bigger than all of Meg's family's rooms. Gilded angels the size of small dogs hovered in each corner, suspended above thick gilded moldings.

Meg and Mr. Dickens looked at each other; Mr. Dickens's eyebrows arched in exclamation.

Mrs. Bogle came mincing heavily into the hall, as excited, it seemed, as if Father Christmas had been announced. She was wearing a gold-colored gown that fit the décor of her gilded hall, as if she were one of its cherubim fallen. And she wore, of course, her gold-charm hat, as if another chandelier to brighten the room. She held her hand out to Mr. Dickens, as if he would put a ring upon one of her fingers. Mrs. Bogle, Meg saw, was all "as if." There might or might not be a real human being in their presence, it was impossible to tell under the weight of the "as if." She was all "as if" and no "is."

"Mr. Bights, I presume, how delightful," Mrs. Bogle trilled, as if a wind-up bird.

Mr. Dickens took Mrs. Bogle's out-stretched hand and pressed it firmly to his lips. Mrs. Bogle blushed crimson.

"Mrs. Bogle. How kind of you to consent to receive we poor waifs. You are as commendable as your late husband, Mr. Podsnap, may God bless his soul"—Mr. Dickens crossed his heart with his hat—"always claimed you were. And twice as lovely."

She blushed again, turned her head away, its gold charms clacking.

Meg stood still and silent, as instructed. She was not used to being overlooked so, and wanted badly to blurt all the questions that she held. But Mr. Dickens had been clear. In such a house, a girl like herself would not speak unless spoken to. If their plan was to succeed, Meg had to hold her tongue—a frustrating turn, to play the part of the refined young lady.

"You are too kind, sir," Mrs. Bogle said. "But it is a true distinction to receive one of my dear Podsnap's old friends. How, prithee, came you to know Mr. Podsnap?"

"Society," was all he said.

"Ah yes, society," she said. "He was such a man for society. Such society. And tell me, how did you find Mr. Podsnap?"

"Quite easily, I assure you."

Mrs. Bogle was struck dumb.

"For when that dear man," Mr. Dickens said, "was not by my side, we were side by side in our hearts. He is greatly missed, I assure you."

"O indeed. Greatly missed," Mrs. Bogle said. "But what I mean to say is, how did you find him as a man of society?"

"Ah," he said. "There was no other like him. He was greatly satisfying, and greatly satisfied with himself. What more can one ask?"

"That is my Podsnap, to the last detail. What great friends you must have been."

"Forgive my manners," Mr. Dickens said. "Allow me to introduce my beloved daughter, Miss Constance Bights. For it is on her behalf I attend you today."

"Madame," Meg said, with a French accent. She offered a deep curtsy. Mrs. Bogle deigned to lower her head, a miniscule acknowledgment.

"Mam'selle," was Mrs. Bogle's reply. Turning to Mr. Dickens she continued, "And how may I assist Mr. Podsnap's dear friend?"

"My daughter and I have been abroad some years, you see, on the Continent. Since before Mr. Podsnap's passing"—again his hat covered his heart—"and have only now returned. We shall soon establish a residence in near-by Albion. Alas, without the guidance of my dear wife, Prunella"—hat over heart again—"I fear Constance shall be lost in London society."

"Poor dear," Mrs. Bogle said with a chuckle, and she actually reached out and grabbed Meg's chin.

"Now, wherever I go in London society, I hear nothing but the name of Miss Bogle, who seems to be the charm of all England. No one speaks of Miss Bogle without reverence. And when it was un-covered that Miss Bogle was Miss Bogle née Podsnap, I hoped beyond hope that my dear old friend's daughter might be the guiding light for my own. Might it be possible, I wondered, for Miss Bogle née Podsnap to teach my own daughter in the ways of London society."

"Georgiana?" she asked, with a tone of astonishment.

"Georgiana. Yes." Here Mr. Dickens put his hands together in a little prayer.

Meg vividly conjured the image of the forlorn Miss Bogle—in the carriage and at the Hanover Square rooms—and found it nearly impossible not to laugh at the moment. Miss Bogle as the charm of anything? She had seemed barely alive.

"*My* Georgiana?"

Mrs. Bogle's expression seemed to indicate that she was also having a difficult time imagining her daughter as the charm of anything.

Mr. Dickens nodded vigorously.

"Why certainly, Mr. Bights. If you say she is a jewel, my daughter, she must be. I am most satisfied with her. Let us introduce our two daughters now—no delay. You will join me for tea, while Miss Bights visits Miss P—Bogle—in her rooms."

An entirely other maid was summoned with a silver bell. Mrs. Bogle whispered instructions to her, and she tore off to whisper the same instructions, no doubt, to yet another maid. Meg was instructed to wait. Mrs. Bogle and Mr. Dickens repaired to the parlor.

"Yours is a most lovely home, none other like it," Mr. Dickens said.

"O, sir, you flatter me. But I wished you had seen the house we demolished to make space for ours. It was only ten years old, but it was exquisite."

Before he shut the doors behind him, Mr. Dickens

caught Meg's eye and gave her a mischievous wink. Their plan was working to perfection. Mr. Dickens had hoped to have time alone with Mrs. Bogle, Meg time alone with the Miss. They were to flatter the Mrs. and the Miss, in hopes of finding out more about the Mr.

Yet another maid, with the equally haunted demeanor of the rest, glided into the entrance-hall and led Meg up one of the grand stairways. O how Meg longed, from the top of the stairs, to glide down the sweeping banister. She was no longer a child, yes, but maturity and experience shouldn't stop one from craving silly things like sliding down banisters. What a lark it would be!

Down long, mirrored hallways the maid guided Meg, turning left and right, several times in each direction, until at last they came to a door that stood ajar.

The maid turned to Meg.

"Miss Bogle is dressing for the afternoon, but consents to see you." The maid opened the door, and without entering, called, "Miss Bights for Miss Bogle, miss."

Meg entered. The room was a riot of color. Vases of fresh-cut flowers adorned every surface, from white lilies to violet irises. Orchids hung in baskets in every corner. Gilt and pink frosting decorated the rest of the room. In the midst of all this sparkle and blaze, there was only one small, plain, unadorned object—Miss Bogle herself.

Surrounding Miss Bogle was a trio of maids, who even in their drab uniforms and tired expressions, seemed all color and wit by comparison.

"Miss Bogle," Meg said. *"Je suis enchantée."*

"Moi aussi," came the drab voice.

"I'm sorry to intrude."

For Meg saw clearly that she was intruding, but leaving now seemed only more rude. Miss Bogle was, for the moment, dressed only in her under-garments, plain white but frilly. Yet Miss Bogle seemed not to care; she said nothing, nor looked at Meg.

The dressing continued. Miss Bogle was, as Meg remembered her, a young woman of high shoulders and low spirits. Her elbows, Meg perceived, seemed chilled.

Meg stood motionless for several long moments, and still Miss Bogle did not speak, nor acknowledge her any further.

"Perhaps I should wait downstairs," Meg said. "I seem to have offended you."

"How offended me?"

"You've said so little."

"O," Miss Bogle said. "Very kind of you to consider. But I don't talk. Ma talks."

And with that, Miss Bogle stopped talking.

Meg felt as if she should leave, but was unable to. A most fascinating device had been introduced into the room.

It was a cage. Meg knew what it was, and how it was used, but seeing it like this, out of its proper context, and so nakedly, it seemed a thing, not of fashion but of prisons. It was a cage-crinoline, a series of metal hoops, each covered in horse-hair and connected one to the other with fabric tape. Into this cage Miss Bogle would be placed, over which her gown would fall, offering her figure the bell-shaped form that current style demanded.

Every woman in London above a certain age and a certain class must wear such cages, Meg knew. She and Aunt Julia were immune from such dictates, because of their social status, and they wore petticoats instead.

Miss Bogle stepped into the cage, and it was fastened about her. She seemed more machine than woman in this, and Meg had a strong urge to steal Miss Bogle from her captivity. She wondered if Miss Bogle—Georgiana—was ever allowed the freedom Meg had so recently experienced when running free through the streets of London in boys' breeches. Meg doubted this had ever happened, or ever would.

Once the cage was established, the trio of maids continued the ministrations, buttoning and enlacing and otherwise stricturing and shaping Miss Bogle. When all was done, Miss Bogle stood serenely in a blood-red gown that seemed to float above the floor of its own accord.

Miss Bogle dismissed the maids with a tired wave.

"I suppose we must conversate, miss," Miss Bogle said. "Sit, do." They sat at a delicate table near the garden window, perched on delicate chairs.

Miss Bogle was truthful when she stated that she did not talk—she did not. Meg prattled on, hoping to evince some life from Georgiana. She asked questions, in answer to which she received shrugs that were once or twice accompanied by the phrase, "I don't talk, but Ma does." Meg told stories of her years on the Continent, as the fictitious Miss Bights, about which Georgiana had no questions.

So, Miss Bogle did not talk. Until she did.

Meg was in the middle of a story she'd invented—how easily such fables came—concerning a certain street in Paris where the blood-stains of the Reign of Terror were still visible seventy years on, when Miss Georgiana Bogle erupted.

"Do you know what I should like to be?" Georgiana said. "I should like to be a chimney-sweep."

Meg was confuddled. Out of the vast silence that was Georgiana Bogle, this whimsical, almost cheerful thought had arisen with no warning. Perhaps Miss Bogle did not talk because no one had ever shown the patience required to get her to talk. A chimney-sweep? Who would ever have guessed?

"And do you know why?" Georgiana asked. "They seem to enjoy it so. Just imagine, a chimney-sweep. What fun."

Meg laughed. Miss Bogle had made her laugh! Meg had never before considered that a sweep's life was an enviable one, but the sudden sparkle in Miss Bogle's face convinced her otherwise.

"And I dare say," Meg said, "you would make a fine chimney-sweep in that dress. If you were to climb down a chimney in such a contraption, it would be a spick-and-span chimney when you finished it."

Georgiana laughed and clapped, and showed herself

from under her silence, and from then on, her words tumbled out.

Meg and Georgiana talked about everything, though Georgiana did most of the talking now. These ridiculous dresses, this horrible house, her mother's incessant talking, and her father. No, not her own father, dear Mr. Podsnap, but her *step*-father, Mr. Bogle. She had admired him at first; now he was nothing but the Railway. Day and night, it was the Railway, and what a tedious topic. If you would not speak of the Railway, you should not speak, so her step-father believed.

"The Railway, you say?"

"Do you know," Georgiana said, clasping Meg's hand in hers, "that he goes there every night? He thinks I don't know but I do. I have had him followed. He goes to the tunnels every night and watches their progress. It's a secret, I believe. He would finish his blasted tunnels and Railway in record time. And I know this, too, so please be confidential. They're not to work at night—boys have died there. It's unsafe. But he is like the Railway itself, a machine that needs no sleep. And if he won't sleep, no one will. I loathe the Railway."

Georgiana grew quiet. She withdrew into the cage of herself.

Meg also remained quiet, but not out of timidity. She was suffused with contrasting emotions—horror and hope. She was horrified to discover that boys were truly working, secretly, in the tunnels at night. Some of them had died?

Meg had pictured Orion working there, but now she saw only too well that, yes, Orion probably was working there. What a clever place it would be to hide him. She was horrified by this vision of her brother's life. But horror quickly veered into hope. If Orion was, in fact, working in the tunnels at night, then they knew where to find him. The Marylebone tunnel was the only active excavation in London, for the moment.

"I have spoken too much," Miss Bogle said. She glanced about. "And I fear I have tired you. It's time for my hair now, and that is too tedious for even me. Good-bye, Miss Bights. As you see, I really don't talk."

All cheer had left the room. Miss Bogle—no longer Georgiana—rang a small bell, spoke the word *hair* to the room, and the trio of maids appeared as if by magic.

Miss Bogle turned away. Meg's audience was over.

Unescorted, Meg stood in the hall and pulled her notebook from her bag. She wrote these words: "tunnels at night—a secret. Orion is there!" She knew that she would remember all of this, but the writing down of the simplest details had become a habit for her. Then she moved through the tomb-quiet halls until she came to the stairways.

No one was in the entrance-hall, so why shouldn't she? Who would ever know?

She side-saddle leaped onto the wooden banister and slid down it, her speed increasing, her momentum exhilarating. Yes, why shouldn't she? In a house so tied-up, so enlaced, she felt compelled to ride the banister, if only to shake off the strict order of Bogle Manor and claim the glee that coursed through her. She flew down the banister; she felt free.

At the last moment she leaped from the banister and landed with two clops on the marble floor. Only to find herself face-to-face with Mr. Bogle himself.

He was tall and severe and dressed all in black. His eyes, too, were black, unsettling. His nose was as thin as the blade of a knife. He stared at Meg, removed his pocket-watch, checked the day's hour, then replaced the watch.

"Who might you be?" he asked, as grave as the undertaker.

It took all of Meg's restraint to not say, "I might be the Queen herself, but I am not." Instead: "Miss Constance Bights."

"What gives you permission to invade Bogle Manor?"

Before Meg could offer any answer, the parlor doors opened, and Mrs. Bogle scurried out, Mr. Dickens trailing.

"My dear Mr. Bogle. How fortuitous. I'd like you to meet an old family acquaintance, Mr. Bights, and his charming daughter."

Mr. Bogle tipped a perfunctory nod, but did not shake Mr. Dickens's offered hand.

"Mr. Bights wishes to have our own Georgiana, you see, usher Miss Bights into the world of London society. To study, if you will, under her charm."

"Georgiana's charm?" asked a befuddled Mr. Bogle. He gathered himself. "How kind. Now, if you'll excuse me."

"One moment, sir," Mr. Dickens said. "I am a man newly returned from the Continent and in search of new ventures. Perhaps we might discuss such a venture someday?"

"Perhaps." And with that, Mr. Bogle stepped around Mr. Dickens.

Meg intercepted him. He looked down at her, sternly, as was his nature. He refused to say a word. She withdrew the counterfeit bolt from her bag.

"Mr. Bogle, sir. Excuse me, but I found this near your carriage today, and I believe it might be important to you. I'd like to return it."

She held out the bolt to him. Meg had not planned on showing him the bolt; the gesture was an impulse. But she expected, or at least hoped, in that moment, that the bolt would somehow frighten Mr. Bogle, startle him. She wanted Mr. Bogle to know that she knew what he was about.

He looked at the bolt with a rather queer expression on his face, as if it were a living creature. He picked it up from her hand and inspected it, turning the top of the bolt towards him. He examined the letters *M* and *R* rather closely.

"Hmph," he said, then returned the bolt to Meg. "Nothing of mine." He brushed past her, disappearing into the dark recesses of the lower floor.

He'd seen it, Meg knew. He'd recognized the bolt, and all that her possession of it meant. He had flinched.

Mr. Dickens shot Meg a knowing glance.

"You'll excuse him, Mr. Bights," Mrs. Bogle said. "He's

a dear man, but so very busy, as you know. The name of Bogle is everywhere in London."

"Quite so," Mr. Dickens said. "I have seen the name of Bogle everywhere myself. But we have taken up too much of your valuable time already. Until next week then, madam. With our humble thanks.

He bowed and pressed her hand to his lips, then escorted Meg to the door, which he opened before the out-of-breath maid could get to it. He and Meg stepped out into the day.

"Adieu," he called.

"Adieu, dear friend," Mrs. Bogle said. A great disappointment seemed to establish itself in her posture. She stood in the open door of Bogle Manor as if her fine house might disappear without someone there to admire it.

Chapter XX

The mouth of Hell; the gates of Heaven

THIS IS NO TIME to halt the train of carriages—let the carriages roll on! Let each carriage fly more swiftly than the one before!

In the rattling, tumbling carriage that returned them to Tonson Lane, Meg and Mr. Dickens compared notes, and together arrived at a conclusion they had each reached independently: Orion was hidden in the tunnels, working through the night.

Ma talked, all right, as Georgiana had said. So satisfied was Mrs. Bogle with the name of Bogle and the man, her new husband, who bore the name of Bogle, that she just couldn't talk enough. Mr. Dickens learned from Mrs. Bogle that Mr. Bogle was such an important component of the Metropolitan Railway that she shouldn't be surprised if it were named the Bogle-politan Railway instead. So devoted was her husband, Mrs. Bogle exclaimed, she doubted the Railway would be completed without him. It was a sacrifice that she, Mrs. Bogle herself, was willing to make on behalf of all London. Mr. Bogle's devotion to the Railway kept him away from Bogle Manor day and night, but such was the price one paid for wedding such an important person. Her sacrifice, Mrs. Bogle said, while great, was nothing compared to the sacrifice her husband—Mr. Bogle—made.

It was so true to say Ma talked that Mr. Dickens believed he might expire of old age on the sofa where he had sat listening to her. He had been on the verge of inventing an excuse to leave, when Ma's talk turned ever more interesting.

You see, Mr. Dickens told Meg, Mrs. Bogle was so impressed with her husband's sacrifices that she forgot to keep his secrets. Mrs. Bogle relayed to Mr. Dickens that "certain corners had to be cut," if Mr. Bogle's sacrifices were to benefit all of London. She told Mr. Dickens about the boys in the tunnels at night, and what a sacrifice it was for Mr. Bogle—dear, conscientious man—to miss so many evenings at home with his beloved family, while he labored in his offices. It was a benefit to everyone, Mrs. Bogle claimed; such labor for an impoverished boy was good for his character, was it not? Mr. Bogle's charity, it seemed, knew no bounds.

Meg's story matched with Mr. Dickens's to the letter. Orion, they agreed, was more than likely being worked in the tunnels they had visited on Sunday. While many other

Railway branches were planned, this was the first to be built, and the cut on Marylebone Road was the only one in progress. For now. Meg shuddered at the thought of how many more children would be required to finish London's grand project.

"And besides," Meg said, "you saw his expression when I showed him the bolt. He was unsettled; he flinched. And he's not, I daresay, a man given much to flinching."

"Yes, I saw," Mr. Dickens said. "I do believe he was quite flustered. But that was a dangerous ploy, Meg, tipping our hand. If Mr. Bogle suspects us too greatly, he may move Orion again. Or worse. Georgiana told us: Boys have died. By accident, by neglect, but dead all the same. I'd put nothing past Bogle and his henchmen."

"I am so sorry," she said. "I hope I have not endangered my brother."

"Let us hope not. We must fly, though, to protect him."

Meg's stomach tumbled. But Mr. Dickens rescued her.

"Having said that, let me add this. I enjoyed, as much as you, watching that man's face turn even more sour. I do believe I saw a streak of fear in him. It was a risky maneuver on your part, but it cements our knowledge. We know, more than ever, that he is our mysterious Mr. B."

A silence entered the Hansom cab, like a third passenger.

"I hate that man," Meg said.

"As do I, Meg."

She shook herself.

"But our hatred will not help us now, will it?" she asked. "Our brains must push aside our hatred."

"For the moment."

Meg and Mr. Dickens burst in on the Pickels in the print-shop. Information was un-spooled; plans were rolled up tightly. All were agreed: the Marylebone tunnels. But first: preparation. They must be quick, but not foolish. And besides, they had until night-fall to return there. If what Miss and Mrs. Bogle said was true, adult laborers worked the tunnels during the day, as expected. The child tunnel-workers did not work until darkness concealed their existence.

Another carriage took Mr. Dickens away; another brought him back, some hours later, hours that were excruciatingly long to Meg. When Mr. Dickens returned, another carriage took Aunt Julia away alone. Yet another carriage arrived shortly, engulfing Meg and Mr. Dickens and Meg's father and Tobias, and a very stubborn Mulberry who insisted on accompanying them. This last carriage shot off into the gathering twi-light—"Driver, Marylebone Street near Park Crescent. All haste!"

"Charles, tell me," Meg's father implored in the noise-wracked carriage. "Are you certain? Do we not rush too much?"

"Father," Meg said. She grabbed his sleeve and looked into his eyes with great force. "I know. I've read all the signs: He is there."

Meg's father gazed at her, inquiring. She would not relent, not now.

"Good, then," her father said.

The coach rolled and creaked and zigged and zagged through the thick evening traffic. Mulberry held his head out the window, reading the novel of London's air.

Mr. Dickens was once again Mr. Dickens. He had rinsed the theatrical black from his hair and beard and moustache, and wore again his customary attire—indubitably Mr. Dickens. The only unusual bit of his costume was a walking stick, sleek and ebony with a plain silver ornament for its head.

Meg showed concern that he should be recognized.

"I would be known tonight, Meg," he said. "Let them know that the Great Man is watching."

The carriage shuddered to a halt, and our party climbed down. There was the tunnel's entrance, the great cut-and-cover ditch. But nothing stirred, no workmen showed themselves. The day's travail was finished. Had they been wrong?

All around them, London continued its incessant business—carriages to-ing and fro-ing, troops of pedestrians, the commerce of it all. The lamp-lighters lit the street-lamps, and the glow of eve-tide London struggled to obliterate the certain coming of night.

Our party stood at the wooden barrier and stared into the work-site. No one—not even Mr. Dickens—seemed able to speak. Where were the workers they had expected to find? Tobias leaned his head against Meg's shoulder. Her father pulled her head to his shoulder. Mr. Dickens tapped his walking stick ever so gently.

Only Mulberry moved, prompted to action by a secret scent. He barked once, jumping a little on his front paws. Everyone looked at him, and he looked at them. He barked again—short and sharp—as if to express his incredulity at their lack of comprehension—why couldn't humans understand? He shook his head with a mild disgust, then trotted away from them, towards the black hole of the tunnel's mouth. All followed timidly.

Mulberry stood above the entrance to the tunnel, and put his front paws on the barrier, staring down into the trench. Thus situated, he commenced a great storm of barking—silly humans!

Meg trotted to him and put her hand on his head. She shushed him and looked into the black mouth of the tunnel, where she saw nothing but blackness. The others caught up.

"Do you think, Charles?" her father said.

"Does he think what, Father?" Meg asked.

"I'm wondering," her father said, "if Mulberry doesn't smell something in the tunnel. Perhaps it's not deserted after all. During our last visit, we only ventured so far. Perhaps the night-work is more secretive than we imagined."

Meg looked up at Mr. Dickens.

"Well," he said. "The nose knows. When was the last time Mulberry, or any dog, for that matter, was wrong?"

"He's in there," Meg said. "Orion is in there. Mulberry knows it, and now I feel it. We must go."

"No," her father said. "I had not expected this; it frightens me to go farther."

"Campion, please." Mr. Dickens put his hand on his arm. "Let us stay with our plan. You and Tobias stay here. Aunt Julia will arrive soon with the police. Meg and I will set out first."

"No, Charles. Not Meg. Not you. We all can wait for the police."

"And show them what? An empty work-site? A vacated tunnel? No, they must have cause to rescue us—else they'll think we're mad."

"Charles—"

"Campion. The time has come, too much has been risked. Meg and I will be fine. Mulberry here will protect us."

Upon hearing this, Mulberry paddled furiously with his hind paws, until his claws achieved a purchase, and he climbed straight up and then straight down the wooden barrier. He barked for the others to join him. Mr. Dickens scrambled over.

Meg's father put his hands on her shoulders.

"Be safe, Meg," he said. "Find him."

She kissed his cheek, then vaulted over the barrier in one smooth motion. She imagined Georgiana Bogle attempting such a feat in her cage-crinoline; she could never surmount even such a paltry barrier.

Meg's father handed her two globed lanterns, and she

slid down the fresh earth of the embankment. When she looked back up, her father and Tobias waved broadly. Tobias, Meg saw, even in the purpling twi-light, was jealous of being left behind.

Mulberry led the way to the mouth of the tunnel, his nose all a-quiver. But he was silent now, and stepped warily through the construction rubble.

Meg, Mr. Dickens, and Mulberry, all three stood at the very entrance of the tunnel, not an inch closer, not one toe over the imaginary line there. The solid blackness of the tunnel, betraying nothing of what resided in that blackness, threatened them. Meg felt that if she stepped one atom closer, the great void might swallow her.

Mr. Dickens struck a match against its box. The sudden flare of the phosphor, white-yellow, showed the ribs of the tunnel's mechanical frame, then the flame retracted. Meg opened the lanterns' faces, and Mr. Dickens touched the match to the wicks. The light swelled again and enveloped them. Mulberry—only then—marched forward into the tunnel. Meg and Mr. Dickens followed their most excellent and bold companion.

It shocked Meg to see that two such tiny flames could illuminate this vast abyss. But the whole of the tunnel was suddenly visible to them. The great skeleton of the tunnel surrounded them, and they followed the spine of the fresh-laid railway tracks deeper into the earth. They were in the belly of the great beast.

They stuck close together as they walked. Mulberry

deciphered the rich, dank air. Occasionally he uttered a low growl, as if mumbling to himself.

The darkness continued several hundred yards into the tunnel. It crooked off to the left, where Marylebone Road turned north into Euston Road, and from around that slight bend, another light seemed to glow forth. Meg just made out the distant tapping of workers at work. Mr. Dickens heard this, too, and our three adventurers moved forward at a brisker pace. The dim glow intensified with each step.

They all stopped at once. Ahead and to one side, two dim figures rested against the tunnel's frame. One rose in attention; the other slumbered. The vigil was a dog, and Meg saw it clearly now, up on its four legs, ears cocked back, hackles raised. It was a white English Bull Terrier, broad of chest, with a blunt muzzle and a black spot that circled one eye. It locked on Mulberry. Both dogs growled low, nearly inaudible.

The other figure was a man, a sleeping man, a dead-asleep man, obviously a victim of drink, insensible of the world. He wore lace-up half-boots over drab trousers, and a black velveteen coat pulled snugly around him. From the pocket of his coat, the unmistakable handle of a dueling pistol emerged.

Mr. Dickens put a hand on Meg's shoulder, and urged them all forwards. The man in the black coat jostled in his sleep, uttered, "Right," then turned on his side, pulled the coat closer, and sank back into his pool of slumber.

As they walked past the guard and his dog, they did

not hurry—though, to be honest, both Meg and Mr. Dickens wished to run. Only a great discipline, inspired by a fear of the strange dog, kept their pace steady. Mr. Dickens, Meg saw, found a tighter grip on his walking stick.

Neither Mulberry nor the bull's-eye dog moved towards the other, but merely allowed their heads to track. They were only feet apart on passing. The other dog's growl grew louder, deeper, and its sharp teeth showed a macabre grin.

Mulberry's growl matched this, and his teeth showed, too. Then Mulberry snapped at the air. The other dog relented, easing back onto its haunches, releasing its growl. Our party passed.

Meg looked back once, to find the bull's-eye dog laid down again, its head on its paws but still watchful.

Had the two dogs fought, lunging and biting and tumbling, Meg was certain Mulberry would not have been victorious—the other dog's size and strength would have overcome. But Mulberry was too smart, though smaller and weaker. Meg had seen small dogs make grossly larger dogs back down before. It was, Meg knew, a matter of strategy. The dog that won was always bolder, if not wiser. Given this, Mulberry could not be driven away.

When they made their way through the bend of the tunnel, the light they'd been walking towards exploded into a white fury. It took a moment for Meg to adjust to this new brilliance.

Ahead of them was the opposite of where they'd come

from. All ahead was white and light and filled with activity. Hanging from and perched upon scant wooden scaffolds, scores of ragged boys were affixing white tiles to the interior of the tunnel's frame. The tunnel was being finished here, moving forwards from King's Cross, inexorably forwards.

The image of Mr. Bogle flashed through Meg's mind. In her imagination Mr. Bogle checked his pocket-watch—impatiently, of course.

They had all stopped, our heroes, and were watching. Mulberry sat down.

As the scene clarified in Meg's reasoning, she began to scan the crowd of working boys. Meg looked down at Mulberry; he returned her gaze, panting and smiling.

Mr. Dickens held his lantern still, as if his one small flame had achieved all this brilliance. Not one of the several overseers, and none of the downcast worker-boys, had spied them yet.

Meg scanned and scanned. She could not find Orion. But how would she recognize him out of all these boys, these boys who wore clothes no one should wear, more rags than clothes, and who under the grime of their unwashed hair and faces and limbs were indistinguishable from one another? None of these boys had names any longer, they were merely "boy."

Rashly, she knew, she rushed forward. The time had come; she would wait no longer. If he was here, it was time to call him home.

"Orion!" she yelled out. "Orion, Orion, it's Meg. I'm here, Orion. Come forward." And she was running before the first "Orion" was out of her mouth, running deeper into the tunnel, into the crowds of "boy."

Mr. Dickens sprang after her with "No, Meg," but he could not keep up. Mulberry ran ahead of her, and joined her call with his own canine version of "Orion."

In the first instant of Meg's breakaway, work in the tunnel continued, but once her calls began to rebound, silence ensued, as all the worker-boys and their overseers turned to stare at the strange sight of this new and unusual "boy" and her dog coming towards them, apparently being chased by a dapper older gentleman brandishing a black stick.

The tunnel erupted into other noises. All the boys dropped their tiles and tools and began yelling, if for no other reason than most boys will yell when there is yelling they might join in with. And the overseers were shouting now, calling, "Stop" and "Ho there" and "Help." Yet none of them moved, and Meg continued.

Then out of the noise and jumble he came, moving towards her, and Meg knew him instantly.

Though she had no reason to know him. He was skeletal. The rags he wore would have taken it as a compliment to be called rags. His face was near to black. It was only when the figure drew nearer and their eyes met that his face was overcome by a vast smile—the smile Meg had longed for so often. Orion's smile glowed out of the shade he had become. But the smile was authentic—Orion at last.

He was upon her and they were embracing, and he whispered, "Meg, Meg, Meg," into her ear. Mr. Dickens let out a great whoop and strode towards the reunited siblings. The roaring of the boys subsided, and they watched in silence as sister found brother.

"Back, back!" yelled a strong voice. "Away from him. Both of you."

A man came close and pulled Meg from Orion, then pushed Mr. Dickens away. He was not Bumble, nor was he Sampson, nor anyone Meg recognized. He was merely a man, and he would not stop them.

Meg hauled back and kicked the man's shin as hard as she could. He bent to his leg, while Meg and Orion moved away from him and towards Mr. Dickens. Mulberry barked in circles.

When the man rose again, all agony, he brandished a truncheon and lunged at Meg.

Orion moved in front of his sister, to absorb the blow, but this was not necessary. The ebony walking stick of Mr. Dickens intercepted the truncheon and sent it flying. Mulberry leaped in and bit at the shin that Meg had recently punished. The overseer slumped to the ground, wailing.

But the other overseers—there must have been six or seven—were now circling them, truncheons raised. Even Mulberry went silent and still.

One of the overseers opened his mouth in a nasty grin,

about to speak, when from the darkness of the tunnel-bend came a stronger voice. The white bull's-eye dog trailed behind its master, skulking in the dark shadows. It would neither approach nor look at Mulberry.

"What have we here, eh?" the voice asked in mocking tones. "Well, well, well. What a sight."

The man in the black coat came towards our heroes, offering a malicious grin and a drawn pistol. The pistol was clearly aimed at Mr. Dickens.

"Ain't this a tender moment?" he sneered. "Come to find our little boy, are we? Come to take him home to his ma? I'm right touched, I am."

"Sir!" Mr. Dickens said with vigor.

The man in the black coat pushed the pistol closer to Mr. Dickens. He drew back the hammer; cocked it.

"I am afraid I ain't no 'sir,' sir," the man said. "And you won't be no sir either, I'm afraid. No, sir. We can't have trouble-makers."

The man raised the pistol until it was directly in Mr. Dickens's face.

Mr. Dickens raised his walking stick and pointed it at the man. As if it were the superior weapon.

"Do you know me, sir?" Mr. Dickens asked. "Do you recognize my face?"

The pistol remained steady.

"I do, I do, sir, though only by your face, not your books. Alas, your face is of no use to you now."

"Then if you know me, all of London surely does. And

more importantly, London knows where I am at the present moment. And London, in the guise of its police, will be here soon."

"I care nothing for your fame, nor does my pistol."

Mr. Dickens turned slowly from the pistol's barrel, and faced the overseers and the boys. He was facing his audience.

"I am Charles Dickens," he called. "And you, all of you, I dare say all of London, know me."

There was a gasp, a silence, a muttering. They did all know him.

"If this thug murders me, surely one of you will step forward, my kind readers. My death or disappearance will not go un-remarked."

He turned back to the pistol, which did not waver.

"And if you kill me, sir, and kill every witness, too, it will still be too late for you. Too in vain. For my face is nothing, my name is nothing, even my corporeal being is nothing. But my words, my words shall last for-ever."

The pistol, Meg noticed, was shaking.

"And what are words to me? Speak them to my pistol's own report."

Mr. Dickens stepped closer.

"Know this. The account of my murder, in the Marylebone Road tunnel, in the middle of the forbidden night, and all in the name of Bogle—that report has already been filed with my copy-boy. And should I not return tonight, tomorrow's special edition of *All the Year Round* will create,

I should think, quite a stir. And your years as a fugitive, *sir,* would be much less pleasant than you might be imagining."

The pistol seemed to nod.

"You're bluffing, ain't you?"

"A fair copy of the report of my demise, here in this illegal work-site. As witnessed by Og Ogleby, copy-boy. I have it right here."

Mr. Dickens pulled a sheaf of papers from his coat and handed it to the man with the pistol. He took them with one hand, while trying to steady the pistol with the other. The more he read, the more the pistol faltered in its gaze, and soon it hung by the man's side.

Orion gripped Meg's shoulder; Meg watched Mr. Dickens. He was shaking, but his gaze remained steady.

"Orion, Meg, Mulberry," he said. "It's time we returned to the living world."

Mr. Dickens placed his walking stick to one side of the man in the black coat.

"You may keep this manuscript, my good man, as a token of our meeting. Just think. You now possess an original work by Charles Dickens. It will be valuable someday."

The man in the black coat took a step back, and our heroes moved towards the tunnel's exit.

They hadn't gone a dozen paces when the glows of several swinging lanterns appeared, approaching them. Meg could make out the shapes of several policemen first, then

Aunt Julia, Tobias, and her father. Mulberry barked ahead, then Orion broke away, holding Meg by the hand and dragging her along. Mr. Dickens followed at a leisurely pace.

Behind them erupted a cheer from the boys in the tunnel.

Chapter XXI

A debate concerning the true end of a story

O HOW HAPPILY IT ALL ENDED, Meg thought. After a long evening at the tunnels, during which the police became more and more involved, Orion was returned to his family without question. And Meg believed for a brief time that this was the end of the story.

But complications arose. The police—two of whom were the same as had begged autographs of Mr. Dickens during their previous visit to the tunnel—took into custody the man in the black coat, a Bill Sikes by name. The brandishing of a pistol anywhere in London was considered a serious breach of the public safety. Along with Mr. Sikes, the other overseers were rounded up for questioning.

Mr. Sikes and his companions claimed that it was all a misunderstanding, and that Orion, whether he'd known it or not, had always been free to go. As was true of the other boys. Everyone in the tunnel, according to Mr. Sikes and Co., was a voluntary and well-paid employee.

This conversation was held in whispers, far out of range of the children who worked in the tunnel, those "willing" employees. And couldn't the police see, Sikes and Co. wanted to know, that no criminal activity was being undertaken? They were building a tunnel, weren't they? They certainly were not attempting to steal the tunnel—that would be madness.

Yes, yes, the police agreed. Building was being undertaken. Still, they had some few questions. By whom, the police wondered, were these men and boys employed? It's the Metropolitan Railway that done hired 'em, innit? Yes, but why were they working so late into the night, and in the cloak of dark's secrecy? Deadlines, miludds, Sikes and Co. protested, the Railway had its deadlines, and they would be met. These were, after all, modern times, and progress would not be stopped.

Reasonable enough, the police collectively agreed. Though the police continued to be troubled by the pistol and why it had been drawn. Did Mr. Sikes have an answer to that question? A grave misunderstanding, was what Mr. Sikes said, and he was more than willing to make the appropriate apologies. He certainly never meant to threaten the Great Man himself. P'raps, said the police.

Meg watched all this from where she and her family huddled around Orion. She was unable to know what the police were saying and what the man in the black coat was saying. But she was worried. Grown-ups had been known to overlook the most obvious wrongs, satisfied to have an easy answer. Meg was overjoyed to have Orion once again in the fold of the family, safe from harm. But what of the other boys?

Boys, happily, will be boys, and as the conversation between Sikes and the police whispered on, one of them crept away from his station and noiselessly approached the knot of men who were deciding his fate. He cocked an ear and listened in, and then he exploded.

"'T weren't no misunderstandin'!" the boy yelled. He was all in rags and blackened like coal, but his furor shone through it. "He was going to kill Mr. Dickens, he was. Because Mr. Dickens wanted to set us free. Bill Sikes is a liar, and a thief, and I very much want to go back home."

The other boys in the tunnel, seeing the courage in their tiny companion, began to shout out, too, and the tunnel was a din of accusations. They all wanted to go home, they all loathed Mr. Bill Sikes and Co., and they were every one of them exceedingly hungry. The police, to their credit, took note.

It is true that some—but only some—police are corrupt. And if it had been one policeman or two speaking with Bill Sikes, these policemen might have been paid to forget everything they'd seen, and being thus paid, might have slunk off into the darker bye-streets of London with their ill-gotten bribe-monies. But on this evening in the tunnel, there was too much light, too much noise, too many witnesses. Corruption—which may be found in any walk of life, not merely in the police ranks—corruption survives only in darkness and silence. And there was too much light and noise in the Railway tunnel for anyone to "look the other way."

Orion rushed from his family's side and joined the other boys in telling their stories. The police eventually heard enough, declared that something was certainly fishy, that it was getting late, and that in the morning they would get to the bottom of this mess.

Meg watched with a warm glow as Bill Sikes and Co. were taken into police custody. Sikes and Co. were to spend some long time in the jail, while the boys, all thirty-seven of them—excluding Orion—would be housed in various police stations about London until they could be reunited with their families. The tunnel was closed for the night, all parties accounted for, and Orion and family were sent along home.

Surely, Meg thought, *this* was the end of the story. But as the carriage trundled all of them home to Tonson Lane, Orion began to unreel for his family and Mr. Dickens the tale of his last six months. There was still more story.

"And then," Orion was saying, "the Sampsons surrounded the two boys and swept them away like so much water in the gutter. Charlie and I hid ourselves, wisely, I must say, just long enough to give the Sampsons false security, and leaping from our hiding spots, we followed, as stealthy as shadows . . ."

Although Meg knew this part of the story from Orion's notebook, she thrilled to hear it again, in Orion's own words, Orion's own *voice*. Orion's telling, she felt, was even more exciting than one of Mr. Dickens's novels.

Yet hardly had Orion begun to recount his captivity when they arrived at the print-shop, and his captive's tale had to be postponed for a matter of most pressing urgency—more than anything else in the world, Orion would have a hot bath. It was what he had most looked forward to in all his time away. That he had not bathed once since he'd been press-ganged, Meg was most aware of the moment they'd entered the carriage together. While she was anxious to hear Orion's tale, she was more anxious that he bathe and wash away the foul odor of his captivity.

A bath was drawn by Meg, while Aunt Julia prepared a supper for all, and after Orion emerged from his bath, he and the family repaired to the roof-garden for the continuation of Orion's adventures.

It was another mild night, a gentle and clean breeze flowing up from the Thames. Around them London glowed in its gas-light, Cheapside still alive with traffic. The sky and its stars were hardly visible. Meg held Tobias under her arm, where he slept, and Mulberry sat at her feet, his keen eyes fastened on Orion, as though he might be taken again. Orion sat between her father and Aunt Julia, and while Meg longed to be close to her brother, she could not stop watching him. The truth was before her eyes—Orion had returned to them. Each time this phrase leaped to her throat, *He is here,* she nearly allowed her tears to spill over.

Meg watched and listened, and Orion finished his tale. The whole of it bloomed before her.

Once he and his new friend Charlie had stumbled upon the Billingsgate work-house, they'd begun to poke around, and what they found led them to asking questions, and these questions all had answers with the name of Bogle floating about them. It was soon clear to both boys that this Mr. Bogle—they only ever saw his name, never his face—was running a press-gang operation. Mr. Bogle employed the Sampson gang to round up stray boys and press them into service in any number of his work-houses. All over London, they discovered, Mr. Bogle's press-ganged boys were toiling in intolerable conditions for the profit of Mr. Bogle and his name.

Charlie and Orion had hoped to expose Mr. Bogle's despicable dealings in well-written accounts in a London newspaper. The two young reporters had also wished—here, Orion blushed, embarrassed at his vanity—to establish themselves as reporters of courage and skill. However, they wished to write the most damning reports possible, so they continued their investigations, striking out for the darkest corners of Mr. Bogle's evil empire.

Until one day a question led to an answer that included the words *work-house, Mr. Bogle,* and *Metropolitan Railway.* Our two reporters had discovered that Mr. Bogle, who was officially tied to the Metropolitan Railway construction, was becoming even richer by producing counterfeit materials with slave-labor. This last answer they received—linking Bogle and Railway—had drawn undue attention to all the questions they had been asking. They had been found out.

On the night he disappeared, the night of the first snowfall, after Meg had bid him good night, Orion left the roof-garden and made his way to Charlie's house, near-by in Pudding Lane. A well-tossed pebble roused Charlie, and the two of them made off to Billingsgate. Here they were discovered peeking into peek-holes where they ought not to be peeking.

The Sampson gang, intimates of Mr. Bogle, were waiting for them, and discovering Orion and Charlie peeking where they ought not to be, forcibly detained them. And for the next six months, they were forced to participate in the gang's activities. Charlie and Orion were never out of range of a Sampson pistol or truncheon. The pistols were never employed, but the truncheons were often unleashed. Orion and Charlie were under-fed and over-worked. They participated, unwillingly, in many criminal ventures. Nights they were shackled to the walls of their prison, a dark basement somewhere near the Tower.

Try as he might, Orion could not get any message to his family. His only hope of communication—hopeless, he believed—was to leave his mark—the constellation of Orion—wherever he went. He had hidden a piece of chalk in the lining of his pants, and when the gang moved him about the City, from one crime to another, he left his mark where and when he could. He prayed that his father or Meg or someone would see it, and know that he was, at least, alive if not well. Those were months of great despair for Orion, and had they gone on much longer, he feared he might lose his mind, or worse, his soul. He was stranded on an island of ruffians in the vast ocean of London.

By listening closely, Orion pieced together the picture-puzzle. He and Charlie had been press-ganged to keep their intrusive questions about Mr. Bogle silent. But as boys, they had value, through labor, to Mr. Bogle, happily worth more alive than dead.

The days passed, to Orion's knowledge, only through the ringing of the bells—one more hour, one more hour.

Until the night at Satis House. There the gang had been spotted. No, not by Meg. Orion had not known she was there, and had left his mark only out of desperate habit. No, Mr. Dickens had been noticed spying through the sky-light and was, of course, recognized. A few days later, one of the many Sampsons—there were, all told, five of them—had followed Mr. Dickens, but was thrown off the trail, and quite easily. Mr. Dickens was not to be found in his usual haunts, and the intelligence on the street was that he was in France. So he was forgotten.

To be safe, however, and at Mr. Bogle's bidding, he and Charlie were taken first to the Billingsgate Market, and from there were separated. Orion was put into the tunnels; he had not seen Charlie since their separation and was terribly worried. He feared for his friend's life.

Mr. Dickens interrupted Orion's story here, placing a solid hand on Orion's knee. He assured him that the police had already been told about Charlie, and that Mr. Dickens himself would do all in his power to retrieve him.

In being moved about, Orion had seen and read Meg's broadside—with immeasurable joy. Since then he'd fortified his intention to escape, knowing as he now did that his family had not given up on him. He was only in the tunnel a few days when he was rescued, when he heard Meg's clear clarion-call.

"Surely," Meg's father said, "we are concluded. Our story is done, the world has been put right again. And happily."

"No, Father," Orion said, obviously weary but upright now and determined. "I will not rest until Charlie is found."

"And then we'll be done, I pray," Meg's father said. "I wish only for a plainer, duller life again."

"No, Father," Meg said. She laid Tobias softly down on the bench. "We will not be done until we find and free all of those children Mr. Bogle keeps hidden."

The two halves of Meg that wrestled over every topic and emotion arose. Yes, she dearly wished the end of the story had been reached, so that she and her family might return to their "normal" lives again—though she suspected their lives would never be "normal" again. But no, she would not have the end of the story arrive simply to offer herself comfort or ease. Meg would not rest until the other children—the tunnel and work-house children—had been returned to their families. The story must not be allowed to end too abruptly.

"And then?" her father said wearily. "Will this tale be finished then?"

"No, Campion," Aunt Julia said. "I am afraid I will not rest until the name of Bogle, and the man who bears that name, is brought low and exposed to all of London."

Mulberry went to Meg's father and stood before him. He barked once, then turned and went back to Meg's side. Mulberry's opinion was clear—story not finished.

Meg's father looked about in apparent frustration. His fatigue was evident, even in the midnight hour.

"Charles, please," he begged. "You are the writer. Help me here. Surely we've reached the climax, the finale. Surely the end is nigh."

"No, Campion," Mr. Dickens said. "I must disappoint. There is no ending here. This is not, after all, a novel. It shall not be concluded by a death, nor by a wedding, nor by the discovery of some fortuitous document, nor even by a happy reunion. This is no novel; 'tis life. And as such, it shall continue long after the last page is written. There will be no stopping life. Tomorrow—we continue."

As is possible only with Mr. Dickens, at precisely that moment London's bells began to chime, the last hour of this day, the first of the next. The roof-garden's party all heeded the bells, save Tobias, who slept. The bells ran their course, and then their leaden circles dissolved into air. Meg had never heard a sweeter sound—a new day begun and her brother home.

After Mr. Dickens departed that night—still refusing to say where he went to—and all the rest were asleep in their beds behind the drawn curtains of their chambers, only Meg continued awake. Even Mulberry slept, hard and fierce by the hearth, his paws in motion, continuing the one rabbit-chase that seemed to haunt all his dreams.

Meg stayed awake for a long hour. She had not been sleepless since that first night at Satis House, a little more than a week ago. The ardor of her pursuits in that time had tumbled her quickly, each night, into the arms of Morpheus. But tonight she willed herself to stay conscious, if only to enjoy the knowledge that the world, at least her small corner of it, was for the moment restored. She crept from curtain to curtain, and listened to the soft, regular breaths of her family. Her entire family. A heavy but happy weight seemed to settle in Orion's chamber. Meg could almost feel what a delicious sensation it must be for her brother to sleep once again in a true bed.

But it was not, Meg realized, her entire family that had returned. Her mother, of course, was still gone, and Meg missed her achingly. To ease herself of this melancholy, she stayed awake for some time longer, and in the dim light of one candle, wrote in her notebook a long letter to her mother, telling her all that she had missed, and how much she herself was missed. Meg did not believe that her mother could read such a letter, but it did offer comfort to write it. Writing to her mother was as close as Meg could come to speaking with her, and for now, it would suffice.

Eventually, Meg crawled into her own bed and fell happily to sleep.

As Mr. Dickens had predicted, life went on. And with considerable vigor.

The morning after Orion's return saw the first of many visits to and from the police. Much was learned.

The boys freed from the tunnel were all returned to their families, though in some cases it might take days to find them. Mr. Sikes and Co. continued their restful jail stays, while the police continued to seek ways of prolonging said restful stays. A visit to the Billingsgate Market revealed a suspiciously empty work-house, and the police increased their efforts to track down the living-dead children.

The officials of the Metropolitan Railway declared complete ignorance of any night-time tunneling, and were hard-pressed to answer why Bill Sikes and Co. and their waifs would wish to work on the tunnel, having not been hired to do so. And while all fingers seemed to point to Mr. Bogle, the name of Bogle remained unsullied. After examining the paperwork at the Metropolitan Railway, and especially those papers that connected the Railway with Mr.

Bogle—a legitimate connection to all appearances—the police declared that all relevant paperwork was in order.

The most startling and welcome news of all was the return of Charlie. He simply walked into the print-shop two days following Orion's return. Meg was shocked to discover that Charlie was almost exactly as she had imagined him—bright ginger hair and green eyes, and an easy way about him. How could she have known? She thought she saw, too, something of the same spirit in Charlie that she'd seen in the spirit of young Dick Whittington—the eternal boy. Happily, however, Charlie's unsullied spirit resided in the living world.

After being separated from Orion, Charlie told them, he'd been attached to a crew of late-night stevedores, loading and unloading ships that did not seem to exist during day-light. But rumors had spread among the boys on the docks, and Charlie took courage at the news of Orion's escape. Last night, just before dawn, he lowered himself into the Thames and swam away. Police, upon hearing yet another fantastical tale of false imprisonment, were investigating.

Orion had been happy in those first days of return, but he had been haunted, too, smiling on occasion, but obviously elsewhere in his thoughts. When Meg saw him embracing Charlie, lifting him off the ground and spinning him around, only then did she find all of Orion returned.

While this fury buzzed about the print-shop and Meg's life, London buzzed about it, too. The city of London, unconcerned while all these children were missing, now seemed aghast at the possibility of such occurrences. Embarrassed editorials ran in all the newspapers, each one calling for an end to such practices. But editorials are only opinions, and change nothing in the world. Nothing would change, Meg knew, until the name of Bogle was firmly attached to the deplorable practices the newspapers objected to. Mr. Bogle had to be found out.

And so each evening, after she had concluded her home-studies—her father insisted on this, insisted some sense of "normal" be restored—Meg and Orion and Charlie set off with Mr. Dickens to his rooms to prepare their story for publication in Mr. Dickens's *All the Year Round*.

Since his first appearance on the roof-top of Satis House, Meg had been curious about Mr. Dickens's lodgings, but he would never speak of them. She had imagined his rooms—as befitting the Great Man—to be a grand suite of elegant decor in a most imposing hotel. Where else would such a man stay? She could not have been more mistaken—Mr. Dickens's rooms were practically a disgrace. And they were practically around the corner from the print-shop, which surprised her as well.

Forgoing a carriage, Mr. Dickens suggested they all walk to his rooms, and so the four of them, Mulberry making a fifth, set off north, passing Satis House, and from there, crossed Gresham Street to Guildhall, behind which they found Aldermanbury Square, and off which they found a tiny bye-way, Hedge Row. Down Hedge Row they tip-toed—the hidden nature of Hedge Row seemed to call for silence—until a narrow doorway appeared—the Boar's-Wine Inn. I say appeared because that is exactly how it seemed to Meg. The Inn's doorway appeared, in one instant, where before there had only been the blank walls of two other buildings. It was as if, Meg considered, the Boar's-Wine Inn were magically concealed between two other buildings, and only appeared when Mr. Dickens uttered this magic spell, "Ah, here we are."

Upon entering the narrow door, they were received into a dismal and dis-colored courtyard, around which rose three flights of dismal and dis-colored rooms. Up the creakity stairs they went, along the warped arcade, until they found the splintered door that Mr. Dickens claimed as his own. This was not at all how Meg had pictured Mr. Dickens's rooms—these were more like a gloomy scene from one of the Great Man's own novels.

But the instant Mr. Dickens flung open the door to his cramped and poorly constructed rooms, Meg understood why he had chosen this place. These were perfect rooms, she felt, for a writer.

On his desk, he had laid out what he called his "big box of writing"—his *Ardoise* paper, his goose quills and sharpening knife, and a bronze sculpture of two frogs dueling with swords. Without these things he could not write, he said, these and a vase of fresh-cut flowers. The rooms themselves were dingy, and the unmistakable stench of horses and their business rose up in the steam of London summer, but Mr.

Dickens had carved out a perfect spot for himself. His desk, with his paper and pen and good-luck frogs, was immaculate, orderly. And from his one window, open at all times, there was a view of St. Paul's Cathedral, majestic and solitary.

Chairs were brought in for them all, and Meg and Orion and Charlie sat about, comparing notes, drawing connections, finding the irrefutable ties between the name of Bogle and its crimes. Their plan was to finish Charlie and Orion's report on Bogle, enhanced by all that Meg and Mr. Dickens had gleaned in the last week. It would take some days to complete the report, but when they were done with it, when they had firmly attached the name of Bogle to the man behind the gangs and the work-houses, Mr. Dickens would print the story in *All the Year Round*. London, meaning all the world, would know the truth.

Lavish meals were brought in, including the obligatory plates of oysters—Meg was still unsure about oysters—and the four of them worked feverishly, though not hungrily. Together, they wrote and re-wrote, then re-wrote again, until the words clearly revealed the truth they all knew.

Mr. Dickens was most often the scribe. His pen flew over the blue-white paper, pausing only to dip into the ocean of ink, breathless to continue the river of words. Mulberry seated himself at Mr. Dickens's feet and rested comfortably. Meg noticed that whenever Mr. Dickens was at a loss for a word or a phrase, he would reach down and scratch Mulberry's ears, then instantly resume writing. It was as if Mulberry were somehow communicating the truest, best words to the Great Man.

During one of these nightly sessions of writing and remembering and reporting, when Charlie and Orion had stepped out for a breath of air, Meg watched intently while Mr. Dickens continued to work.

"Sir?" she asked politely. "If I may. I'm inclined to believe you are no longer haunted. I'm inclined to believe you have found your book."

He looked up, surprised, a rare expression for Mr. Dickens.

"Why, Meg, I believe you may be correct. Why, yes, the haunting that brought me to you, it does seem to be gone."

He stretched and looked about. He smiled.

"Is it your book then? A new one?"

"Oh, yes," he said. "I've found that. And I'll give you the title. Soon, you'll have pages. But for now, let me just say this: Our Mutual Friend."

And they both smiled. Mutual friends, indeed.

"But . . ." Meg felt there was something yet unsaid.

"But," Mr. Dickens said. "But it's more than my book. It's these children, Meg, what you and I and Orion and Charlie are doing right now. We will save these children. Of that I am certain. And that is my un-haunting, Meg. To know again the great moral purpose of my life, which is this: All children must have a better future than is allowed them. To know this, that I work for a better tomorrow, that is what's restored me. I am no longer haunted, no longer the

Great Man, no longer the writer. I am simply Charles Dickens, a member of the human race, and I am doing what we all must do—make tomorrow better."

And with that, he turned back to his furious pen and paper.

By Friday evening, they had completed their report, and they knew it was solid enough to bring down Mr. Bogle's apparently porcelain empire. Meg wondered whether to be happy for young Georgiana Bogle or to weep for her. Perhaps both.

All was done except for the headline. They had worked so hard on the story, the title now eluded them. Nothing came to mind, and Mr. Dickens insisted it had to be perfect. Their words were to be published, and the public must be drawn to the words.

If they could finish tonight, a fair copy could be got to the printers, for a Saturday rush-order. Time was passing, more time for the name of Bogle to check its watch in peace. The bells outside were ringing—eight bells.

Meg picked up her reporter's notebook—it was nearly filled now—and sketched quickly with her carpenter's pencil. She made the letters large and bold, as with a headline, then shaded them for emphasis. Without a word, she turned the notebook to face Mr. Dickens and Orion and Charlie.

"BOGUS BOGLE!" Mr. Dickens read. "Meg, you quiz! That's it."

They all laughed, and then Mr. Dickens went out to the gallery and called for a carriage. They were done, for now at least. The story would continue, but one ending had been achieved.

Just before leaving his rooms, Mr. Dickens stopped them. Meg could tell by the set of his body that he was about to perform a theatrical maneuver.

"Meg, Orion," he said, with great solemnity. "It has come to my attention that, while Orion has been brought back to us, he lost along the way something you both consider important."

And already Meg knew what it was. But she waited with anticipation. It was difficult to resist Mr. Dickens's theatrics.

"For you," he said. "For the both of you."

And he put into Meg's hands the third volume of his own *Great Expectations*. Meg smiled and blushed and looked down at the book. Orion's hand fell on her shoulder. Meg clutched the book to her. Perhaps this was the ending she'd been awaiting.

"A gift from the author," Mr. Dickens said. "But on one condition. Orion, it was you who lost the book, I'm afraid. So it must be Meg who's allowed to finish it first."

And they all laughed.

Outside the narrow door of the Boar's-Wine Inn a carriage accepted them all—Mulberry, too—and they set out for the offices of *All the Year Round*.

Charlie and Mr. Dickens sat on the banquette across, jabbering voraciously of their report and the image of Mr. Bogle bathed in shame. As she listened to them talking,

Meg imagined Mr. Bogle in the parlor of Bogle Manor, taking his leisure. At some hour tomorrow, Meg knew, he would check his watch, and then he would pick up the new issue of *All the Year Round* and see the headline BOGUS BOGLE! She hoped he would check his watch one more time, calculating how quickly it would take the rest of the world to learn of his crimes.

Meg and Orion sat next to each other and watched the London evening flash by the carriage windows. They were oddly quiet—Meg felt they'd been talking without pause since Orion's return, and they had. It was good to be quiet for this moment. In one hand she held her brother's, and sensed that the world was returning to the best parts of its past. In the other hand she clutched the fair-copy of BOGUS BOGLE! and sensed that the world was also going forward into the future, the best parts of the future.

She stayed quiet for some time, while all around her London wheeled, and the carriage, all jangle and speed and never-ceasing motion, moved on.

Children and Charles Dickens

WHEN HE WAS TWELVE YEARS OLD, Charles Dickens was sent to work in a "blacking" factory. His father, who was never a good businessman, had been sent to a "debtor's" prison until he could raise enough money to free himself. There was no other choice for the family but to send Charles to work. And work he did, ten hours a day, six days a week, earning just enough money to keep only himself alive.

Warren's Blacking made shoe polish and was housed in a tumble-down, rat-infested warehouse. Dickens was placed, all alone, in a cramped wooden cubicle that looked out over the Thames River. Except for two short breaks, he did nothing all day but wrap pots of shoe polish, first in oil paper, and then in a decorative blue paper that he secured with string, and over which he pasted the company's label. It was mind-numbing, body-breaking work for anyone, but especially traumatic for a young boy with the soaring ambition and imagination of young Charles. And all for a pot of shoe polish!

Though he only worked there for two months, the experience was so painful that Dickens later only ever told one person about it, his closest friend, John Forster. But the experience left its mark on Dickens. Many of his biographers believe that his time in the blacking factory was what made Dickens a writer. He had experienced firsthand the cruelties adults often inflict on children, and set out to write about it.

In 1839, Dickens published *Oliver Twist,* the heartbreaking story of an orphan who is tossed from one cruel institution to another—from workhouses to criminal gangs. *Oliver Twist* is virtually the first novel in literature to have a child as its main character. Many of his later novels had children as main characters, too—*David Copperfield, Great Expectations, The Old Curiosity Shop*—and every one of his novels has children as important characters. While many of Dickens's children find happy endings, such endings only come after long and difficult struggles. Those who do not find happy endings die. By writing realistically about the lives of children in his world, Dickens hoped to change their lives for the better.

The world of Dickens's England was not a pretty place for children. At that time, they were thought of much differently than they are today. Most people thought of children as small versions of adults and treated them so. Many thought of children as property, property that could be put to good use, especially when it came to arduous labor. Children were used as workers in every type of manufacturing, often given the most tedious jobs, and they were used, too, in the coal mines of the day, feeding the great hunger of England's industry. Since there were no laws regarding child labor, children were forced to work terribly long hours in horrifying conditions. They were ill-housed, poorly fed, rarely paid, and often suffered severe injuries. In nineteenth-century England, fewer than one child in three was sent to school, and those few who did go went to pitiful "ragged" schools, often leaving before their educations were complete.

As a reporter, and later a novelist, Dickens closely followed the plight of children, and he wrote continually about them, urging his readers to change the way of the world. He also became personally involved in campaigns to raise money for schools and orphanages and hospitals, and he worked to institute new laws that would protect the welfare of the country's least-powerful citizens. His writing did have its effects, and English society began to change its treatment of children. It was a slow progress, but progress nonetheless.

Dickens knew, however, that imaginative literature had a special power to change the way people see the world. And that this power could last for centuries. When we read Dickens today, we are still moved by the plight of his child characters, and see our own world differently.

Just before he wrote his most popular story, Dickens read a shocking report on the working conditions of children in coal mines. He was horrified by the death and despair the report painted. *A Christmas Carol* is, in part, a response to that report. Tiny Tim's crippled legs are braced by iron cages, and for Dickens, these braces represented the prison of cruelty and injustice that so many children suffered. It is no surprise, then, that in this happy ending, Tiny Tim is offered the promise to be healed so that he may walk freely, as a child, through the streets of London. Dickens would have it no other way.

Source Notes

ONE OF THE GREAT TREATS of writing a book like *The Haunting of Charles Dickens* is all the reading I get to do as research—everything from the history of London, to the construction of the first underground trains. "The novelist must know everything," the writer John Irving has said quite rightly. It's not enough to simply say a book is set in a time and place far removed from our own, but the writer needs to know what people wore there, and then, how they greeted one another, what sorts of shops were in a particular neighborhood, what the sound of gaslights was like, etc.

Here are some of the books I read while working on this novel, put together for the reader who becomes interested in Dickens's own words, or who wishes to learn more about the great man himself.

BOOKS BY CHARLES DICKENS

Each of these is referred to in *The Haunting of Charles Dickens*. It might be a character or a place, but the clues are there.

A CHRISTMAS CAROL—Even if you've never read anything by Charles Dickens, you probably already know the story of miserly Ebenezer

Scrooge and how he rediscovers the spirit of Christmas. There have been countless movie versions, both live action and animated, and the name Scrooge and the phrase "Bah, humbug!" have become a part of Christmas lore. This is one of the great short stories of all time, and it never fails to make me cry.

OLIVER TWIST—The heartbreaking story of young Oliver's life in the workhouses and on the crime-ridden streets of London is considered the first novel with a child as the main character. There are many film and animated versions of this book, as well.

GREAT EXPECTATIONS—Pip, another of Dickens's orphans, has a mysterious benefactor who arranges a new beginning in London for him. Pip is beset by cruelty and lies at every turn of his journey, especially by the mad Miss Havisham and her protégée, the often-cruel Estella. Young Pip loves Estella, but he can never have her.

A TALE OF TWO CITIES—Set against a backdrop of the guillotines of the French Revolution, this story of betrayal and sacrifice has one of the most famous opening lines in all of literature, "It was the best of times, it was the worst of times."

THE OLD CURIOSITY SHOP—Dickens often published his novels serially, that is, a few chapters at a time. American readers were so obsessed with this story of Little Nell that thousands of them gathered at the docks in New York when the climax of the book was published, all wanting to know if Little Nell had died. When they discovered she had, the crowd burst into tears.

LITTLE DORRIT—In the England of Dickens's lifetime, people could be put in jail simply for being in debt. Raised in a prison with her family, Little Amy Dorrit shows great courage in holding fast to her ideals.

DAVID COPPERFIELD—The quote at the beginning of my book is from *David Copperfield*, which is the most autobiographical of Dickens's novels. Its chapter on young David's time working in a horrible factory echoes Dickens's own time as a twelve-year-old in a blacking (shoe polish) factory.

THE PICKWICK PAPERS—The comic adventures of the Pickwick Club and its rather inept membership was so popular in its day that people all over England wore Pickwick Club pins in their lapels, much the way we might wear a T-shirt showing our favorite movies or bands.

BLEAK HOUSE—My favorite first sentence of a novel comes from *Bleak House*: "London." It's concise and vivid at the same time. *Bleak House* tells the tale of a lawsuit that's taken so long to move through the courts, no one can remember precisely why it was started in the first place. A perfect cast of evil and hilarious characters.

OUR MUTUAL FRIEND—Dickens's last completed novel, this is part murder mystery, part comedy, as well as a warning of how wasteful human beings can be and how we ought to care better for our planet.

THE UNCOMMERCIAL TRAVELLER—Charles Dickens was a voracious writer, and was a reporter and essayist, as well as a novelist. This is a collection of short reminiscences by Dickens, and from these funny and charming pieces, I learned a good deal about Dickens as a child and how he found a way of seeing the world with fresh eyes.

BOOKS ABOUT CHARLES DICKENS

Dickens's life is as entertaining as one of his novels. He rose from a rather impoverished beginning to become one of the most famous people in the world. He was, truly, a rock star in his time. And today, he continues to be written about and studied, nearly two hundred years after he was born. These are the books that most helped me understand his life and times.

DICKENS by Peter Ackroyd
THE LIFE OF CHARLES DICKENS by John Forster
CHARLES DICKENS A TO Z by Paul Davis
CHARLES DICKENS by G. K. Chesterton

Thank you for reading this
FEIWEL AND FRIENDS book.
The Friends who made

The Haunting of Charles Dickens

possible are:

Jean Feiwel, *publisher*
Liz Szabla, *editor-in-chief*
Rich Deas, *creative director*
Elizabeth Fithian, *marketing director*
Holly West, *assistant to the publisher*
Dave Barrett, *managing editor*
Nicole Liebowitz Moulaison, *production manager*
Jessica Tedder, *associate editor*
Ksenia Winnicki, *publishing associate*
Kathleen Breitenfeld, *designer*

Find out more about our authors and artists
and our future publishing at
www.feiwelandfriends.com.

OUR BOOKS ARE FRIENDS FOR LIFE

MLib
2/11